LAST DANCE

OTHER BOOKS BY
JEFFREY FLEISHMAN

My Detective (A Sam Carver Novel)

Promised Virgins: A Novel of Jihad

Shadow Man

LAST
DANCE

Jeffrey Fleishman

**BLACK
STONE**
PUBLISHING

The characters and events in this book are fictitious.
Any similarity to real persons, living or dead, is coincidental
and not intended by the author.

Printed in the United States of America

First edition: 2020
ISBN 978-1-982517-32-8
Fiction / Mystery & Detective / General

1 3 5 7 9 10 8 6 4 2

CIP data for this book is available
from the Library of Congress

Blackstone Publishing
31 Mistletoe Rd.
Ashland, OR 97520

www.BlackstonePublishing.com

For Monsignor Terrance M. Lawler

CHAPTER 1

She lies pale and light as shaved ice. Her hair spreads like a black flame across the pillow. Classical music plays in whispers. Schubert, I think. The place is scattered with toe shoes, tights, diet pills, opioids, suitcases, dresses, scarves, and empty bottles of Stoli. I snap on gloves and kneel beside her, study the small, nude map of her body. Taut, muscled, delicate except for her blistered and misshapen feet. A ballerina's feet. I want to cover her but I cannot change the scene, and so she lies among strangers—taking her picture, bagging her things, reconstructing the final moments of her life. She is a broken bit of magic fallen from a music box. I imagine her dancing, a flash in a spotlight on a distant stage, or maybe here across the polished floor of this Spring Street loft. I saw her face last night on the side of a bus when I arrived at LAX, her arms thrown back as if flying through a winter's dusk. I rise. My eyes go back and forth over her. No bruise, no blood, but a slight frozen shiver on her face, as if she were bracing against a sudden wind. I walk to the large, arched windows. I press down a yawn and take a breath. The air is cool, and the light is the way it is in that fugue time of in between.

"Name?"

"Katrina Ivanovna. Russian or some shit, I guess," says the uniform. "Here's her passport. Think she might be famous."

I flip through it.

"She's been around," I say. "What are you guessing?"

"Smothered, maybe. Not an OD."

"Why?"

"Face looks a little surprised, don't you think, Detective? Not peaceful, you know."

"A lot of pills. Vodka."

"Yeah, but doesn't feel that way."

"Who called it in?"

"The guy who comes to feed the cat."

"I don't see a cat."

"There is no cat."

"You sure?"

"Hardly any furniture. Where's it hiding?"

"There's a litter box in the corner."

"Cat shit but no cat," says the uniform, eyes scanning. "Must have run out. Cats are like that."

"Where's the guy?"

"Antonio Garcia. In 503."

I cross the hall and knock. A slender man in a blue silk robe, white T-shirt, and tight gray pants opens the door. He blows smoke sideways from a cigarette and invites me into a loft of half-dressed mannequins, sewing machines, drawing boards, swatches of cloth, and boxes of sequins, lamé, and glitter. A pincushion rides like a watch on his wrist. His hand is shaking, and he takes another long drag on the cigarette, bites a lemon, and downs an already poured shot of tequila.

"Did you see her?" he says.

"Yes. I'm Detective Sam Carver."

"Poor girl. Do you know Katrina?"

"A ballerina."

"Not *a* ballerina. One of *the* ballerinas." He rubs his nose and wipes away a tear. "She moved in a few years ago. She's not in LA much." He flicks ash, looks over my shoulder and out the door to the cop faces in the hall. "Her *Giselle* opens next week. The *Times* did a feature on her. Do you know ballet, Detective?" He's shattered but smug, his ponytail black and slick. He pours another shot. "We became friends. Soul mates, really. I advised her on costumes. I design, as you can see."

"You were feeding the cat?"

"Nishka. A stray she picked up in Cairo. I don't know why she kept him. Black, short-haired. Not a pretty thing. She was often in and out. She gave me a key and asked me to feed him." He lifts his shot and nods toward the window. "Katrina liked the street. When she was home, we'd sit over there and play games with the people below. How they moved. What they wore. Things you talk about over coffee."

He reaches for a tissue.

"This is terrible," he says.

"You found her in bed like that?"

"I thought she was sleeping." He takes a breath. "She was beautiful. I stood there for a moment. I didn't expect to see her." He steps toward me. "She had perfect lines, Detective. I loved making clothes for her. I gave her a dress once as a gift. She put it on right away and took me out to dinner at one of those new places around Seventh, near the one that sells macaroons. Katrina loved macaroons. We once ate a whole box. She could be enchanting that way." He steps back and crushes out his cigarette. He pours a third tequila and looks up at me. "When I came closer to her, she didn't move. I touched her with a finger. She was cold. I wanted to put a blanket over her. But I ran back to my place and called 911. Nishka must have slipped away then. He's always getting out."

"A lot of pills and vodka over there."

"I kept telling her she took too many. She wouldn't listen. She had pain from years of dancing. It's cliché, isn't it? The artist's overdose." He lowers his voice. "I'm sorry, Detective. That sounded cruel, but I was scared of this."

"Did you hear her come in last night? Was anyone with her?"

"I got home less than an hour before I found her. I was returning from Paris. The Louvre had a show of seventeenth-century couture. A minor display, but that fashion is so ornamental. It's a favorite of mine. I had been there a few days." He looks me over as if sizing me for a jacket. "I didn't know if she was home. I was coming to check on Nishka."

"Do you have the plane ticket?"

The request agitates him, but he flashes me the e-ticket and Uber receipt on his cell phone.

"Did you have a relationship with her?" I ask.

"Sexual?" He laughs. "Look around, Detective. What do you think?"

"Did she have a husband? Boyfriend?" I say. "Anyone?"

"There's a cellist," he says. "I don't know much about him. He would come now and then and sit in the middle of her loft and play. She danced around him like a sad angel. I saw them once when I came to feed Nishka. They didn't stop. They were in another world. He was tall, jet-black curly hair. Trim and well built. Hypnotic hands. I had never seen hands like that. So attuned to their craft. Sacred, almost. Do you know what I mean?"

"You notice a lot about bodies," I say.

"I dress them," he says with a glimmer of contempt. "I must."

"Did you get his name?"

"No. I only saw him a few times. I'd hear the music coming from her loft as I passed. The soft scrapes of her feet. They did have a fight once. I heard yelling but couldn't make out the words. One was as angry as the other. They went on for a few minutes, and then the music began again." He sighs. "The cello is the sound of sorrow, don't you think?"

"It's the instrument closest to the human voice."

"Yes, I think that's true."

I hand him my card.

"Call me if you remember anything more about the cellist, or if something else comes to mind."

He lights another cigarette and closes the door. I cross the hall back to the white suits, gloves, vials, swabs, and simmering chorus of voices. They're almost done. The crime scene is not a lived-in place. She was a vagabond. There's no sense of settling in here, no photographs or paintings or even a full set of plates—just a few books, a bed, two chairs, and, along the right wall, a row of mirrors and a barre. She lived like a cat.

Sun shines through the arched windows. The fifth-floor loft is an open stage to the street, and I imagine homeless and hipsters looking up and glimpsing her, a moth brushing against glass. I hear the crinkle, that sound that even after all these years still startles, the same as when a cartridge clicks into a chamber or a needle drops onto vinyl. She disappears into a bag, like the Stoli bottles and her pills, smartphone, laptop, and a couple of glasses. She is lifted and carried away. I walk to the bathroom: black-and-white tiles, the kind in old barbershops and speakeasies. A locket shaped like a swan hangs from the mirror. I hold it to the light, look around, slip it into my pocket. It is my one illicit urge, this thing I do to keep the dead a part of me, so I can see them as they were, feel their slight weight in my grasp.

"We're wrapping up, Detective," says the uniform, C. J. Alvarez. "You got everything?"

"Not much here. Anything in those books? Envelopes? Letters?"

"No. We did bag a paper napkin from that new place over on Olive. The NoMad. Nothing on it though. Think there'd be a phone number or something. Why take a bar napkin with nothing on it?"

"We'll run it for DNA."

"Kinda calm, you know, Detective? That quiet after the vic's gone."

"You catch a lot of homicides?"

"I was in Compton for a while after the academy. Saw my share. When they take away the vic, and the yellow tape goes up, there's an empty-church silence."

"Catholic?"

"Born and raised," he says.

"A medical examiner I know calls that silence the *final equinox*."

"Weird and peaceful."

"Don't get mystical."

"Just saying."

"I get it."

"You been working downtown a while, huh?"

I start to answer, but C. J. Alvarez gets a call and disappears into the hall. I take the elevator down. The sidewalks are quiet except a few dog walkers, a homeless guy talking on a pretend phone, and a weepy man with a trumpet, barely making a sound on the curb. I walk to the coffee shop on the corner and order an espresso and a glass of water. I sit and pull out my notebook and write *ballerina*. I scribble some notes of the scene and look out the window. I sip. The espresso is bitter. A bus passes, and I see her face again, flying through the streets of my neighborhood and toward the edges of where I need to go.

CHAPTER 2

"Shit, Carver, you looked wrecked."

"Only back a few hours when I caught the case."

"OD, maybe suicide," says my boss, Captain Manuel Ortiz, who's too awake for the hour. His espresso cup rattles, and he bites a croissant, brushing crumbs from a blue blazer I've seen too many times. "Stopped by her loft. Not much there. What are you thinking?"

"A lot of vodka and pills. I don't think that was it though."

"She's somebody. I Googled her. There'll be reporters and shit. You a ballet guy? You like classical stuff."

"I've been once or twice."

"Don't know how they do it."

"What?"

"Jump around in those slippers. Gotta hurt."

"They're not slippers. They're toe shoes."

"Whatever." His eyes roam over the café. "Espresso's acidy. I don't know why it's so hard for these places to make a decent cup. How difficult can it be?"

"You have to have the right machine. It's an art." I sip, make a face. "Why you here?"

"I was up. Saw the call come in. Figured I'd come see you. You were gone two months."

He stirs in a sugar. Then another.

"You're checking on me," I say.

"You haven't been right for a while, since, you know . . ."

"I keep—"

"Don't go there, Carver. It's been what, a year? She's gone. It happens, you know that."

"I thought I'd run into her in Europe. On a street. In a museum. I felt I was being watched once or twice. She's over there, or maybe Argentina. Somewhere with great architecture." I sip and pat myself for a cigarette I know I don't have. "I still hear her voice in my ear." I look out the window and back to Ortiz. "I thought she was going to kill me that night. Circling me, talking and crying. I was waiting for it. But she kissed me and left. 'Bye, Sam.' That was it. The words came out like when a marriage ends. I didn't even know her, but I hear those words every day."

"She knocked you out and tied you to a chair. It'd be wise to let it go."

Ortiz shakes his head. He knows the story, the strange, recurring prayer of mine.

"She was obsessed with you," he says. "In that screwed-up mind of hers, you were her savior. The one who would understand. Dylan Cross was a clever, messed-up, vicious broad."

"She had her reasons."

"She had vengeance. Killed two men who raped her, left a third chained in her basement. Vanishes. She wins." Ortiz smooths his mustache. "Probably be a Netflix special on her one day. You know, those long serial real-crime things they've been doing. I hope they don't. I hope I'm retired by then." He leans closer. "You know, they're cutting back on overtime and pensions. All this shit the *Times* has been writing about abuse. They better not touch mine." He takes a breath, studies his hands. "I hate that any doer gets away, but after what those pricks did to her, it doesn't bother me so much."

"Maybe."

"You ever trace the email she sent you after?"

"Tried, but it was impossible."

"What'd it say, again?"

"'Somewhere, someday.'"

"Like that old song."

"A time and a place for us."

"Whatever. Okay, Carver. Past is past. We got new shit bearing down. Dead ballerina. Real-time case. Drink another one of these things. Jolt yourself and do what you do. A man's got to have attitude, know what I'm saying? Not flailing around and thinking what-ifs." He swipes a yawn away. "It's Sunday. I got church with the wife. Bishop's at the cathedral. She likes the bishop. A mass for immigrants and DACA kids, or some shit. I'll let you know what I hear on the ballerina's bio. Katrina something, right? And what the crime lab pulls from her phone and laptop. If she's a Russian national, the consulate will get involved, and you know what kind of deep-shit complication *that* is. Christ."

Ortiz looks at me hard for a few seconds and leaves. It's odd to be back. I order another espresso—the barista's a surly, tattooed Asian hipster in a white apron—write in my notebook, and gather myself. I didn't know whether I'd return to LA. When I was in Berlin, I felt I could live there, wander the Tiergarten, drink beer at Zwiebelfisch, take the S-Bahn east, and get lost amid the galleries and ragged streets of Kreuzberg. A good life. A slipping of the skin. One day, maybe. Or perhaps Rome. Lisbon. Bucharest. I like to think so. I want something new, but I may be too grooved to the self already made. A couple kisses in the window and twirls away past an old man hurrying across Sixth Street with the Sunday paper. I'd like to sit here with a whiskey, read Milosz or Eliot, and let the day spin away—a man with a bit of money and no cares. Can't do that. That is pretend. I'm back with a new case. Dylan Cross is out there, though, strolling the ruins of an old continent, drawing buildings in the sweet air, as if in a film or hallucination.

Her words linger: "*Bye, Sam.*"

CHAPTER 3

It's still early. No one's around. I enter through the backstage door and walk past curtains and ropes to the wings, where I see Andreas Stein sitting alone center stage in a spotlight, scrolling on a laptop and listening to music. He's oblivious to the empty seats and the shadows around him. I had read about Stein in the *Times*—an indolent eccentric who made a name for himself years ago at the Joffrey but has since bounced through the ballet world like a lost boy wonder. He is a man of tantrums and tenderness, or so dancers and critics say. He wears a sweater and a scarf and tight jeans. His face is lean, like Beckett in his later years, and his hair is bristly gray-black. A shorn figure from his own mythology. The scent of cologne drifts off of him. His eyes are closed, a slight smile of contentment on his lips. I stand for a moment, watching. He opens his eyes, startled, and hops up.

"Jesus, man! Who are you? Sneaking around like a phantom." He smiles at the allusion. "Are you the lighting fellow? These lights are terrible, not one decent beam." He studies me closer. "You don't look light a lighting man. No. The lawyer, perhaps. As I've said, I'm not signing until we fix the indemnity clause." He shakes his head. "But you don't look like a lawyer either. Hmm . . . You know what you look like? And don't take offense: a cop. A relatively suave one—I can see a bit of style in you. That's a smart shirt. Yes, I think you're a cop." He winks. "Have we burglars? Some untoward sexual mischief in the wings? My dancers are not here. Alas, I am alone for you to question."

"I'm Detective Sam Carver."

"No? I'm right, then? Wonderful. I like guessing about people. A proclivity of mine. I'm quite good at it, most days." He laughs. "Do you have a badge?"

I flash my shield.

"I haven't done anything illicit; I assure you. I've been working nonstop on our ballet. *Giselle.* Do you know it?"

"Brokenhearted girl dies and is resurrected by virgin spirits."

"Close enough. How may I help you?" He looks at me, quite pleased with himself.

"When did you last see Katrina Ivanovna?"

"Our Giselle," he says. "We had a rehearsal yesterday afternoon. Ended about four. She left in one of her moods. Volatile temperament, that girl. Worse than most. Very difficult. The great ones are, of course." He takes a breath. "She's aged, you know. Can't do what she once did. That's confidential, mind you. They say that about me too. She and I took this on to prove we could still do the things we did back when everyone wanted us. She's lovely but, as I said, quite difficult. Has she done something?"

"She's dead."

His eyes narrow. He turns his head toward me, swallows, looks down, then out to the dark theater. He takes a step back, steadies himself on the chair, lifts a hand to his lips, closes his eyes hard. The lines of his face pull tight, and as with so many who are given such news, words, for a moment, escape him. Tears run; seconds pass.

"Oh, dear," he says. "Was it an overdose? She had been taking pills. She was in great pain much of the time." He wipes the corner of his eye with a finger. "The body is fallible to the dream. She used to say that. I think she picked it up from an old teacher. This is not right, this news you're giving me, Detective. How?"

"We're looking at everything. There were pills and vodka. We're not sure yet. We found her alone in a loft over on Spring."

"She bought it years ago when real estate was cheap downtown."

"So you last saw her around four p.m.?"

"She walked across this stage, did a clumsy pirouette just to goad me, and left out the backstage door."

"Did she leave with anyone?"

"Not that I saw."

"Was she close to anybody in the company?"

"Not really. She was brought in to dance this part. She's not part of our troupe. The dancers will be here later, if you wish to talk to them."

"I do. Did she seem upset or preoccupied? Anything bothering her?"

"She was losing her talent, Detective. That upset her very much. She still had enough to occasionally dazzle, but the sharpness was blurring."

"Was she close to a cellist?"

"Detective," he sighs, "she was close to cellists, oboists, violinists, maestros, and, when the mood struck her, ushers and set designers. Men or women. It didn't matter. She had a ravenous nature."

"With you?"

"Oh my, you are direct. Once or twice over the years. Not recent."

"A neighbor said a cellist came to her loft and played while she danced."

"As I said, she knew many musicians. I don't know who this cellist could have been."

Andreas Stein sits down and squints in the spotlight. Says nothing. He rises and slides the chair into the darkness. He wipes his eyes and tells me when he first saw her, years ago in Paris: how she moved, the flare of her grand jeté, the grace of her adagio, the fine line of her neck, her slender jaw, delicate as spider's thread, and how they went out for drinks after rehearsals—she drank Campari then—and walked the cobblestones until morning, confident and amazed of what was in them, their gifts that demanded everything but rewarded them with the indelible lie of beauty, and how after the last performance, they couldn't sleep, so they wandered again through the city and ate bread and jam for breakfast and watched the boats on the Seine and the way the morning light slipped over the steeples and into the gardens and through the mist of fountains. He will never have that again. I have just met him, but I can tell he never will. He is living on embers. He looks at me, embarrassed, as if he has committed a sacrilege to memory. But I know how he feels, how it all can seem so splendid and useless.

"We've lost our Giselle," he says, staring into the empty seats. "What will we do?"

CHAPTER 4

I call the medical examiner's office. No answer. The crime lab is backed up and won't get to Katrina Ivanovna's phone and laptop until tomorrow. "It's the weekend, Carver, you know how it is," says the curt voice when I call. Some asshole a year from his pension. There's no security video from her building. Ballerinas from Stein's company offered little except to say that Katrina kept to herself and was often in a haze—until she danced and, as one of them said, "became this wonderful thing."

I head to Malibu to see Stefan Petrovic, a one-time gunrunner and drug smuggler turned art dealer and global financier. Stefan has long intrigued the feds but has never been arrested. "I have the best lawyers, Sam, but truly, what have I done?" He helped me on a case years ago after I made detective. He appeared at the Little Easy, sat beside me, slid a slip of paper toward my drink, and left. He has become an occasional drinking partner and off-the-books confidential informant. I have told him that I'd arrest him if he broke any laws in my jurisdiction. "How incestuous it all is, don't you think, Sam?" he said once while ordering martinis at the Biltmore and waiting for a performance artist (that's who he told me she was) from Prague. "The line is not so straight between good and bad, no?"

The air cools with the night, and by the time I hit the coastal highway, the full moon is bright over the ocean. Planes lift like dark angels from LAX, and the last of the surf boys are peeling off wet suits near cars parked on the roadside, their dope sweet on the breeze. I curve north. Santa Monica falls away in my rearview. I slide in a Balkan CD Stefan gave me—fast-moving Romani music spliced with dirges that bring to mind broken furniture and regret. The music is sly like Stefan. He was born in the mountains north of Sarajevo, the only son of a Serbian father and a Muslim mother. His parents were killed by each other's tribe in a war I remember watching on TV as a boy. Markets spattered with blood and shattered fruit, men marched along rivers, girls raped and shot in fields and forests. It was distant and exotic: mosques and churches, red-tile roofs, tanks aflame, orchards, and old ladies running with groceries and dodging sniper fire on the fringe of Europe.

I wind up a hill and stop at Stefan's gate. Luksala, an African Stefan saved from some unending genocide, buzzes me in. The eighteenth-century Belgrade-style villa is dark. The front door is open. It feels as if guests have fled a party. Luksala whispers, "Mr. Stefan no good tonight. Sitting out back by himself, drinking. Drinking all day. Anniversary of mother's death. He like this every year. Come."

He leads me through the foyer and living room, out to the back patio, past the pool, and to the grass, where Stefan sits in an Adirondack chair, staring at the ocean, his white robe aglow.

"Sam, how are you? It's been a while."

He crosses his legs and lights a cigar.

"You're out of your neighborhood, Detective," he says, waving me to sit beside him. "I told you, though, I've gone respectable."

"It's not a good time. I'll come back."

"Stay. You must have a case."

Distant boats and a few tankers slide past in the moonlight.

"Do you know the ballerina Katrina Ivanovna?"

He looks up as if deciphering the night sky.

"I met her once at a Harvey Weinstein party. Before all that shit came out about Harvey. When he had power and people were scared of him. I used to set him up with money guys for his movies. Harvey was always looking for money. He was a scavenger dog." Stefan blows a plume of gray. "Katrina Ivanovna danced at the party. Everyone watched. I still remember. A piano played and she moved like a tiny creature from a fairy tale. Does that make sense? I had never gone to the ballet. But that night, I thought I might start." He looks in his glass and then to the sea. "I told her how good she was. We talked a little, and she disappeared through the crowd."

"She's dead," I say. "We don't know if it's an overdose or if she's been killed. Pills and vodka, but it doesn't feel right."

He shakes his head, brushes ash from his robe.

"Who would kill . . ." His voice drops. He pinches the bridge of his nose, sits quietly. He looks at me, then away. His eyes are bloodshot, but they are for his mother and from a long night of drink. "Katrina Ivanovna," he says. The name hushes in the air. He starts to say something but stops. He hands me a glass and a bottle of bourbon. He offers a cigar.

"I quit smoking," I say.

"I'm quitting tomorrow," says Stefan. "You think I might know something?"

"A famous Russian ballerina dies. You travel in certain circles. She arrived in LA a few weeks ago to rehearse for *Giselle*."

"I've heard nothing," he says. "Could be too many pills. You read it all the time. This country is a big medicine cabinet." He puffs. "Russians, though, huh? Stealing your election. Poisoning spies and dissidents in Europe. They are busy people, the Russians. When did it happen?"

"She was found this morning. Why do you think she danced at Weinstein's party?"

"I don't know. That was years ago. Maybe she thought she'd get into a movie. Harvey was a man of promises."

"You think . . ."

"No, Sam, she wasn't Harvey's type."

"I didn't know he had one."

"Is he in jail yet?"

"He's in New York, facing all kinds of charges."

Stefan leans back and takes a long sip.

"That night at the party, I wanted to reach out and touch her. To see what she felt like, you know, like a little girl and a woman in the same body." He glances toward me but doesn't wait for an answer. "If I hear anything, I'll let you know. Serbs and Russians are alike, Sam. We are, how to say, *dark and misunderstood*. Yes? It's in our books and histories. We are brooders and fatalists. A little like you, Sam."

We sit in silence. A gust shoots along the coast; the air goes calm again. Below, all is quiet. Faraway lights move here and there as if the world had turned to another part of itself and left us alone at the ocean's edge. I breathe in. A shiver runs through me, a recognition of those moments that, over the years, gather unknown inside you, appearing from time to time like a heaven of misplaced stars.

"How's your mother, Sam? Still bad?"

"She doesn't know me anymore. Her mind is gone."

"In Boston?"

"With my aunt. I need to get back there soon."

"I'm sorry. Forgive me, but may I ask, does it feel like she's dead?"

"It feels like she's hiding in a place I cannot reach."

"That may be worse."

Stefan recrosses his legs, wipes the corner of his eye.

"My mother used to get up before it was light," he says. "Our house was near a stream. We had a raised, open porch. A *deck*, I think you call them here. She would sit with a coffee and a cigarette—she was a European Muslim, not a Middle Eastern Muslim, so cigarettes were permitted—and all the world did not move, except the stream. Did you ever listen to a stream? It's hypnotic. One morning when I was little, I went out and sat on her lap. She sang an old Balkan song about a king and his lover. Then she stopped and said, 'This is my favorite time. See how the trees step out of the darkness.' We watched together as it became light. We left the porch and woke my father. He drank a lot of plum brandy but was a good man. He was a surveyor. I think I told you that before. He was not a lunatic nationalist like so many Serbs. When the war came, we thought we'd be no part of it. But it found us."

The cigar ember lights his face. The moon is high, incandescent; you can count its countries.

"Muslims from a village in the valley came one night and took my father. I never saw him again. Two days later, Serbs who once ate in our house and danced at our parties came for my mother. You would not have believed it then, Sam. Killing became the only way." He lets a long while pass. "I was asleep. They tied her to a tree. I hope that she blocked it out by listening to the stream, but I don't know. They shot her and went away. I cut her down. I washed her in the stream and buried her. I took my father's gun and went down the road. I killed the first Serb I saw. I didn't even know who. I emptied the gun on him. I threw it down and ran into the mountains."

He crushes out his cigar.

"I felt hate but also a boy's thrill at the power in my hand. I can't explain what it was, but the feeling was over when the gun emptied. All I remember of that day, really, was washing my mother, and the blood running from her and into the stream. She would have liked that. To be part of the stream and carried to the sea. I dug a grave so that if you saw it from the sky, you would think that God had made it."

I turn toward him.

"You okay?"

"Yes, Sam, fine. Those times stay deep, you know?"

"Yes."

I hear him sip.

"I can still see her dancing," he says.

"Your mother?"

"No, Sam. Katrina."

"Made an impression."

"Some . . ."

His words trail off. We sit a bit longer. Stefan finishes the bottle and falls asleep. Luksala comes to rouse him, but it is no use. Stefan is lost to the drink and the night and the tragedies that have made him. I stand.

Luksala takes my seat. "I stay with Mr. Stefan. In a few hours, light."

I head to my car and back to the city. The highway's almost

empty. LA is quiet, so unlike itself, except to those who cannot sleep, who know that this is the true city: a metropolis of spirits and distant lights, a cool, dark place of lies that spin along the coast and blow across the desert. I get off the 110 at Fourth Street and park. No one's in the lobby; the security guard is on his rounds. I take the elevator to my apartment, pour a drink, sit at the piano, and pull out Katrina Ivanovna's locket. I hold it to the light and, with one hand, play a soft, meandering tune of the kind I imagine she may have danced to with the cellist. I'm not a very good pianist, but I have these compositions in my head, unrefined lines that rise and lose themselves. I stop and put the locket in the inlaid box that holds belongings of all my vics: tooth, business card, newspaper clipping, rosary, quarter, key, photograph— mementos that tell me the dead were once here among the living. From a tiny piece, you can trace a life, its yearnings and failures, its sublimities and its empty hours. I shower and sit by the window with one more drink. Esmeralda is not there tonight. She's getting weaker and might be in a shelter, although she hates them, the way they crowd in on her, dispossessed eyes wanting to steal her things and take her soul. That's what she says. The sidewalk is not the same without her shopping cart and clutter of possessions. I open my laptop and click to a photograph of Katrina Ivanovna, looking out from the wings of a theater in Budapest years ago, her hair pulled tight, her face poised, expectant, waiting to dance into the light. I push the laptop aside and sit in darkness, thinking of my mother, who no longer knows me, this woman who bore me and gave me a name and ran with me when I was a boy, across the coves and beaches of New England.

CHAPTER 5

I open my eyes. I'm in the chair. Day is on me. My head hurts. Horns, voices, the whine of a bus, clack of a skateboard, girls laughing. Midmorning. I stand, undress, and head to the shower, glimpsing myself in the mirror, disheveled and in need of a shave and a haircut. I look closer. A few threads of gray stretch back from the temple. I imagine how I might age, incrementally and then suddenly, the lines deepening, the hard cut of the face softening, the skin paling—a washed-out me with a ghost inside pushing out. I smile at the inevitability of it and summon a less-than-inspired defiance. I swallow three aspirin. It's been a rough, lost time lately, but I've known it before, although now, after Dylan Cross, the scrambled pieces don't go back so easily anymore. I feel like a painting where shadows shift unexpectedly. Screw it. I face the hot water and baptize myself for a new day. I wrap a towel around me and head to the stove and French press. I throw away the empty scotch bottle, open the kitchen blinds, water the plant I have killed, notice the suitcase I haven't unpacked, and check my phone: twenty-three missed calls from Ortiz.

"Hey."

"Don't fucking 'hey' me, Carver."

"Sorry, phone was off. I'm still a little jet lagged. Listen, I . . ."

"We're in a shit storm."

"What?"

"The ballerina's gone," he says.

"Gone?"

"Fucking gone."

"She's dead."

"She's gone too. Kidnapped from the morgue."

"How?"

"Middle of the freaking night. Three thirteen a.m. Two cars explode in the parking lot. Everyone runs, doors opening, chaos, lights flicking. All kinds of batshit. Total breakdown in security." Ortiz is breathing, and I know he's smoothing his mustache the way he does when he's anxious and pissed. "Two guys dressed like morgue drivers and wearing pulled-low ball caps sneak in, slide her out of the tray, and put her in a bag. Disappear. Real quick and smooth. I'm looking at the video now. Amazing. So ballsy, it worked. I mean, who would have thought of someone stealing a stiff? Everyone's thinking terror attack or some shit. It's bad, Carver."

"But . . ."

"It gets worse," says Ortiz. "It was the weekend, right? Busy weekend. A lot of bodies, short staff. So . . ."

"*No.*"

"Yup. They never examined her. No autopsy. No nothing."

"No cause of death."

"Bingo. Don't know if she's a homicide, suicide, OD, or what."

"This isn't happening."

"It has happened."

"What do we do?"

A pause. A breath.

"I'm thinking no one steals a body unless . . . fuck, I don't know; it's more sinister than an OD," he says. "Still, technically, no body, no crime. Of course, the body's been stolen, so that's theft, minimum. But we got to treat it like a homicide. Got to. The Russian consulate called the chief. FBI's coming over. Someone leaked it to the press. TV cameras all over the place. International incident. We look like idiots."

"It is a great story—I mean, from their perspective."

"Don't be a wiseass, Carver. You have a tendency to be a wiseass at the worst times."

I sit with a coffee and look out the window. A woman on a bike glides through traffic. She's wearing a skirt, sneakers, and a white T-shirt; her blond hair is blowing in the wind. She's young, pedaling toward palm trees in Pershing Square, as if she has come down from the hills to buy fabric and flowers from those cheap places near Skid Row. My eyes follow her. She turns left, the last flash of her hair disappearing around the corner, out of sight and into eternity. A sudden joy fills me. Slips away.

"Carver. Carver."

"I'm here. You think a cop or someone from the ME's was involved? How'd they know where to go—where, exactly, the body was? It was quick, right? They had to know the layout. What were they driving? What kind of explosives?"

"Everyone's being questioned," says Ortiz. "I don't think one of ours is involved, but who knows? I don't know why, but when you see this video, it's just too weird, you know?" He clears his throat. "Fire marshal and bomb guys are trying to figure out it all out. No one hurt, thank God, but Jesus! You get any leads?"

"Just the cellist I told you about. The one who came to her apartment and played while she danced. They had a fight a while ago, according to a neighbor. Maybe something there when I find the guy. I didn't get much from Andreas Stein, her choreographer. The dancers didn't know much either. She slept around. Took pills. She aged out of her prime and was trying to get it back."

"Can't do that," says Ortiz. "Impossible."

"Imagine having the life she had and finding you can't have it anymore."

"At least she had it once."

"She didn't see it that way. Ends up alone and naked in a bed."

"Marilyn Monroe."

"You're dating yourself."

"I'm old, so fuck it."

"Whitney Houston drowned in a bathtub in Beverly Hills."

"Big voice."

"Lost it, couldn't get it back."

"We could go down the avenue of the doomed all day, Carver, but we've got a ballerina to find. My guess is, we're not the only ones looking. I keep replaying this video. It's unbelievable 'cause you're seeing it all, kinda grainy and fast, but you're not hearing anything. Just this silence. You want to hear a voice. Something."

He sighs. "Jesus, Carver, we lost a *body*."

CHAPTER 6

Special Agent Azadeh Nazari walks toward me with a pinot noir, a smile, and a file folder. She sits, stares me up and down, inhales a vape, and watches two women, one in a tight dress, the other in motorcycle leather, kiss in the twilight. She sips and lets her black hair down. We're on the roof of Perch, overlooking the city in the purple-orange flare of a dying day. A lot of pickup lines and pretending are going on, especially among the young who have valeted their Priuses and Mercedes and are thinking how clever it is to be a trust-fund baby, tech geek, B film actor, wardrobe designer, gallery curator, or portfolio manager at Citibank. They drink Grey Goose, eat sliders, and pass around iPhones, laughing at their tiny movies, oblivious of the moon and the coming stars.

"Why'd you pick here?"

"It's close for both us," says Azadeh. "I like it. Don't you live, like, right across the street? Besides, I wasn't going to let you drag me to one of your dives."

"My places are respectable. One was in a Michael Mann film. They have character."

A breeze lifts. She sips and can't help a grin.

"Lose anything lately, Carver?"

"Don't give me shit."

"It went viral."

"Ortiz says he doesn't think it's one of ours. Too *surreal*, he said."

"He said *surreal*? *Ortiz*?"

"Not verbatim, but that was the gist."

She looks at the menu, puts it down. She opens the file.

"Katrina Ivanovna. How much do you know?"

"I read the obituaries," I say. "Let's play nice and pretend the FBI and the LAPD get along and are, you know, collaborative. She's a famous pill-addicted ballerina with a cat and a loft on Spring, a lot of lovers, who, in a few days, was going to be Giselle."

"That's what I like about you, Carver. Concise. Pack it all into a sentence."

"I'm not as informed as you."

Azadeh looks around, lowers her voice, and leans toward me.

"Katrina trained with the best dance teachers in St. Petersburg and Moscow. Her father, Anton, was in the KGB but not in the field. He pushed paper. An analyst of some sort. Knows Putin, but not close. He retired early and spends his time at a dacha outside Moscow. Her mother is the interesting one." Azadeh finishes her pinot. She waves for a waiter and asks me if I want another—on the Bureau, of course I do. "Maria Ivanovna is the daughter of one of Boris Yeltsin's best friends. Went to the best schools. There's a gap we don't know much about, but she ended up in petroleum. She's connected to Gazprom and has a link to a gold mine in Guinea. She's not an oligarch but she knows their secrets and hunts reindeer with them in Siberia. She sleeps around, like her daughter. But discreet. Very plugged in. Definitely a Kremlin insider."

"Is it a hit? Poisoning job like those murders in England? Plutonium in the tea, or something, wasn't it?"

"We don't think so," says Azadeh. "Maria's in good standing. Anton's just a gardener. But who knows, right? Maria has serious cred. Could have angered someone, run afoul, I guess. Katrina and her mother weren't close. They stopped speaking years ago— best we can tell, anyway. We've asked the CIA for an assist, but you know what it's like trying to squeeze a nickel out of them. Of course, if we had the—"

"Don't go there," I say. "We don't have her body. At the moment."

Azadeh smiles. The waiter sets down the drinks and leaves.

"You saw her, right?"

"Pills and Stoli bottles," I say. "Sad ending."

"So?"

"Didn't feel like that though. I'm thinking she was smothered, or someone forced the OD. No marks, no blood."

"Suspects?"

"A cellist."

"Hmm. Not the usual."

"He played while she danced. They argued."

"That's it?"

"Hey . . ."

"Sorry."

"Did she get back to Russia much?"

"No. Pretty much cut ties there," says Azadeh. "Lived all over Europe. South America. That place on Spring. She was a wanderer."

"Of dying talent."

"I watched clips of her on YouTube before I came here. She was lovely. Full of grace."

"You sound like a prayer."

I smile. Azadeh rolls her eyes.

"I wanted to be a ballerina when I was a girl," she says. "I'd twirl in my bedroom and through the halls. Humming. I was a great hummer, Carver. I was very young."

"A Valley girl, weren't you?"

"My parents moved there after they left Iran, right before Khomeini and the mullahs took over."

"The Great Satan time."

"My father got out with his money and his faith. 'Islam,' he used to say, 'doesn't want little girls to dance.' He wasn't a fanatic. That's just how he thought back then. He was cosmopolitan at heart and became quite American. But he kept this false hope that one day he might go back. A lot of older Iranians out here think this. At least, they used to. We call them the 'burned generation.'"

"Between worlds. What does your old man think of your wife? Elsa, right?"

"I've turned him into a progressive. Lesbian daughters can do that."

"Or make you a fundamentalist."

"He goes to the mosque. Trump has pushed him closer to God. I think it's more out of defiance than religion though."

"Our president has that effect."

I met Azadeh when I was starting with the cops after Berkeley and she joined the FBI after Yale. She was a prize for the Bureau back then—a clever, gay, multilingual daughter of Islam who listened to the Ramones and skateboarded on weekends. We went to Venice Beach once, strolled along the canals, smelled the marsh air and the money, and, at night, walked to the shore with a six-pack and a candle that wouldn't stay lit, looking at the moon and listening to the waves and the homeless, drinking until fog covered the sand. We were wet and cold by morning, shivering and huddled against each other, but in no hurry to leave. We shared a damp cigarette, a bag of cashews, and the last beer. We fell into each other's stories, two people on the brink of new lives. I remember the voices of surfers at dawn—their laughs, the slap of boards on the water, and the way the mist lifted and the sky hardened and fishermen cut bait on the pier and a girl with a guitar and a broken amplifier sang hymns in front of a boardwalk café that had yet to open.

"Katrina danced at a Weinstein party," I say.

"That creep."

"What if it was something like that? Jealousy. Abuse. Slept with the wrong guy."

"With her, could be a lot of wrong guys. She got around. I wouldn't #MeToo this thing. But stealing a body is occult, fetishistic, don't you think? It's more than covering up a crime."

"We don't know what the crime is."

"And with no body . . ."

I shoot her a look.

"Sorry, Carver, but it really is a clusterfuck."

"What's *clusterfuck* in Farsi?"

"Sanctions."

We laugh. Azadeh pays the bill.

"You get anything from her phone or laptop?"

"Not yet."

"We'll talk."

She closes the file, waves, and is gone. Perch is full. Voices, rattling glasses, high heels. Scents of dope and magnolia. I look west over the city, past Pershing Square and palms brought here long ago when they began making movies and believing in things not real. Los Angeles is a crueler place than that though. It leaves you thinking so much more is beyond your grasp than you once thought. But you stay, with your inlaid box of strange souvenirs, among killers and naked ballerinas and young couples drunk in the night, pretending. I stare at the unfinished twelve-story mural across the street: angels floating around a tribal child, a girl of the land's first people, who looks with white-flecked eyes into darkness. I finish my drink, frisk myself for a nonexistent cigarette, and take the elevator down. A stoned redhead kisses me in the lobby. "This is awkward," she says. "I thought you were someone I came with. I seemed to have lost them all." She wobbles away. The valet looks at me, expectant, but I shake my head, turn right, and head up Hill. I see Esmeralda leaning against the Hotel Clark, wrapped in scarves, her shopping carts and bags a fortress around her. I sit next to her on the sidewalk. We listen to each other's breathing. She turns toward me.

"Give me ten dollars."

"No."

"Whiskey?"

"Don't have any."

"Why you here bothering me, then? I got to sleep. You always be coming around at all hours. Like a snake. A snake is what you are. No money, no whiskey, just a snake."

"How have you been? I didn't see you last night."

"Had me at the hospital."

"You okay?"

"I left," she says. "That's where you go to die. A hospital ain't a place for living. Any soul worth a shit knows that. They gave me a shower. Held me under real long. Scrubbed me like a dog. Hate them, hate them all."

Two Harleys roar past and stop near the corner. The riders join other bikers who are drinking canned beer and tequila and whistling at Latinas waiting in line at La Cita. Bouncers get nervous around this time. Winds blow down from the San Gabriels, carrying voices and intentions from all directions. A cop car slows but keeps going, and on the other corner, a bus drops off a batch of cleaning women who disappear up the hill toward the financial towers and a billboard advertising for accident and personal-injury lawyers: "Stopped Getting Screwed. *Se Habla Español.*"

Esmeralda coughs.

"You've been on the streets too long," I say.

"Shh!" she whispers. "You see that man over there? Sitting, yellow eyes."

"Where?"

"Right there across the street. Sitting there smiling with his yellow eyes. He's been staring at me for a while. I'm hiding from him, but he finds me. Always finds me somehow. How do they do that? Big-ass city, but they find you. You got a man with yellow eyes following you?"

"Not lately."

"He'll be there. They come when you don't think they will. Like snow. They had snow where I used to live. I think they did. Somewhere not from here. A cold place with a bad sky."

She pulls her scarves tight. Face black, eyes bloodshot, she looks like a gourd, withered, her hands long and knotted, knees pulled to her chest, lost in a pile of rancid clothing. She turns away from me; her breathing changes. I wait until she sleeps, staring into the few lighted windows left on the street, searching for the yellowed-eyed man of her crazy dreams.

CHAPTER 7

How can a body get lost?

Where does it go?

I see her, lying still in the bed. Veins like blue ink beneath pale skin. Her bruised ballerina feet. Her eyes open, her mouth a slight flash of teeth, as if locked between syllables. Something she wanted to say, a final thought, a revelation. No, something more frightening, I think—a recognition, perhaps lasting less than a second, that it was ending; a train of faces whooshing past, girls and dancers, the way they moved year after year, like painted saints on chapel walls, always there, spinning around her. No more.

Ortiz slides me a coffee. He's breathing in the slow, labored rhythm he has when he's mad and mystified, letting it build, running a hand through his thinning hair, looking out the window of Demitasse to the edge of Little Tokyo. He's put on a little weight over the years, but his eyes are quick and clear. He starts to stay something, bites his lips, sips espresso, stirs in a sugar. Licks the spoon. Sighs.

"Don't talk to any reporters, Carver."

"I know the drill. I'm pretty reticent, don't you think?"

"Why do you say shit like that? *Reticent*. Why can't you just say *quiet*? Words people actually use." He slides his spoon into the cup. "You weren't always so *reticent* either. You got too close to that pain-in-the-ass reporter. What's her name?"

"Susan Chandler."

"Yeah, her. I don't like her, Carver. Has a way of getting phone numbers and shit she shouldn't have."

"She's gone. Took a job at the *Washington Post*."

"Good news," he says. "I guess it doesn't matter. Story's out. Headlines. Social media. Jimmy Fallon. We're a punch line. Trump even tweeted about it. 'LAPD can't stop illegals, loses ballerina. SAD.' I hate that guy."

"Anybody from inside?"

"We've grilled the MEs staff, all cops connected, morgue drivers, janitors—the bunch of them. Nothing. We gotta go further back. Former employees. I'm still thinking no though."

He reaches for another sugar packet, decides against it.

"You see the security video?" he says. "Two men in uniforms and ball caps running through the halls with a body bag. They knew where to go."

"They looked lost a couple of times."

"Happened fast. A ballerina doesn't weigh more than a bird. But why kill someone and leave a body behind in a loft and then steal it later from the morgue? Makes no sense. Get rid of the body right away. No body, no crime, no clues."

"Maybe the killer and the thief aren't the same."

"C'mon, Carver. What are we looking at, then?"

I don't answer. Ortiz exhales. The barista brings him another espresso. "Thank you, Mariella," he says in the voice he uses only for her. I shoot him a look. He leans close. "What? I'm married. I know. I can imagine. No harm." A girl opens a laptop on the counter, puts on headphones, and peers into her screen, smiling at a virtual labyrinth that unfolds into a paradise and then into the black and stars of deep space.

"You see the stuff they pulled from her phone?" says Ortiz. "They're still working on it, but it's a start."

"I'm heading there now. You know the guy?"

"A writer or some shit."

"Ghostwrites biographies for celebs."

"Our ballerina had a story to tell."

"Could be. She met him for a drink at the NoMad a little past eleven the night she died. He's her last text."

"What about the cello guy?"

"Haven't found him."

Ortiz stares out the window.

"Hey, Carver, you gotta get a new car. Jesus, man, look at that thing."

"It's vintage."

"It's a wreck. What year?"

"Late eighties. I thought you loved my Porsche."

"I do, but still. It's one of those character things with you, isn't it? You know the way you are. Righteous. Not the annoying kind, although at times, maybe, yes. Sticking with something out of spite or a sense of devotion. You're kinda like a dog that way, Carver."

"I just like my car. It runs fine."

Ortiz shakes his head.

"Get over to that writer guy," he says. "I'm gonna finish this. The Russian consulate's coming over in an hour. Wants a brief."

"They probably already hacked us."

Ortiz stops in midscowl and smiles.

"Go be useful," he says.

I take the 101 north toward Los Feliz, get off at Hollywood, and head up the hill toward Griffith Park, turning left on a street of sycamores. I check the address. The door to the Tudor-style house is half open. I knock. "Come in," a voice yells from the distance. "Be right there." Bombino is playing soft, wiry blues from Africa, which gives the living room, with its antiques, leather chairs, framed maps, pulled shades, and reading lights, the feel of a desert outpost in the waning days of a colonial empire. I imagine poems in the wind, scarves blowing from the necks of horsemen. That mystique changes, though, when my eye catches two Warhol-like paintings of Audrey Hepburn—topless, beaded in sweat, a whip in her hand—and Lady Gaga, a debutante in black dress and pearls. They hang on opposing walls, sizing each other up, playing tricks with preconceptions.

"I almost did a book with her—Gaga, of course, not Hepburn. Ah, but Hepburn would have been something, another era chicer than this one. The Gaga deal fell through. You get used to it. Fickle bunch, the famous. Always need tending. Like a garden. Stubborn too. You can buy a lot of stubborn with money." He opens his arms. "Welcome to my home."

"I'm Detective Carver."

"I've gathered."

Michael Paine is muscular and short, toweled blond hair, shaved face with the pinched tightness of a recent eye tuck. He's wearing a Lou Reed T-shirt, black jeans, and beat-up loafers with no socks. He seems a precocious adolescent who stumbled into adulthood and doesn't want to be there. His words come in bursts. He twirls a finger and points, leading me through the kitchen—deep sinks, stained glass, flowers drying upside down over butcher block—to a patio that rolls into a yard of honeysuckle and bougainvillea. An Aztec statue of a kneeling man looking skyward peeks from ivy. "My spirit brother," says Paine. He pours iced tea and nods for me to sit.

"The writing life is good," I say.

"Gaga aside, not bad, Detective. I'm a laptop for hire. The famous have an insatiable need to be taken seriously. I bring their epiphanies, for lack of a better term, to the page. You'd be surprised at how many of them can't express two articulate thoughts. Makes you wonder. But then some of them—ah, some of them are glorious, really smart. Drink, Detective, drink." He offers a plate of cookies and biscotti. "I started out as a novelist, but novels don't pay. Amal and George do. Look around. It's rather excessive, I know. Children are starving somewhere. But these are our times." He smiles. "Have you noticed, Detective, I tend to talk a lot? I don't think I was listened to enough as a child. Cut in any time. You look like the quiet type." He laughs. "What movie is that from?"

"Katrina Ivanovna."

"Ah, right to business. Direct." He bites a cookie. "A tragic loss. And then to *be* lost. How does that happen, exactly?"

"We're looking into it," I say.

"I would think."

"You met her at the NoMad. Her text to you was her last."

"She texted she was running late. She appeared minutes after. Swept in like an exquisite piece of candy. She had the faint scent of weed about her. We ordered two dirty martinis and found a place in the corner. The NoMad's become popular with a certain kind. Downtown is suddenly hip. For a time, I suppose. West Hollywood has become passé. So few things feel new there anymore. Perhaps that's age and cynicism talking. What do you think? Of course, I live here in Los Feliz—hardly scandalous, but still."

"Who set up the meeting?"

"Her agent is friends with mine, and yada yada, phone calls were made."

"She wanted a book?"

"I gathered she'd been thinking about writing her life story for some time. 'Russian Ballerina Conquers World.' Could be marketable with all the Moscow intrigue these days. Ballerinas aren't my coterie, if you know what I mean. I tend to stay away from the classical world. Talk about weird diets, egos, and insecurities. Wow. But she was intense. Agitated. She said she had a tale that would shake things up. 'Could be exposé.' That Russian accent, you know."

"What kind of exposé?"

"Wouldn't say. She said she wanted to get to know me better. She asked to arrange another meeting. Quite mysterious. I was getting interested. I kept studying her. She was as thin and delicate as a martini glass."

I wince.

"I thought she was an 'exquisite piece of candy,'" I say.

Paine smiles, puts a hand to his lips.

"Sorry, Detective," he says. "I'm prone to metaphors. Writing habit. Her hair was down and wild, and she wore a Thai shirt with pretty buttons, and tight black pants. I could tell she had been crying. I had read about her before we met. Drugs and lovers. Nude photos on yachts. The crash and burns. She mentioned *Giselle*. She said it would bring her back. So many of them are like that, you know. Unable to accept the inevitable. The turning wheel."

"Like West Hollywood."

"Touché, Detective."

Hummingbirds buzz around the honeysuckle. Paine bites into another cookie, pours tea, crosses his legs, and points his face to the sun. It's still early. The sky is a yellowish blue of heat and smog that scrims the San Gabriels and stretches to the ocean, making the air bristle and tricking you into thinking rain will come. The backyard is quiet. It is never this quiet downtown, never a veil of silence, except maybe in a church or in my apartment around 3:00 a.m. But even then, a siren or a madman's screech can find you.

"Where did you go after?"

"We had two drinks," he says. "We agreed to meet again. She'd call me. She kissed me on the cheek and left. I watched her go out the door to the sidewalk. She stopped and talked to a tall man with curly black hair and a cello case—too big for a guitar, too small for a bass; I'm assuming it was a cello—strapped to his back."

"What did he look like?"

"I barely saw his profile. He turned toward her, and they were gone. Curly hair, as I said, a little long. He was tall, lean, but put together well. I immediately thought of Eastern Europe, if that means anything. The dark hair. That's really all, Detective. I didn't see his face."

I scribble in my notebook.

"What did you do after?"

"Ah, the alibi. The alibi is the currency of my trade." He laughs, pleased with himself, but he'd be easy to break. "I stayed for another drink and called my agent. She lives a few blocks from the NoMad, over near Grand. She wants me to do a book with Lindsay Lohan. That'd be a handful. We drank a bottle of wine, and I Lyfted home."

Paine stands, lights a joint, watches the birds.

"Did you guys find her diary, Detective?"

"Diary?"

"She told me she had kept a diary for years. It was all in there. 'My sins and sins done to me.' Said it just like that, in her accent. I can still hear the inflection when she said *sins*. She told me that if she trusted me, she'd let me read the diary, and we would tell her story."

"Didn't give you any hints?"

"She was circumspect," he says. "A tease. But anxious, you know, like someone with stolen money."

"Another metaphor."

"The dope makes them a bit sloppy. Want a hit?"

"I'm working."

Paine leads me back through the house. Lady Gaga's eyes follow me across the living room. She is lovely, dressed in retro elegance—another disguise—and I wonder, even if Paine ends up writing a book about her, will he get the truth? He opens the door. Sunlight fills the foyer hung with old Hollywood photographs. Louis B. Mayer. Charlie Chaplin. Valentino. Mary Pickford. All in black and white. Dark eyes and young faces. Chaplin mischievous, like a child playing in a bowler hat and tails, and Valentino, a busboy who became a sheikh, looking seductive and not at all like a man who would die of ulcers at thirty-one. They seem faint flames reaching out from burial grounds. They watch and soothe, and for a moment I feel suspended with them, insubstantial in the light. When I was a boy, my mother took me to old movies at the Jane Pickens Theater in Newport, Rhode Island. We were often the only two there. We'd laugh, the projector clicking and the screen silent, my mother putting her arm around me as if we were two conspirators on a winter's afternoon. It was in the years after my father died.

"My wall of ghosts, Detective," says Paine.

I slip out the door and walk to my car.

CHAPTER 8

"I feel like I'm waiting for the oracle to speak."

"Gather your men, Odysseus. We sail at dawn."

"Not what I was hoping for, Detective Carver," says Dr. Louis Markle, a department psychiatrist. "This could help, you know. You're too resistant."

"I don't have a problem."

"Ortiz thought it would be good. He feels you're not yourself since the Dylan Cross incident."

"The *incident*," I say. "Sounds ominous."

"You can categorize it any way you wish, but these things, these traumas—and you did experience trauma—stay with us. They don't just go away."

I'm fifteen minutes into my second required session with Dr. Markle, who, because of Ortiz, wants to rummage through my demons, which, like all of us, I have. But I'd prefer to keep them hidden in my subconscious, where they are comfortable and quiet at the moment. I tell this to Markle. He is not pleased. I don't want to be the bruised, tight-lipped (reticent) cop, but Dylan Cross is sacred to me—my mystery and riddle, the one who got away. I still feel her kiss, taste the wine on her lips, and see her standing at my apartment window on that long night when she explained it all and left. I knew even before then. I had seen the video of what they did to her. I understood her vengeance. And I knew why she left me a picture of her playing tennis from her Stanford days. She wanted me to know the prodigy she once was: fierce blue eyes locked on the ball, long muscles, the ease of her backhand. It was the best of her, a glimpse at near perfection, taken before they turned her into something else. She wanted me to know that, to see her as the world once intended. She's gone. Killed two men; let the third, the weakest one, live. She thought he was a victim, too, and perhaps, after all the blood she let, she allowed in a moment of mercy, though none had been granted her.

"It's been about a year," says Dr. Markle.

"Yes."

"She gave you a nasty blow to the head. Any residual problems with that? Vision? Pain?"

"Headaches for a while. Nothing now."

"Every time I read the case file, I'm amazed. She broke into your apartment, knocked you out, taped and tied you to a chair. Talked with you for hours. And left. She believed you were her confessor, that you would condone what she had done. You were her moral equation, Carver. If she could convince you that what she did was justified, she would be absolved."

"Christ, you're *enjoying* this," I say. "Three men raped her. It wasn't difficult to sympathize."

"Yes, but not condone. That's what you had to deal with. That's what she wanted from you. Absolution. She knew you, Detective.

She had hacked your laptop. She scrolled through all your secrets. She knew your history. She knew about your murdered father. How do you feel about that?"

"How would anyone feel? Exposed, violated."

What I don't tell Dr. Markle is that I didn't feel violated for long. After she disappeared, I felt she was carrying something of mine, pieces of me that mattered and that, otherwise, I would never have shared. There was peace in knowing that someone—a killer, yes, but someone—understood me without ever having to ask. She saw me unadorned. I don't know that I could arrest her now. I tell no one that. I like to believe that I'd cuff her and bring her in. I'm a good cop; I know my duty. What the hell good are you if you can't do the thing that defines you? Am I only a cop though? There is more to me: the piano in the night, a half-remembered saint, a line from Akhmatova at the prison walls, the sounds of Tashkent and Marrakesh, the calm beyond the breakwater when my father took me sailing in the year before he died. They must accumulate into something. The things Dylan knows. I like that she's out there, wandering with me inside her. Wherever she is, I'm sure she's drawing buildings. She's configuring the math of the architect, the beauty that can lift and slant from a line, like the church she designed in the high desert near Joshua Tree, where I drive on weekends and sit amid the stones, wondering whether she believed in God or whether it mattered, and whether she had the same feeling I do when twilight falls against the stained glass, and the old man sweeps and crosses himself with holy water before locking the doors for the night.

"She knows everything about you," says Dr, Markle, "and you know everything about her."

"If we were children, we'd be even."

"Are you worried she'll come back to . . ."

"She won't be back," I say.

"You're probably right. Why would she? The perfect crime."

"No. We know who she is."

"But from what I know about her—all from your case file, Detective—she's the kind who can stay lost."

"It'll be up to her. It's always been up to Dylan."

"You sound resigned."

"No, we'll get her one day."

A silent second passes.

"How's your mother?" he says. "I know she's been ill."

I must look startled.

"Ortiz told me," he says. "He's worried about you. He's a good man. Old school. Do you know he collects old maps? It takes him away from the job. We all need time away from what we do."

"I've seen his maps. He spread a few out in front of me once and said, 'Look, Carver, see this road here becomes this there and then this road. Roads make us.' He's philosophical about his maps."

I look out Markle's window to city hall. How many cops over the years have sat where I'm sitting, waiting for it to be over?

"My mother's mind is gone," I say. "She's forgotten my name, my voice. It's as though I never lived."

"How do you feel about that?"

I shoot him a look with a bullet in it.

"Stupid question," he says. "I didn't mean to degrade it. Just wanted to know how you're feeling. There's a lot balled up in you."

"I find that's true with everyone. You wouldn't want to unravel most people."

He smiles, looks at his clock, caps his pen. Another quiet second passes.

"We did okay today," says Markle.

"I feel much better."

He laughs, but there's no joy in it.

"Ortiz was right. You're a wiseass, Carver. I'll see you in a couple of weeks."

CHAPTER 9

The cellist streaks out of the Ace Hotel.

I take off after him, following his black, curly hair down Broadway, past old movie houses and Latino stores selling boom boxes and tuxedos. He's quick. Long strides, shoulders back, arms pumping, his bow flashing in his right hand like an arrow. Two uniforms in a cruiser try to cut him off on the sidewalk, but he slides across the hood and keeps going, block after block, crowds parting, stepping out of his way, shooting him the finger, as if a squall arose out of nowhere. And this being LA, no one is sure whether it's the real thing or a movie shoot. People are looking for cameras, stars, and helicopters, as if the Rock is going to sprint out of an alley and take down a stuntman standing in for Chris Pine, right before a car catches fire and a gunfight erupts on the corner of Sixth, just up from Clifton's, where a cartel deal is going down, and Al Pacino is waiting on makeup. It happens. Sirens wail, and three uniforms join the chase and—back to real life— the cellist is a good twenty yards ahead of me when he cuts into

Grand Central Market and disappears among tourists, hard hats, hipsters, lawyers, and office workers in lines for ice cream, *pupusas*, tacos, Thai noodles, and falafels. He passes the Golden Road beer counter and runs out of the market onto Hill, crossing the street near Angels Flight and racing up the stairs toward California Plaza. My legs are burning; my breath is squeezed. Someone yells, "Catch that fucker!" A young uniform breaks ahead of me, chasing the cellist up the stairs, which, even in this fury, smell like piss and dust. The uniform tackles the cellist, who slips free and bounces up but trips and tumbles down the stairs, stopping at my feet in a tangle of torn clothes, blood, and sweat. Everyone's clapping, thinking Al Pacino is going to shove me aside and get hysterical right before a director yells "Cut!" The world goes silent. Then everyone returns to their lunches and Instagrams, pleased with their LA moment, not exactly sure what happened but guessing it could be in a movie or a new series on Amazon.

"Let me cuff this motherfucker," says the quick uniform, L. Crenshaw. "Why you running like that, man? Look at my pants. Tore up my pants."

He clicks the cuffs tight, yanks the cellist to his feet, pushes him against the fence. A helicopter circles and flies away.

"What's this?"

"He's a cellist. It's his bow."

"Fuck that. See how he plays with it shoved up his ass."

L. Crenshaw winks and hands me the bow. His radio crackles.

"You're pretty fast, Detective," he says. "But you started slowing once you hit the steps."

"Thanks."

"When did he start running?"

"Ace Hotel."

"Damn," says L. Crenshaw, adrenaline still flowing. "Serious distance. Wouldn't think a cellist could do that shit."

We both look at the cellist. He stares back, unblinking, as though he's been here before. Or I'm imagining it, but I don't think so. He stays silent. Sweat drips from his black, curly hair; his nose is banged up; his neck is scraped. I sit, catch my breath, reach for my notebook, slide it back into my pocket, check my shield, gun, and wallet. Intact. I'd love a drink, but that's hours away. A breeze curls up the stairs, cooling me, blowing papers and cups, specking the air with grit. I stand.

"Take this guy, right?" says L. Crenshaw.

"Read him his rights, process him, and put him in a box. I'll be there soon."

"What about this bow thing? Could be a weapon."

"Made of horsehair."

"Who thinks up shit like that?"

"Take it."

I head back through the market and buy bottled water from a taco stand. I splash my face and feel a stillness inside, as if peeking out of the back end of a storm. Tranquil, almost. Content to have run like a madman over all those blocks and come away with a suspect. I walk to the station, take the elevator up, turn left, and see Ortiz ferreting toward me, file in his hand, tie loosened, glasses perched on his forehead.

"Hey, Carver, heard you took a little jog." He laughs. "Wish I could have been there."

"Don't mess with me."

"Looks like the Ace thing panned out."

I had gone to the hotel earlier after cross-referencing musicians' guilds, orchestras, opera, and chamber society websites for cellists.

I scrolled through bios and photos and came across Levon Sokolov, a Russian American born in West Hollywood. Thirty years old. Curly, black hair. Impressive résumé: Colburn School, the Royal College of Music in London, and the Moscow Conservatory. He performed with ensembles in Europe, returned to LA to play on movie soundtracks and occasionally with chamber quartets. Lately, he's been a cellist for hire, working weddings, brunches, a petting zoo, and a yoga retreat in the Palisades. He's had gaps in his bookings, but the asterisk stood out: he had performed with "the incomparable" Katrina Ivanovna. A wider Google search found he was playing at the Ace with a pianist and a violinist as part of a downtown cultural series. I took a seat in the back. He was tall, slender, and in shape. His tux was tailored, not rented, and an air of privilege came off him—a fallen grace, perhaps, but that may have been the score, his half-closed eyes and his gentleness with the bow, which moved across strings in slow, slanting angles, the music sounding like someone awakening in darkness to an unexpected frost. I approached him after the recital. He had a small fan club, mostly girls taking pictures, and an elegant woman with a tapered scarf and silver-black hair. She kissed him on the cheek, whispered in his ear, and left. I stepped closer, complimenting him, easing my way in, but when I identified myself, he bolted before the last syllable of *Carver* hit the air.

"Why did you run?" I say.

He looks at me from across the table. A Band-Aid covers the bridge of his nose. His neck is raw and bruised. His jacket is off; blood speckles his white shirt, which is torn at the right shoulder and sleeve. His hair is wild, and his dark eyes move over the box: table, three chairs, two-way mirror, cameras in corners, black scuffs kicked onto walls over the years by suspects who had run out of answers. Ortiz calls the box the ultimate personality test, the place where a man factors his equations, weighs his sins, calculates his truths and lies and the nuances in between, and makes a play for walking out the door and back into the night. Most don't know how doomed they are. Levon's eyes stop on the black scuffs—all their eyes do—and then scan on, rolling over the ceiling and settling on me.

"Why did you run?" I repeat.

He says nothing.

"You play well," I say. "The ending adagio was inventive."

He leans forward, puts his hands on the table. They are clean, unscarred—long, slender fingers drawing you in, tempting you to admire their symmetry. Antonio Garcia was right. Levon's hands, pale in their splendor, are attuned to their craft. He watches me. He knows their power. He slides them back and rests them in his lap.

"You're a musician?" he says.

"I play a little."

"What?"

"Piano."

"I Imm."

"Why did you run?"

"I didn't know who you were."

"I identified myself."

"Who knows who is who these days?" A slight crack in his voice.

"You're on edge," I say. "A man who runs from a cop, something's wrong there."

"People come up all the time. You never know."

"I don't believe you. You knew what I wanted."

He runs his hands through his hair, shakes his head.

"Tell me about Katrina Ivanovna."

"I want a lawyer," he says.

"We can do it that way."

I let him sit, think about it.

"Let me just ask you one question though," I say. "When did you last see her?"

"That night . . ."

"What night?"

"The night she died."

"How did you know it was the night she died?"

"Because the next day it was all over the web."

"Where did you see her?"

"I want a lawyer."

"You're doing fine," I say.

We sit in silence. I nod toward the mirror. Ortiz walks in with the cello and the bow. He leans them in the corner. Levon goes to them. He lifts the cello, runs a hand over it, plucks a string. He sets it down and examines the bow. He bends and slides it across the strings—a single forlorn, vanishing note. He sits.

"I've had it since I was a boy. It's a Stradivarius. My great-grandfather played it in Saint Petersburg. He died. My parents brought it when they came here during communist times." Ortiz leaves and closes the door. "I can't believe I left it behind." Tears edge at eyes, but he swallows and composes himself. "I don't know what I'd be without it."

"You played for Katrina?"

He bites his lip. I think he's going to ask for a lawyer again, and if he does, I'll have to relent.

"Just the two of us," he says. "In her loft. Only there. She loved the way I played. She'd take my hands and kiss them and say, 'Play it sweet.'"

"What did you play?"

"She didn't want ballet music. She liked David Lang and Bach. She'd dance slowly around me for hours. I think it took her away, you know? I'd get tired, but she wouldn't allow it. She'd yell at me to keep playing, and when she was done dancing, she'd collapse on the floor and cry. We'd drink vodka and do it again."

"Why so intense?"

"She said it was like floating away in the night. She said it with a Russian accent, and it fit, you know, the whole Russian dark-soul thing."

"She drank a lot, took a lot of pills."

"I don't know how she kept going."

He keeps looking at his cello, wanting to touch it again. He starts to stand. I shake my head no.

"She was hoping for a comeback," he says. "She kept telling me she wanted one more great performance."

"How did you meet?"

"Our parents had mutual friends back in Moscow."

"Were you lovers?"

He looks around the box, down at his hands.

"No. I only held her on the floor while she cried."

"You wanted to be a lover?"

"Anyone who knew her wanted to be her lover," he says. "She had a lot. She just wanted me to play."

"You saw her that night."

"She texted me. She was going to the NoMad to meet someone. She wanted me to come by. I had written a piece of music for her. She wanted to see it. I was with an old teacher of mine from Colburn. We were going to see a soprano he knew who was having a late dinner at the Eastern Building. We met Katrina in front of the NoMad. She walked a block with us. I gave her the score. She hugged me and walked toward Spring."

"Alone?"

"Yes."

"And you?"

"We went to dinner," he says.

"What's the teacher's name?"

"Michel Avanti."

I leave him alone in the box. Ortiz and I sit on the other side of the mirrored glass. We stare at Levon. It's like watching a still life. He sits, hands on table. Nothing moves. He must be exhausted. The tightness, nerves, scrapes, and bruises. His wondering about where things are headed. He pushes his chair back and goes to the cello and bow. He sits and plays. I don't recognize the piece. Perhaps it's the one he wrote for her. His eyes close.

"It's like listening to the past," says Ortiz.

"What do you mean?" I say.

"The things you don't get back."

We let Levon play for a while.

"He's grown but he's like a boy," says Ortiz. "How old is he?"

"Thirty," I say.

"Kinda in-between."

Levon pulls the bow slow; the music almost disappears, so faint, and then returns.

"First cellist we've had in the box," says Ortiz.

"We had that sax guy a while ago."

"He didn't play though. It all changes when they play."

"What are you thinking?" I say.

"I'm going to call Michel Avanti right now," says Ortiz, stepping into the hallway and leaving me alone with the music.

I'm tired. My joints are stiff. I feel my bruises too. It's late. It's always late in this job; day slides into night in a trick you never see. Levon plays. I think of *Madman Across the Water* and how long ago it was when I heard the name Levon for the first time, sung from my mother's record player, the small one she kept on her dresser and listened to when she couldn't sleep.

"Alibi's good," says Ortiz, poking his head in the door.

"What now?"

"Gotta cut him loose."

I step back into the box. Levon leans the cello against the wall.

"I think there's something you're not telling me," I say.

"I don't know anything. I played for her. We were friends."

"Did she talk about her family? Russia?"

"Never about her family," he says. "Two men came once. They spoke Russian. I speak a little from my time in Moscow, but not well. I was sitting with my cello. They looked at me. She took them outside to the hall. I went to the door and listened. I didn't hear much."

"Why would you listen?"

"I could see she was uncomfortable. When she came back in, she went to the window to see if they had gone. She stood there a long time."

"What did they . . ."

The door opens. Ortiz steps in with a man in a blue suit and a hurried, perturbed look about him, as if he'd been rousted from bed and thrown in a shower. He smells of talcum and cologne and has the manicured arrogance of a man who charges a thousand or more an hour and knows half the sins committed in Beverly Hills on any given night. His hair is black, his business card tastefully sparse. He moves right to Levon, holding a finger up, demanding silence. Levon, I can tell, has never seen Bernie Mathias, of Mathias, Epstein, and Raines, before.

"My client will say no more."

"He didn't call a lawyer."

"And yet, as you can see, Detective, here I am."

"We're not holding him."

"I know you're not."

"We'd like to talk to him a little more," I say. "He was just telling me—"

"We can arrange a time later. Right now, he's been through an ordeal. He's tired."

"He ran from the police."

"Are you charging him?"

Ortiz and I look at each other.

"No," I say.

"Collect your things, Levon."

He lifts his cello and bow and disappears out the door. I follow.

"Levon, you didn't tell me why you ran. Was it those men?"

"Detective, this is over," snaps Mathias. "Say nothing, Levon."

He and Levon step outside and walk toward a Mercedes. Levon, his torn white shirt bright in the night, looks a mess, disheveled and rushing across the plaza, laying his cello in the trunk, and slipping into the backseat—I can see inside—next to the elegant woman with the silver-black hair who whispered to him after the recital. The door closes. The car speeds away. Levon turns, his face, pressed against the window, disappearing in a light rain, the kind that falls in the sleeping hours and is gone by dawn.

CHAPTER 10

Lily Hernandez is curling barbells, listening to a global hip-hop mix, and looking at me the way she does when I'm late. I step through the half-open door of her Boyle Heights apartment, not far from the café, opened by two white artists, that set off the latest outrage among Latinos over gentrification and race in a neighborhood that was once the entry point for immigrants—Jews, Salvadorans, Mexicans—in a tiny, ever-changing nation in east LA. Rents are going up, accents changing. Neighborhood activists are throwing real shit at gallery walls and phoning death threats to bohemians and start-up geeks. The protesters want to keep these streets from changing beyond what they can afford, but you can't keep what you don't own the same. The city is fluid, stretching and blurring in changing patterns of pastel, stucco, brick, wood, stone, edging out from the center toward ocean and desert in endless languages. I mention this to Lily. She is not amused.

"Eighteen, nineteen, twenty." Her muscles tighten and shine. She drops the weights and starts sit-ups. She'll do a hundred a set, five sets, before stopping. Up and down like a piston. She's a cop with six years on the beat, a daughter and granddaughter of cops, living on the second floor of a wood-sided house painted white and trimmed in blue. I step to her back porch and look to a garden and a small arbor of grapes, tended by the man downstairs, a retired teacher in a beekeeper's hat. Rust blooms from the steeple cross at St. Mary's on the corner, and the air is hazy and heavy, rolling west toward the skyline in the late quiet of a Saturday morning.

"What is it with you and time, Carver?" says Lily, into her third set.

"The dead-ballerina case," I say, sitting in a porch chair by the door.

"The lost-body case," she says, not even panting.

"Not you too."

"Irresistible. Lose a body, Carver, you'll get shit."

"I didn't lose it."

"Your case. You own it. Besides, you'd be late no matter what."

"I'm here. I'm ready. Where today?"

"Short one. Five miles. Then a shower and later dinner."

"I'll cook."

"We'll see," she says. "You're a man of good intentions, anyway."

She hops up, her short, black hair is wet, as if she had stepped in from the rain.

"New shorts?" she says.

"You like them?"

"If they make you faster."

"I know you're in great shape, but I keep up."

"Get real."

We run to the corner, take a left on First Street, passing the taquería I like near Felipe Bagues Mortuary, and keep pressing west. Girls in dresses file up the stairs at the Bethesda Tabernacle, where a preacher stands in amber light, fans whirling overhead. Skateboards skim past, and a half-dressed mariachi band sits in the plaza shade beneath the Virgin of Guadalupe, her robes blue and green and flung with stars. A girl holds up a crying baby, a dog scatters doves. Lily pulls ahead. I find my pace. We fall into our rhythm, her looking back to keep the distance between us respectable. Two boys yell, "Lilyyyyy." A mother waves, and a skinny man in a cowboy hat and curled boots sprints off the sidewalk and runs ten yards with her before fading. Lily is refracting light—a cop, an Ironman competitor (she finished third in the women's division in Australia a few years ago), and the girl they watched grow up, making confession, taking communion, dancing at her quinceañera, burying her father, who was killed by gangbangers. We pass the mural of Lily's face, painted two years ago on a café wall by a boyfriend who refused to scrape it away after they broke up. It is gray and black, the color of ash, of something purified by fire: her black eyes drawing you in, a red bandanna around her neck, a rose in her hand, looking like a rebellious *campesina* from a long-ago war. Her old boyfriend says it's not Lily, but a dream of all the women below the border. Everyone knows it's a lie, and when people stroll by it, they smile, knowing the story.

Lily crosses Boyle Avenue and runs down the hill along the tram tracks. I cross Boyle a minute later, thinking about stopping for a latte at La Monarca Bakery but knowing that this wouldn't be a good idea. I see the speck of Lily turning right along the river. I pick up the pace, my breath coming easier. I feel a slight lift from the endorphins and I like the prospect of leaving it all behind for a few hours to roam the ragged backside of a city that these days is colored by wrens and graffiti and signs of stirring life. I run past tattooed men at the river's concrete edge, speaking Spanish, polishing car fins, listening to Selena, and drinking beer.

Lily knows about Dylan Cross. She was the uniform on duty at the murder scene of Dylan's second victim, Paul Jamieson, a smug, talented rapist architect. Lily studied the knife wound, walked around Jamieson's apartment. I was impressed by what she drew from the clues and the setting of things, knowing that a murder is its own universe. I told Ortiz she would make a good detective. We started working out together, and many nights I appear at her apartment, sitting on the back porch with her, drinking beer, talking. We listen to the sleeping street and feel the wind rush and die and pick up again, on and on out of the stillness. Lily sleeps with me, not out of love—at least, not yet—but out of necessity. We are loners with needs. We understand this about each other—the limitations, but the unexpected moments, too, when we catch each other's eyes and feel a kind of grace. We were raised in the church. We drifted from it, but we know the narrow space between the sacred and the profane, although that may be overstating it, but I don't think so. Childhood hymns play somewhere deep, and when Lily says, "Make love to me, Carver," it sounds like both plea and prayer.

Lily is doing push-ups and jumping jacks at a bend in the river. The sun is high and hot. We are drenched and happy. She kisses me on the cheek, and we walk toward the Arts District.

"Not too bad today, Carver."

"I felt a second wind at the end. How far?"

"Just over five."

"Felt farther," I say.

She rolls her eyes and skims the sweat from her hair.

"How was Europe?"

"Something I needed," I say.

"Did you see her?"

"She's gone."

"I don't think so, Carver. Won't be gone till you arrest her."

"Might not happen."

"Then she'll always be there," says Lily.

We trace railroad tracks and walk a hill, crossing the First Street bridge, a thread of water running beneath.

"How's your dead ballerina?"

"We don't have much. Made to look like an OD, but it's not. She kept a diary, and I think she wanted to tell a story."

"You get the diary?"

"Not yet," I say. "Her parents are well-connected Russians. Putin level—at least, the mother. Katrina had lots of affairs with men and women around the world. Did whatever she wanted because of her talent. An *enfant terrible*."

"Brought back some Europe, huh? Your accent's shit."

"Points for trying," I say. "It was strange to see her dead. I've seen a lot of stiffs, but something about her, I don't know. We're looking at a cellist who played for her. Maybe not the doer, but he knows something."

Lily slaps me on the back.

"That's right, Carver. I heard you chased a guy through town."

"That was him."

"I hope you caught a cellist, Carver. Please tell me a *cellist* didn't outrun you."

"He almost did. I had help."

Lily laughs, sly and innocent, the sound of a charmer.

"No more work talk," she says. "Let's wander and see what we see."

"Get coffee too."

"Then dinner."

"I'll cook."

"Carver, let's just grab tacos. It's Saturday."

We walk, our sweat drying, the day as it should be: a pause, a breath, hours of living the way you see other people live. The sun is high, the mountains hard behind us, the city luring us to its center. Lily jumps on my back, bites my ear, tells me she wants to be my partner when she makes detective, and I say I don't know, and she says, "With me, no one will ever outrun you." I've worked alone for so long. Ortiz indulges my "weird aloofness." I like to follow a case on my own, to let it seep into me, to go where I am pulled, chase the odd angle, not having to explain or get drawn into things that don't matter. My father, the boxer, was that way. Always on edge, a distant creature, running by himself for miles, turning up at all hours. My mother said it was like "keeping vigil for a Bedouin." I tell Lily maybe. We order lattes at Hauser & Wirth gallery and head back over the bridge to the taco place, where we buy a bagful and walk to Lily's and sit on her back porch, listening to Chavela Vargas, looking at the moon, getting up and showering together, me holding her in the water, nothing more, and then climbing into bed half-dry, Lily, the brilliance of her warmth under my arm, her body stretching along mine, both of us staring out the porch door to palms blowing in the black beneath the cross at St. Mary's.

CHAPTER 11

Cello between his legs, head drooped. The bow leans against him. He seems a sleeping puppet in a leather chair. His hands, scrubbed and mesmerizing, hang still at his sides. A syringe and a bent spoon lie beside him. A belt on the floor. Bare feet, tuxedo pants—the old kind that musicians wear to Armenian weddings in Glendale and bat mitzvahs in Hancock Park. Is this what a prodigy comes to? All those years of work and unforgiving stages in cities not stayed in for more than a night? I snap on gloves and kneel next to him, Levon—a cautionary tale in a West Hollywood apartment, a shambled place of sheet music, take-out cartons, and half-smoked joints. Beer bottles and an old Soviet flag with a frayed yellow star and sickle; a picture of Pushkin in the snow; a poster of Pussy Riot, scowling through pink ski masks, stomping in army boots, setting fire to a photograph of Putin.

Cello music lifts from a speaker. I read the playlist. "The Mustard Seed," by Icelandic composer Hildur Gudnadóttir. The

TV is muted to a TMC black-and-white Western. The curtain is open, the hills hard in the night. Lights streak from canyons. I search the arm with the rolled-up sleeve. A prick of dried blood. No other tracks. A single prick. His face is serene. Not like Katrina's, who saw death coming and resisted. Levon welcomed it; at least, that's what it looks like. It can be a comfort, I suppose, to go numb, to feel the warm flood, the gentle surge. That's too easy though. That didn't happen. But his face does not betray the crime. His black, curly hair has been cut short. He looks more like a boy than a man. A tall kid, a recruit, with a scalp of bristle. The white-suit guys are bagging things. Cameras flash. The apartment fills with strangers. The clatter of cabinets, drawers, gloved hands rifling through clothes. I step to the table by the window and pick up a scrap of paper scribbled with a few bars of music. I slip it into my pocket. Levon is part of me now, another too-soon ghost, the young man whom I chased through the city only a few days ago.

Buzz. I answer.

"It's him."

"Shit," says Ortiz. "What's it look like?"

"Staged overdose. Heroin, probably cut with fentanyl. He wasn't a user."

"Like the ballerina."

"Same MO," I say.

"She could have OD'd. She was pretty screwed up. Not on heroin, but on pills, right?"

"She was killed."

A pause. An exhalation.

"We don't have a body to prove it," says Ortiz.

"Better not lose this one."

"Don't talk like that, Carver. It's not helpful."

"The last we saw Levon was three nights ago when he left the station. I called his lawyer, that Mathias guy, the next day to set up an interview. He never got back to me. Then Levon disappears. His parents are not around either."

"That woman in the back seat of the lawyer's Mercedes. Who was she? His mother?"

"No. There's a picture of him with his parents online. It's not her."

"Why is someone killing Russians in LA?" says Ortiz.

"Technically, he's an American. He was born here. But is that a rhetorical question?"

"Fuck you. Find out."

Ortiz hangs up. I drive to Century City to see Bernie Mathias, Esq. I don't like Century City. It's a soulless glass dreamland of suits, agents, and bistros floating west of downtown and bordering Beverly Hills. A twentysomething secretary in a mint-colored dress and blown-out caramel highlights meets me in the lobby. She reminds me of my first crush in middle school: Alice Cheevely, who played Dorothy in our production of *The Wizard of Oz*. I was a flying monkey with a hose for a tail and wings sewn by my mother. Charlie Sheen bursts through the door, yelling at a man shuffling papers and scrolling iPhones. An actress from an Avengers movie is hitting on a vape and reading a script. A tall woman, an Iman knockoff with a Maltese peeking out from her purse, sweeps past with a chattering entourage. I feel as though I need new clothes. That's what happens to you this far west—a soul starts taking inventory.

Mathias's office is on the tenth floor. I thought it would have been higher. The secretary—Carly, originally from Santa Cruz, who sings at night in a retro punk band—hands me a cup of coffee and puts me in a conference room.

"Bernie will be with you soon," she says. "He's finishing up with a client."

She smiles and leaves. I reach for my notebook, jot down Bernie's name, time, place. I stare out the window and write what I see: terra-cotta rooftops, swimming pools, Fox Studios, Bentley, gardening truck, empty sidewalk, the sky north orange and gray with the latest brush fire. The winds are not yet dry, but there's been little rain, and the fires dance. A helicopter skims south; a thin layer of smog reaches to the ocean. I write like this often, a memoir of each case—not only the facts of the crime, but also what lies before me. I find comfort in placing myself in a scene. Shadow, time of day, the way light hits a window, the impermanence of the smallest detail, a flash and speck of gravity that holds it together in the mind's eye, like the man below stepping into a church with a bouquet of flowers.

Footsteps, indiscernible voices. The door opens.

"Sorry you had to wait, Detective," says Bernie. "Busy day."

"When did you last see Levon?"

"Get right to it. That's good. The night at police headquarters with you. I called him the next day after you phoned me, to set up the interview. He didn't pick up."

"He's dead."

Bernie sits.

"You don't seem surprised," I say.

"How?"

"Overdose."

"He was troubled."

"More likely someone troubled him. How did you get the call that night you came to the station?"

"Detective, there is a thing called attorney-client privilege."

"Not so much anymore, I think. There's only one of you now. We can do this here or downtown."

"That always sounds ominous in the movies. But, really, you know . . . oh, never mind."

He leans back. Takes a moment. Straightens his tie.

"His parents called me that night," says Bernie. "They were frantic. They came here from Moscow in the eighties. His father does something with software, and his mother is an interior designer. Not wealthy, but flush."

"Why you?"

"Our firm represented the father on a trade case a few years ago. I handle our criminal work."

I take notes. It slows things.

"Levon had been sliding," says Bernie. "The music thing wasn't working out. He was supposed to be first or second chair in a major orchestra by now. Lot of pressure on the kid. His parents had friends in Russia who knew Katrina Ivanovna's family. They were hoping for contacts, help. They reached out to everyone. Insular world. Like here. Levon ended up playing for Katrina. You know this already, Detective. I don't think I can help you out much more. Like I said, I got a call late at night."

"That's taking a lot in for a late-night call. What do you know about Katrina?"

"Only what I read. She's dead and lost." He smiles, quick as an arrow.

"Who was the woman, the tailored, classy one in the back seat when you picked up Levon?"

"Friend of the family's from Russia. In the music-dance world too. That's what she led me to believe. She didn't say much. I picked her up at the Peninsula before we drove downtown. Her name was Zhanna. Strong accent. You're right, though, Detective. She was lovely but terse, like an aristocrat from old Russia—at least, that's what I imagined. I wonder what it was like back then."

"Where is she now?" I say.

"That was the only time I saw her. I dropped her and Levon off at the hotel. It was before dawn."

Bernie relaxes. He's coy, but I don't think he knows much. He's a power in Hollywood—rescues celebrities from unseemly headlines and reputation-ending confessions—but Levon and Zhanna have taken him beyond his element. Trim and in his late fifties, Bernie has the money and reputation earned by those from the best schools back east who arrived here decades ago to reinvent themselves, surf, smoke a little dope, and find their niche among the privileged. Accountants, lawyers, fixers live off this town's sins and insecurities. They have homes in the hills with end tables of framed photographs of them at some benefit with Julia Roberts or Jennifer Lawrence. They are a class of men whose fathers read Dreiser and Fitzgerald and taught their sons that life is a shifting bargain between wonder and treachery.

Bernie stands and walks to the window.

"You like these long pauses, don't you?" he says. "It makes people want to fill the space. People don't like unfilled space. I'm curious. Do you get a lot of confessions?"

"Never enough."

"I suppose not." He laughs. "I tell my clients, never talk. A misplaced word, thinking you're smarter than the guys with the questions—that's poison. Just sit there and don't fill the space."

"Seems like you want to fill it."

"I want to be helpful. I feel bad for the kid."

"Why did Levon run from me after the recital?"

"You know why. He told you before I got there."

"The two Russian men—at least, they *spoke* Russian—who came to Katrina's apartment. They spooked her."

"He started to talk about it in the car, but Zhanna cut him off. She said something in Russian. I think it was, anyway. It was curt, you know. She saw me glancing back in the rearview and said in English that she didn't think it rained in Los Angeles, and that her friends back home would be disappointed and surprised when she told them." He shakes his head. "She wasn't good at small talk, but she knew her power, if you know what I mean. She could make a lot of money in this town. Levon didn't say anything. He looked out the window like a scolded child. We got to the Peninsula. They got out. I drove away."

"What about his parents?"

"Never met them," he says. "I only talked to his father when I got the call. I phoned later, but no answer. I sent someone to their home, but they were gone. As you can see, Detective, I was involved in this matter for about three hours, just to get a kid out of your box." He walks from the window and sits back down. "I got a call early this morning from Zhanna. She said my services are no longer needed."

"Did you get a number?"

"Came across as unknown."

"You worried?"

"Different kind of people than what I'm used to. What do you think?"

"I'd watch myself," I say.

"That's reassuring."

He walks to a cabinet in the corner, pulls out a bottle and two glasses. He sits beside me and tells me to turn my chair toward the window.

"End of the day," he says. "Best show in town."

He pours.

"Matthew McConaughey's label. He bought into a bourbon distillery in Kentucky. Authentic, you know. All the stars want a liquor brand these days. George has his tequila. Made a billion on it. Matthew and the others are trying to cash in too. You can only sell so much coffee and cologne. Now it's booze. Pretty soon it'll be weed. Cheech is already marketing hydroponic dope."

"I'm on duty."

"The sun's setting, Detective. Have a drink."

I take the glass.

"I read about you," he says. "An old story from the *Times*. You're from Rhode Island. I'm from Connecticut. Groton. How'd we get here?" He sips. "Look at it, Detective. Never tire of it. Fire in the sky, man. Never the same, you know. A second is added or taken every day, every one a new creation. You ever think about that?"

"I do."

"I think about it all the time. The balance. Calibration. It reminds of my imperfections, but in a good way, you know, a way that says, *it's okay. We're human.*" He breathes out, loosens his tie. "'Our worth is in understanding the majesty before us.' A lawyer actually said that in a murder case. No shit. When I was starting out, I used to sit in on trials. This lawyer was the best. Gavin McEdwards. A master of restrained flourish, you know. He said it in a closing argument. He wanted to elevate the victim. To make the jury see her even though she wasn't there. It was a great closing." He runs a hand through his hair. Sips. "I think of all kinds of things when the sun goes down."

He pours us a little more.

"What's the best closing you ever heard?" he asks.

The bourbon warms. I feel oddly content.

"Death penalty case," I say. "The perp was guilty every kind of way. But he was young. He was scared and didn't look like he could do what he did. The defense attorney gets up, walks back and forth in front of the jury. Back and forth, slow. Seconds go by. Minutes. He wants the jury to see his client—you know, really see him. The judge gets ready to say something. But the lawyer keeps pacing. You could hear everything. The sounds you never hear. Echoes out in the hallway. The creak of the bailiff's belt, shuffling shoes. A breath. Then the lawyer says, real soft, 'Have mercy.' It was brilliant. He knew he lost the case but he was trying to save a life."

"What happened?"

"What do you think?"

Bernie finishes his bourbon, sets the glass on the table. He leans forward. I pocket my notebook.

"We never had this conversation, right?" he says.

"What conversation?"

He laughs. We sit in silence and watch the night slip in from the east.

CHAPTER 12

The Little Easy is nearly empty. Lenny is reading the *Times* on the bar. A hipster and his tattooed, silver-ringed, short-skirted girlfriend are kissing in the corner over a bottle of Shiraz and a plate of sliders. I sit. Lenny pours without taking his eyes off the paper. Dinah Washington is playing low. I see myself in the mirror behind the bar. At this distance, I don't look so tired, but I feel it. A siren pierces and passes. I pull out my notebook and riffle through pages. Dinah Washington fades into the funk, rasp sex of Betty Davis—Lenny's favorite singer, reminding him of his club-hopping youth in New York—who hides a razor's edge in every seduction.

"I don't understand Trump," says Lenny, holding up a headline about Russians and Mueller. "Really, I don't. I try, but Jesus."

"I told you not to."

"But he's there all the time, fucking things up. The Russians have him, Sam. Putin owns him. Might never be proved, but it's true."

I cut him a look.

"All right," he says, "no politics." He wipes the bar. "Now that we're changing topics, what's up with the ballerina?"

"Lenny . . ."

"Still lost, I guess."

"Lenny."

He pours me another, loosens his bow tie, rolls up the sleeves of his white shirt. It's near closing. How many nights have I watched Lenny cash out, take stock, and lock up? The soft rattle of glasses; the smoothing of bills, stacked by denomination; the whisk of a broom; and the slow dance of Lenny's rag over oak. Back when I smoked, we'd share a cigarette out front as the last of the homeless wandered past us to boxes and tents over on Main and down toward San Pedro.

"Guy came in the other day. Stoned. I mean, Sam, this guy was three-sheets blurry," says Lenny. "Sat over there, half asleep, real pleasant buzz on his face, as if he had seen the divine. You know the look. Like an after-sex look but more relaxed."

"You have a girlfriend?"

"No. But I remember sex. Anyway, I'm thinking I should start smoking again. Just a little every now and then. Take the edge off. It's legal now, so there'd be no problem with my previous conviction. Who would remember anyway, right? I did my time way back. What do you think?"

"Why not?"

"My thoughts too."

"How long have you been out here, Lenny?"

"Decades."

"You miss New York?"

"I get back now and then," he says.

"A lot of New Yorkers moving this way."

"Guy came in the other day from Flatbush. Thick accent. I thought he was an extra."

The door opens. A breeze runs through. Stefan Petrovic appears in the mirror next to me.

"You'd be easy to kill, Sam," says Stefan, wrapping his arm around me and sliding onto a stool. "Here every night."

"Not every, just most. You drinking?"

"Bourbon, please."

Lenny pours and glides to the end of the bar with his paper.

"What is it with bourbon?" I say.

"It's hip," says Stefan. "Everybody likes."

He lifts his glass. Looks around. Checks the mirror, swivels back his shoulders, combs a hand through his black hair. He looks as if he just came from a workout and a steam. His suit, imported from an Argentine tailor he met in a card game in Milan, hangs sleek and fine. Chin strong, eyes deep set, he has the air of a minor prince, a man of charm who, at any minute, could disappear with your wallet, car keys, and wife.

"Some fires up your way," I say.

"I hope not like last year. Malibu was hell last year, Sam. Almost lost my house."

"End-of-days sky. Nature is beautiful in her fury."

"You drunk?"

"Nearly. You here to kill me?"

Stefan points a finger gun at me and laughs.

"No, I have news for you. I spoke to a friend in Russia. He told me things about your ballerina. Could be interesting."

"What kind of things?"

"Can't say yet. Complicated. Maybe soon you make a trip with me."

"Where?"

"Somewhere not close."

"That's it?" I say.

"For now."

Stefan looks at me, winks, waves to Lenny for another bourbon. I know not to push Stefan. After his parents were killed in Yugoslavia, he was shipped to Belgrade to live with his grandfather, Goran, a mandolin player who trafficked cigarettes and currencies and kept a big flat off the main square near the opera house, where he was visited nightly by a Macedonian soprano with legal problems who offered private arias in exchange for deutsche marks and a fake passport. This is the story Stefan tells. He has many such tales, and it is hard to know what is true and what is not. He's a miniaturist. No detail or bit of color is too small or dismissive. I like that about him. People to him are recurring characters in real and make-believe stories never finished. I know the soprano wore fake diamonds, drank champagne, wept at Verdi, washed her stockings in the sink, and kept in her purse a small pistol that she once fired at a director. But I don't know whether she got her passport and set alight for someplace new. When I ask him about her, he says, "Oh, yes, hers was an amusing end."

Goran took Stefan on smuggling trips across a disintegrating Yugoslavia. They wandered war ruins at night, and his grandfather told him, "Someone must put it back together but also create something new." When Stefan was fourteen, Goran sent him to a French boarding school and later enrolled him at the Sorbonne, where Stefan studied finance, leaving Paris from time to time to join his grandfather, who by then traveled with an entourage that was heisting diamonds in Brussels, and paintings from German castles. "I am giving you two worlds," said Goran. "One may not work out, so you will have the other. We in the Balkans know this. It is our blood."

Stefan spent years running guns but went straight—allegedly—when he started in finance and "growing money for people"—mostly deals in Europe and Asia. "Sam," he told me once, "everybody is a crook, but you can make more money with the legal crooks." There's much I don't know, much I don't ask, about Stefan. Azadeh Nazari warns me about him. "The FBI has a file open on the guy, Carver," Azadeh told me one afternoon at the Water Grill when Stefan strolled past with a Chinese developer. "Be careful." I said, "He helped me out on a case." "Because it benefited him," she said. The case involved a banker who had hired an assassin to stage a burglary and kill his wife. Not too smart for a smart guy. A friend of a friend of Stefan's knew the hit man. Stefan walked into the Little Easy one night and slipped me the killer's name. "I don't like this banker," Stefan said. "This is good for you and me. Check the security cameras on the Santa Monica Promenade. Money exchanged there. Stupid, huh?" He laughed and walked out. The banker had used a burner phone to call the killer, but the killer recorded their conversations for eternal blackmail.

"Two more, please," says Stefan.

Lenny pours.

"I watched Katrina on YouTube," says Stefan. "Unbelievable, really. Someone put together clips of her best performances. Like greatest hits. You can see her age. Just a little. YouTube is like that. When you watch it like that, time makes life short, you know, like all you have is a few minutes. Even the best people can be turned into a few minutes. It's kind of sad, don't you think?" He sighs. "I still remember her from the Weinstein party. I told you, right?"

"Yes."

"You find out any more about her? She had many lovers, I think."

"We're looking into everything. No good leads yet."

"Must have something."

"No."

"Mmmm."

"Why 'mmmm'?"

He looks at me in the mirror, then away.

"She danced at the party slow and lost, like child," he says. "This is what I thought."

"You think this person you know can help?"

"We'll see. You look tired."

"A little."

Stefan sips.

"Tell me about your father," he says.

"I don't want to talk about that now. You know the story."

"Never found them, did they?"

"No."

"Was he a good boxer?"

"He won more than he lost," I say.

"But crazy, right? A little off."

"Yes. He was beaten to death in an alley."

"You were a boy."

"Yes."

"Your first case."

"I was a little young."

"You know what I mean."

"Never solved. They got away."

My long-dead father intrigues Stefan. The story reminds him of Yugoslavia—a bit of glamour and brutality that passed into history. He quizzes me sometimes on how my father looked in the morgue: battered, cut hands, face almost unrecognizable, pale-moon skin; the cool of the room, the scent of him, like acid and soap, and then the sheet falling back over him, and the sound of the tray rolling, the little door clicking shut. Stefan told me once that he and I were "two bruises." He likes that analogy of sharing damage: murdered parents, and my mother, who I am a stranger to, gazing out a window in Boston. When I first told Stefan about my father, he enfolded me in his arms, and I felt how a refugee must feel when the burden of atrocity is lifted for a moment.

"You driving back to Malibu?"

"Why not?" he says.

"You didn't have too much?"

"I am part Serb, Sam. There is never too much."

He stands, throws money on the bar. A big tip for Lenny. He steps behind me, puts his hands on my shoulders. We look at ourselves in the mirror. These gestures are important intimacies for Stefan. In the Balkans, he once told me, it was common for men and boys to touch, to be unafraid of affection, to hear a man's breath. "You know, Sam, they might slit your throat two hours later, but in that second, you are their brother. American men don't do this, I have noticed." He pulls his hands away and disappears from the mirror. The door opens.

"Call me about this trip," I say.

"Soon."

The door closes. The hipster lovers pay their bill. It's Lenny and me. He flips to the sports pages. I walk to the upright piano and play, notes here and there, no structure, meandering like a voice looking for grammar. I close my eyes and see Katrina, as Stefan said, dancing and aging, every spin a year. I leave her suspended there and drift to a poor rendition of Art Tatum's "Someone to

Watch Over Me." I know the lines and pauses, the way the notes slide, shimmy, and run, but they are in my head, not my hands. I can't gather them. I shift to another string of notes and see Dylan Cross. I ride them out a bit but don't linger. I pull my hands back from the keys, and she is gone. I go to the bar, collect my notebook and pencil, and head for the door, feeling an ache in my legs and remembering Levon.

"Hey!" yells Lenny. "Next time you see me, I might be a tad stoned."

CHAPTER 13

It's raining. I'm watching the streets shine black and reading Hemingway's *A Moveable Feast*, which I first read twenty years ago at Berkeley. I bought a copy the other day at the Last Book Store, on Fifth. The pages are stained with coffee and wine, and the cover—a sketch of a bridge over the Seine—is ripped and worn. The scent of age and dust fills me. A plane ticket and a sticky note fall out. The note has no name, message, or time, just a careless ink spiral in the corner. The name on the ticket is A. Riordan—no hint whether man or woman—who left Beirut on August 30 (no year) at 8:50 a.m. Bare clues to a mystery. I hold the evidence to the window and wonder about A. Riordan, their life, what they did, who called while they were out, and why the trip to London. I imagine A. Riordan was or may still be an archaeologist or a spy, someone solitary, clever. It's a composite, a guess from traces left in fading numerals and letters. How did the book get to America? Into the Last Book Store? On that shelf? How many hands and lives had it passed through? I know more about A. Riordan than

I do about whoever killed Katrina and Levon. Nothing to hold to the window. No scrap or trace of the doer, just an excess of drugs in the bloodstreams of unfortunate lives. I turn a page and read: Paris, cold and damp, bars, skiing, whiskey, horse races, poverty, betrayal, a young man writing stories far from home. And this sentence: "All things truly wicked start from an innocence." Hemingway would have made a good cop.

I put the book aside and call Ortiz.

"Anything?"

"No," he says.

"Think about what we have."

"How about what we don't have. A body. Still nothing on who took it. Our guys came up clean. I don't know what we've missed. We'll have to go further back in employment records. One of those guys knew the layout of the morgue." Ortiz sighs. "At least, we have Levon's body. Enough heroin and fentanyl to kill a small army. But let's go on the theory he wasn't a user. We have no evidence anyone was there. No prints, motive. You know what the DA's office will say: suicide or a rookie mistake by a novice junkie. Next."

"They were both killed."

"He says. How about some tangibles?"

"'Tangibles'? Have you been watching PBS again?"

"Screw you," says Ortiz. "What are you doing?"

"Reading Hemingway."

"Christ."

"You?"

"Fishing. We're at the pier in Manhattan Beach."

"You don't strike me as an angler. Hemingway fished, you know."

"I fished when I was a kid. My dad used to take us on a boat off Long Beach. Thought I'd try it again. It's supposed to relax you."

"Isn't it raining?"

"Drizzle."

"Catch anything?"

"Nibbles and stolen bait." Wind in the phone. "Hang on."

I hear voices, the whine of a line being cast, caws.

"Fucking seagulls," says Ortiz. "I'm back. Hey, Carver, we gotta find Katrina's diary and that woman—what was her name?—the one who picked up Levon that night."

"Zhanna Smirnov. That's the name she checked in with at the Peninsula. She checked out the morning after we released Levon. What about the Russian consulate? Ask them about her."

"I will. They call every day wanting updates. I kicked them to the chief's office, but I'll check her name with them. Do we know for certain she's a Russian citizen?"

"We don't. I'm going back to Katrina's neighbor. Maybe he knows about the diary."

"The costume designer guy?"

"Yes."

"I gotta go. Some asshole's tangled in my line."

Click.

Sunday afternoon. Gray. I use A. Riordan's plane ticket as a bookmark. I make coffee, read my notes. I lift Katrina's locket from my sacred inlaid box of stolen things. I lay it by the notebook and pencil, hoping something will connect, a strand however thin. Nothing. I put it back in the box near the other possessions: The ring from the kid who was running his mouth in a barbershop over on Tenth. Kid wouldn't sit still. Wriggling in the chair, yapping. The barber snapped, pulled a .38 out of the scissor drawer. "I just wanted to shut that fucking boy up." The rosary from Maria, hit coming out of church by a stray marked for someone else. She bled out on stairs bright with veils and first-communion dresses. That's how lives end. Weeping, a priest's vestments in the wind. You're there, unaware, and suddenly the warmth of you is gone. It all goes still. I close the box. I run a bath, pour a drink, and soak; close my eyes as if I were floating in the sea, maybe off Lisbon or somewhere like that, somewhere in memory. Not Rhode Island, though—the water is cold there and the currents swift. I dry and call Maggie.

"It's good to hear your voice, Sam. How are you?"

"Fine. How are you guys?"

"Your mother's in her room. Looking out the window. Like always."

"At the birds."

"Counting."

"Has it gotten worse since I was there?"

"Her body is more curled. She's too thin but won't eat. She doesn't talk anymore, Sam. Just looks. She doesn't know me most days. I'm her sister. I'm here with her every day, but she doesn't know me. I've lost her. They told us."

"Maybe it's time . . ."

"Not that, Sam. Never that. She's staying with me. I can handle it. There's a girl a few streets over. I don't think you met her. She's a nurse. Works over at St. Catherine's. She comes by twice a week and helps me bathe your mom. She's good company. She's not married. We sit and have a beer after in the kitchen. Her name's Susan. She's been a godsend."

"It's good you're getting a little help. You need it, Maggie."

"Susan and I talk about all kinds of things. She's very smart.

We both like Nat Geo. In my day, it was National Geographic, but now it's Nat Geo. They have a Twitter thing."

"I'll come soon, and we'll talk and have a beer."

"I'd like that, Sam."

I can imagine Maggie in her kitchen, her long, gray hippie hair. The rebel my mother wasn't.

"You want me to put the phone to her ear?"

"Please."

"Hang on. Let me go upstairs."

I follow her in my mind. Through the living room, past the lace over the couch and the nautical map of Nantucket; past pictures of dead relatives, the most recent in color, the older ones, like my great-grandfather Mel, who worked all his life in a spindle factory, looking out half amused in fading black-and-white; up the stairs—twelve of them; the eighth one creaks—turning left down the hall to my mother's room, through the door (I oiled the hinges on my last trip) and to the window where she sits wrapped in a blanket.

"Okay, Sam. Here she is."

A silence I alone must fill.

"Hi, Mom. It's Sam. Your son."

I hear a single long breath. I tell her I'll be there soon. I promise. I talk about our trips to the beach when I was a boy and how she watched me from the shore. On the way home, we'd stop for fried clams at a shack along the rocks, and it was just the two of us—my father then was running and punching air, a boxer with his own rhythms—and after we ate, we'd drive home, our skin red and warm, and we'd change and walk down the street for ice cream. It was a time before I knew I would have a life beyond her. She would tell stories as we walked home in the dark, wondering if my father would be there, the wild man she loved, the only one who could tip him straight. For a time. She doesn't know me now, but maybe she remembers far-back things. The doctor told Maggie and me that pieces of the past live inside, rising, flashing, unexpected. I call every week, and we go through time. She was a teacher. She wrote short stories, had a few of them published. She drove an old Saab, loved Joni Mitchell and Tim Buckley, went to church when no one was there, and lit all the candles and sat in the light against the statues and Stations of the Cross. I was her only child.

"Hi, it's Maggie."

"Any response?"

"Almost a smile. That's something. I think she's tired."

"I should come back," I say.

"You were just here before you went to Europe. No need, Sam. Really, I'll let you know when you need to come. How was your trip?"

"I had to get away."

"I know you did."

"It was good, Maggie."

"I'm glad," she says. "What are you working on now?"

"We have a dead ballerina."

"Is that yours? I saw it on the news. Terrible. And the body disappearing. What a shame. Who takes a body? She was Russian, right?"

"Yes."

Maggie reads crime novels. She's full of tips and theories. She follows all my cases.

"I still wonder where Dylan Cross is hiding," she says. "Somewhere with a lot of pretty architecture, I'll bet." She takes a breath. "I know you don't like to hear this, Sam, but I'm glad she got away."

"You sound like Ortiz. I'll find her one day."

"But what will happen when you do?" Maggie asks.

I don't answer. We talk about politics and Trump until Maggie, who has marched against just about everything, grows exasperated. "The man drives me to fits, Sam." She tells me about the cold winds up the coast, and the hard rains that have fallen over the past two days, and the fog that settles thick in the dawn. I can see her sitting on the bed next to my mother, the TV downstairs muted and turned to the Weather Channel, the candle lit by the back door, near the basket where she keeps mass cards for dead friends. The radio in the kitchen tuned low to NPR. I know that a sliver of air slides through a crack in the window—I should have replaced it on my last visit—blowing over the sink, through white linen curtains yellowed by years of sun and smoke. The curtains will be gone one day, and the house will be passed to others, its secrets lost. We say goodbye.

CHAPTER 14

The elevator opens on the fifth floor. The hallway is polished, light slants through the window at the end, and the ceiling is painted with angels, horses, clouds, and creatures from a madman's fairy tale.

"Aren't they lovely?" says Antonio Garcia. "A muralist used to live here. He did a lot of meth. Couldn't sleep at night, and in the morning, there'd be something glorious. He moved away about a year ago to Denver, I think. This is his legacy." Garcia opens his door. "Detective, when will they take that yellow tape away from Katrina's apartment? It's very disturbing to be reminded every day."

"It's still a crime scene," I say.

"Crime?"

"Open investigation."

Mannequins in various states of dress are scattered about the loft. They are posed as if at a cocktail party, lingering by the window in 1950s-era gabardine suits and hats, swing dresses, high heels, and pearls, all suggesting Vitalis sheen and postwar confidence. Boxes overflow with scarves, beads, fabrics, scissors, spools, sequins, and other things that glitter. Dress patterns hang on the walls, and a skeleton ("that's Luis") fastened to a hat rack stands in the corner beneath reproductions of anatomical drawings by Michelangelo.

"You can't design clothes, Detective, without knowing bones and tendons and how we're put together."

Garcia unbinds his ponytail; black hair falls past his shoulders. He is not as slight or thin as I remember. I don't remember the angels on the hallway ceiling, either, but I was tired, just in from Europe, on that morning he found Katrina. Garcia cuts a lemon, pours tequila, lights a votive candle ("for Katrina's memory") and a cigarette. He holds a glass up.

"You're on duty, I suppose," he says.

I nod. He puts it down. We sit in two brocaded, French-style salon chairs, a Turkish carpet and a table ("it's from Damascus") between us. Behind him hang a scarlet-and-black vampire cape ("from a crazy Chilean movie"), a nun's crisp, white habit ("some Belgium art-house film"), and, as if completing a triptych, a black-and-white poster of Katrina—on toes, in tights, back straight, arms out, head like a statue. She is crystalline and luminous, burning out like an apparition. Her eyes and mouth betray nothing except youth. The photo must have been taken years ago, probably after a rehearsal, when all the other dancers filed away and she was alone, still, a girl contemplating flight. "She's beautiful," says Garcia, getting up and walking toward her. "Look at these lines, Detective." He traces her with a finger. "Science, math, and beauty conspiring in one body. That's as close to the sublime as we get. Look, she signed it for me. 'To Antonio, fellow traveler.'"

He wipes his eyes and downs another tequila. He walks among the mannequins, pleasantly buzzed, theatrical.

"Don't mind the mess, Detective. It's for a film. A Dean Martin biopic." He bites a lemon. "It would have been lovely to live back then, don't you think? The jazz. The big cars. The thought that it would never end. All the new money and big houses. It always ends, though, doesn't it?"

"By the time we realize it, it's too late."

"Ah, you're a romantic."

"I'm a cop."

"I've heard they can be."

He sits. A cat jumps on his lap.

"Nishka," he says, "making mischief."

"Is that . . ."

"Yes, Katrina's cat. What could I do? I had to take him in."

"I'd like to go over a few things."

I reach for my notebook, hand him a picture of Levon. Garcia holds it up for a long time. I can see the pricks and calluses on his fingers. No wonder he had noticed Levon's hands— he called them hypnotic—when I interviewed him that day. Garcia's hands have no elegance or grace, but, as with Levon's, beauty comes from them.

"He was the one who played for Katrina," he says. "That's him. I'm certain. Did you find him?"

"He's dead."

"What do you mean, 'dead'?"

"Looks like an overdose, but we don't know."

He shoos away the cat and puts the picture in his lap. He lifts it again, stares at it, hands it back to me.

"What's going on, Detective?"

"We don't know. He told us he played for her. Their parents had mutual friends in Russia. They put them together."

"Were they lovers?"

"He said not. He said that one day two men came to the loft. They spoke Russian and seemed to frighten her. You ever see anyone like that?"

"Men would come and go, Detective. Katrina never wanted to be alone." He gets up and lingers between two mannequins, as if eavesdropping on a conversation. "She would knock on my door late at night, with a bottle. We would put on whatever costumes I was making and act out skits. Both of us drunk. She ripped that cape from the wall once and whirled around the room and disappeared out the door and down the hall. I caught up with her on the sidewalk. She wrapped the cape tightly around her. 'I am the night,' she said. 'Come to me.' I coaxed her back inside. The only times I saw her quiet and calm were when he played cello for her."

"Any threats by other men? Anything you might have heard in passing. Did she ever talk about being scared?"

"Not that I ever saw or heard," he says.

"Did a woman ever come here? Midfifties, refined, silver-black hair—"

"Cut just above the shoulders. Exquisite dresser. Lovely lines. Yes, I saw her occasionally. I passed her and Katrina in the hall a few days before Katrina died. She didn't introduce us, but the woman—I assumed she was a relative or one of her managers—had an accent. They changed from English to Russian when they went by. I think it was Russian, maybe Armenian. There are so many of them now. Armenians. Is she involved?"

"We're looking at every lead," I say. "You think you could describe her to a sketch artist?"

He scoffs. "I can do it myself."

He walks to a drawer and pulls out a pad and pencil. He stands at the kitchen island. His hand moves smooth and fast. Gray blurs sharpen into features: nose, lips, eyes, slant of hair across the forehead; a face taking shape. Slow, sensual, looking up, well-bred, moneyed—the kind of woman you would meet for drinks in a bar on a rainy night in Warsaw or Prague. I can imagine her voice, suave condescension, and a laugh that goes through you. It is the face I saw in the back of Bernie Mathias's Mercedes when they drove Levon away.

"That's her," says Garcia. "What did you say her name was?"

"I didn't. But it's Zhanna Smirnov. You got all that from glimpsing her a few times?"

"Look at her. Hard to forget. The soul is out."

"What?"

"The man who taught me to draw when I was a child used to tell me, 'Bring the soul out.'"

He looks at the sketch and back to me.

"Did Katrina ever mention a diary?" I say.

"She wrote all the time in little red-bound books. Small ones you slip into a pocket. I assumed they were diaries. She told me once, in her wonderful accent, 'Antonio, I am making memoir.'"

"Did she give you any details?"

"Not many. I guessed it was about her career. She had them around the apartment. I never touched them."

"They weren't there when she died. Did you see them? You were the one who found her."

"I didn't notice anything that day except her body."

"You didn't take them?"

"I would never."

"Have to ask. They were there. Now they're gone."

We sit in silence. Garcia ties his hair in a ponytail, releases it, ties it again. He stops a tear before it falls.

"This whole thing has taken me apart, Detective. Why is this happening? When I go out now, I crack the door first and look to make sure no one is in the hallway. I don't sleep well. I hear sounds and think about poor Katrina." He rips the page out of the sketch pad and hands it to me. "I thought she OD'd. Now, you're telling me Levon is dead, and her apartment is a crime scene. Maybe whoever is doing this thinks *I* know something. I was her friend."

"What do you know?"

"I've told you all I know."

"Have you? I don't get that sense."

"What else could I possibly know?"

"That's what I'm wondering," I say.

"Well . . ."

"Why you fidgeting?"

"It's just a pencil," he says.

"Seems like fidgeting."

"Is this what they teach you in cop school?"

"Something like this."

"Should I be worried?"

"Not if you're telling the truth."

"I mean, about somebody coming and, you know."

"I don't think so. But stick around. I may have more questions."

I fold the drawing into my jacket pocket. I pass the mannequins and say goodbye to Garcia. The door clicks behind me. I look up at the angels and creatures on the ceiling and wonder how someone finds a face on a blank page. I get into the elevator, the old, slow kind with the wrought iron door you have to close and open by hand. I feel suspended in another time. I descend, thinking of Nishka the cat, the nun's habit, Garcia's cut lemons, and Katrina, young and at the brink of all that would come, looking out from her poster. Garcia never asked about her body. How it could have been stolen. I write that in my notebook. I step on the sidewalk, crossing Spring and glancing up at Katrina's big windows, imagining her dancing while Levon played.

CHAPTER 15

"Zhanna Smirnov is an alias."

"One of many, I bet."

"Yes."

"Who is she?"

"The FBI doesn't know," says Azadeh Nazari. "We think she was involved in the Russian hacking of our elections. Traveled back and forth a lot in 2015 and '16 on multiple passports. We couldn't tie anything to her, though. CIA says she spent time in Ukraine. They won't give us much more. Real pricks, those guys. Don't know if they know a lot or nothing. Homeland Security same." Azadeh sips iced tea on the porch of her craftsman in South Pasadena. Her wife, Elsa, gardens near the sidewalk. "She definitely has Kremlin buddies. Same circles as Katrina's mother."

"So?"

"That's all I have. She obviously knew Katrina. Levon too."

"Can we . . ."

"No, Carver, she's gone. Unless she comes back, you can't touch her. You don't really have much either."

"Levon's parents are still missing," I say. "You heard anything?"

"They haven't left the country."

"Unless . . ."

"Fake passports, maybe. Or . . ."

"That's what I'm thinking."

"The 'or' is always troubling."

"The 'or' is never good."

"More pressing for you though. Have you found Katrina's body?"

"No."

"Well . . ."

"Well, what?"

"Whole thing dissolves on you," she says. "No body, no crime."

"We *had* a body."

She smiles, shakes her head.

"What?" I say.

"I can hear the judge laughing."

I stand in the shade at the edge of the porch, listening to a lawn mower, and two kids pedaling past on bikes.

"You like it up here?" I say.

"Sure. Why not?"

Elsa digs around a bush. Fair, light-brown hair, green eyes. She's a quiet Swede, a mathematics professor at Cal Poly, whose father is a diplomat to Ghana and a former United Nations weapons inspector. Her mother makes documentary films about refugees. Elsa moved to America years ago, coming out much later than Azadeh when, with uncharacteristic abandon, she painted a rainbow on her face and marched topless with a sword and a shield in the Halloween parade in West Hollywood.

"I don't think Elsa likes me," I say.

"She doesn't like anybody who does what we do. She's scared one night I might not come home; you know, she might get a knock on the door. Nothing personal."

"You like that?"

"What?"

"Having someone waiting, watering your roses."

Azedeh stands next to me on the porch. The house is not far from the library and a café on the corner with Save the Planet signs and photographs of missing dogs in the window. You can't hear the train from the porch but you know it's there, running diagonally through town every twenty minutes to points north. South Pasadena is real but isn't—too neat and swept, a map of make-believe. It's what some people want. Sprinklers, pastors, incense, a craftsman to restore on weekends. I have to admit, I like those houses, their slants and porches, earthen colors, eaves, and dark little mysteries. They are sturdy, wise, sitting back, watching. I wonder whether Azadeh's parents, when they escaped Iran and Khomeini, had this in mind for their not-yet-born lesbian daughter: a seven-figure home with a thirty-year mortgage, a Prius and a Fusion in the driveway, a holstered gun hanging on a closet door near a bedroom window that overlooks a gazebo as delicate as a bird's cage.

"I do like it, Carver. You should try it."

"Not for me. It's pretty though."

"You think I've conformed," she says.

"You're a Muslim lesbian with a nine millimeter. Not a lot of conforming there."

"My father would agree. What do you want, Carver?"

"Are you getting existential? I want to catch a killer."

"But after."

"There'll be another one after."

"C'mon, Carver, I can see you shopping at Sprouts, bagging your tomatoes, talking kombucha with lonely wives."

We laugh. Azadeh rubs my arm, and I think it could be like that, but it won't be.

"I see you still have the car," she says, nodding toward my Porsche.

"It runs."

"Needs paint," she says, checking her phone. "Let's go for a ride."

"Where?"

"I'll tell you on the way."

We walk down the steps in afternoon heat. Blowing in from the ocean, mountains, and, farther east, the desert, the winds thread and weave around Los Angeles in unpredictable patterns. The air up here is warmer, until night, when breezes from the San Gabriels descend with reassuring purity over the white orchids and eucalyptus. Azadeh kisses Elsa, whispers to her. Elsa wipes the dirt from her hands and walks us to the car. They kiss again, and Azadeh tells me to drive toward Echo Park. She puts on Sudan Archives—African hip-hop rhythms, a violin, and a woman's voice that sneers and pouts.

"I like this," she says.

"My recent obsession. She's from LA by way of Cincinnati."

"Who's the other one you turned me on to?"

"Bedouine."

"Elsa likes Bedouine. We went to her show at the Bardot last year."

Azadeh rolls down the window, lets her black hair fly like demons, reminding me of a fable I heard when I was a boy, about a desert princess who loved cherries. For her birthday, her father gathered doves from across the land and dispatched them to orchards in a rival kingdom to carry back one cherry each, until the sky filled with white and red, and the princess laughed and danced on her balcony as the enemy king sent out his armies.

"Where are we going?"

"Just drive, Carver."

We drop onto Sunset and park between a barbershop and a tattoo parlor.

"It's like a hipster petting zoo," says Azadeh. "You should get an earring and grow a beard. Get one of those Bogart hats they wore in those old noir movies. You have hipster potential, Carver; I see it." It is a Sunday, and she is happy. "You hungry? Let's get a Cuban sandwich. This place up here has the best."

"What's going on?"

"Relax, Carver."

We order two sandwiches and coffees at the counter and take a table in the corner. The place is nearly empty. A blond twenty-something in yellow-tinted Lennon glasses is typing on a Mac. A guy with a wallet on a chain, and a beard too gray and messy for a hipster is reading Hunter Thompson, shaking his head at the funny parts. A Latina slides us our food, an overhead fan spins, and I feel I've been here before, years ago, but I don't remember. A man in a deep-green suit and striped shirt walks in, slow, five foot ten, fading tan, darting eyes. His black shoes and combed-back hair gleam. Azadeh waves and he heads toward us, winking at the cook, hugging the waitress. He pulls out a chair and sits down. Nobody says anything. I listen to the fan and wait. Azadeh gets up and walks out the door.

"We go back," says the guy, nodding toward her. "She's good people."

"She asked you here?"

He rubs a hand over his mouth, moves his chair closer.

"This young man, this kid, the cellist," he says. "I seen him here a few afternoons ago, maybe last week, sitting right over there with his instrument all cased up. Minding his own business, you know." The guy pulls out a vape, studies me, sits there like a bronze cast, confident, a bit of East Coast Soprano air about him. "Anyway, these two big fucks come in. One of them was really fucking big, like a tower, you know? They move the kid's cello. Sit on both sides of him, squeeze him in like. I'm sitting over there watching." His eyes cut to a table near the counter. "Everything's real nice and slow, no hysterics, but mean, you know. Like this kid's in the shit. I can't hear what they're saying, but the kid is spooked. Confused. They lean in even closer. One of the guys—the smaller one, but shit, even he was big—was packing. A bulge under his jacket. Then things kinda relax. The guys get up, pat the kid on the back, and then, *boom*, out the door, gone."

"Who are you?"

"I'm uncomfortable with identities. Azadeh knows me. She can tell you." He reaches for half of Azadeh's sandwich. "She won't mind. Never seen her eat two halfs."

"Why were you here that day?"

"It's my neighborhood."

"You know what happened to the kid?"

"Azadeh told me. But I'm thinking, kid didn't put that needle in his arm without a little help."

"These guys . . ."

"Sounded Russian—at least, definitely Eastern European variety." He reaches for a napkin. "Good sandwich. Too much cheese, maybe."

"Have you seen them before?" I say.

"Nah. They're not from here, you know. The clothes. Russian clothes. Different fabric, cut. The big guy had a pack of smokes, not the kind they sell here. You know how you can just tell about guys? A kind of unexplainable sense you get. Definitely not Angelenos. But these days, who the hell really is, you know? All kinds of fucking people arriving from all kinds of places."

"What else?"

"What else? I just gave you a boatload."

"Can you describe them more?"

"Already did. Azadeh."

"You know about the ballerina?"

He exhales, shakes his head.

"You guys lost her. All over the Internet. I'm thinking—"

"The same thing we are. You didn't hear anything else, see anything?"

"Just that these guys weren't locals," he says. "So whatever came, came from somewhere else?"

"How would I find out about that?"

"I guess you'd have to know the right people."

"You know the right people?"

"I know a person." He takes the last bite of the sandwich, reaches for Azadeh's coffee. "Oh, she likes it black. I like a little cream. Fuck it." He sips. "Azadeh tells me I can trust you. But this can't come back on me. I mean, shit, I can't have two big, funny-talking shits put me in a squeeze at that table over there, or anywhere. Say I mention a name. No one knows where that name came from. Just a name you happened to hear from the anonymous. Right?"

"Couldn't have put it better."

"Jimmy Krause. Lives in Burbank."

"What about . . ."

"All I'm saying." He checks his phone. "I got a date. I met a girl a few weeks ago. She likes walking around the lake, snapping pics of water lilies and turtles and shit. What the fuck, right? You gotta do what they want, least in the early stages." He stands, brushes crumbs from his suit, tugs his collar straight.

"I like that," I say. "Where'd you get it?"

"Tailor on Beverly out near Larchmont. A bit pricey, but nice work. Armenian, I think. Maybe a Jew."

"What are you?"

"I'm outta here."

He leaves. I finish my sandwich. The blond is still typing away. Girls at a table next to her are sharing Instagrams and laughing and talking about a boy one of them loves but is too shy to tell. They tease her and shovel french fries, and they start talking about Kanye and Kim and why has he been so weird, "talking nice shit about Trump and disappearing to Wyoming or Montana—you know, one of those white-people places." And why Kylie Jenner is making "like a billion gazillion selling lipstick. That girl smarter than the whole bunch—Kim, even." They are from another world, an orbit briefly touching mine. I like listening to them sailing from sentence to sentence through a late afternoon, like a parade that for a moment has stopped. I walk outside. Azadeh is leaning against my Porsche, eating ice cream.

"You didn't bring my coffee?"

"Your guy drank it."

"What'd you think?"

"LA by way of Jersey."

"He can put it on thick," she says. "He's a good CI, though. He's part Iranian. Mother's side. He's a scam artist, sets up money-laundering fronts. He's a fixture here." She licks. "You know how some of them like it. They pretend not to, like it's a chore or we're pulling fingernails, but they like it. He's like that. He likes the whole chemistry. Makes him feel important, like he's working all angles. I love hustlers like that. I've worked him for five or six years. Usually on the mark." I lean next to her. The sky is hard blue behind us. Azadeh's eyes are hidden behind sunglasses; she has chocolate on her chin. "I spread Levon's picture to a few of my people," she says. "Nobody recognized him except him."

"Strange he was in there the day Levon was."

"I know what you're thinking. Thought the same thing. But he's clean, not connected—not to this, anyway. Sometimes you catch a break, Carver. You go with it."

"So who's Jimmy Krause?"

"That's for you to find out. Keep me in the loop, right? In case this becomes a Bureau thing."

"It already is, isn't it?"

"Depends on who you arrest."

I reach and wipe the smudge from her chin.

"It's mocha fudge, Carver. Want a lick?"

"I'll pass. Where now?"

"Home."

I open the door. She slides in. I go around and start the car and ease into the thin traffic on Sunset.

"Why you laughing, Carver?"

"It's just funny."

"What?"

"How it all rides on guys like that. Devious men who know other devious men."

"Makes sense to me."

We get on the 110. Wind fills the car; the mountains rise clear. Azadeh sends a text.

"Thanks," I say. "I owe you."

"You do."

CHAPTER 16

Andreas Stein leads me to the rooftop of a restored Art Deco near Sixth that's been converted into apartments. A violinist is playing. Ballerinas and slight, handsome men are drinking around a pool next to a framed portrait of Katrina Ivanovna. It is twilight, and in the distance north and west, the sky is black and red with rage. It's been like this since the first brush fire flared in Ventura and zigzagged to Bel Air. It is a terrible beauty, fed by dry winds, and from this distance it has the glimmer of the sacred, reminding me of candles burning against stained glass, colors changing with light and heat. Flames rip through funnels of smoke that rise like doomed towers and topple across the horizon. Beneath, in neighborhoods and arroyos, fires feed and howl; sparks spin and scatter, searing the air with orange diamonds as night falls.

"How many acres?" says Stein, standing near the roof's edge, a wineglass in his hand.

"More than two hundred thousand," I say.

"All the way to Santa Barbara. I read that. It's like the *Inferno*.

I suppose that sounds arch or obvious, Detective, but from this far away, it looks like a glimpse of hell, doesn't it? Imagine humankind picking at its sins and wailing through eternity. Dante knew." He breathes, teeters, and waves a hand over the horizon. "I'm sorry. I'm a bit drunk. But look how frightening and majestic it is."

"People call it a lot of things."

He takes a big swallow of wine. Unshaven and weary, his voice cracked, he's not the man I met days ago in the theater, sitting on the stage in the spotlight, reading his laptop and plotting his comeback, his *Giselle* with Katrina. "It seems unreal," he says. "I half expect the flames to stop and the smoke to be vacuumed away. Paradise destroyed and resurrected. The way they do in the movies." He wipes away a tear. "All those flaming palm trees. They look like armies in bright rows."

"You okay?"

"We had to cancel *Giselle*."

"I read."

"We couldn't get a replacement in time. Impossible. We had to do something. The dancers wanted to have this goodbye for Katrina. She made an impression. She always did. They're up here to pay homage. See that man over there, the very good-looking one? He's a choreographer from Paris, and the one over there, a bit chubby in the black suit—he's the money. He was financing *Giselle*, but alas, well, you know . . . I feel as if I'm slurring, Detective. Am I slurring?"

"A little."

"I can't believe she's gone," he says. "She was in and out of my life for so long." He looks at me, squinting, losing and finding words. "I don't know if we could have pulled it off. You didn't know me before, but I had my day, Detective. I wasn't such a wreck I thought Katrina and I might take one more gamble. A reverie." He puts down the empty wineglass. "Are you closer to anything, Detective?"

"We're following leads."

"Ah, yes, leads. Many, many leads, I suppose. Is there a chance you'll get her body back? I dream of her out there, wandering."

"We're doing everything we can. I have a question."

"Please."

"Katrina kept diaries in small, red books."

"She wrote in them often," he says, his eyes scanning for a waiter. "At breaks in rehearsal, she would sit in the back of the theater and write. I asked her once what she was scribbling. She looked at me, and I knew to mind my own business. I haven't seen any. There were none in her locker when we cleaned it out."

"What was in there?"

"Ballerina things. Leggings, toe shoes, you know. A picture of her doing an arabesque, another of a grand jeté. It's rare to have so much strength and explosion hidden in such elegance. Making the body insubstantial until it succumbs to beauty." His eyes widen. "You're looking at me as if I'm crazy." He teeters a bit more. "I am full of myself, I suppose. At any rate, I have seen no diaries." He takes another glass of wine from a passing silver tray. "There is someone I'd like you to meet." He draws me to him; his voice softens. "See that woman over there? Blond hair, black dress? Her name is Molly Ames. Wonderfully American, if you know what I mean. A once-promising dancer ruined by injuries. She managed Katrina off and on. She helped bring *Giselle* together. Follow. I shall introduce you."

He's drunk but walks through the crowd with ease. I hadn't realized before how compact he is, how delicate, like a dancer.

Katrina's choreographer and occasional lover, he is a man, once brash and indulged, whose name I am certain she scrawled into her little red, lost books. Molly Ames turns. She kisses Stein on the cheek. He flits away.

"He's bombed," she says in a Southern accent, the kind I heard years ago in a hotel in Savannah, where I had attended a forensics conference on the art of autopsy and the science of sociopaths. "That man can drink, honey. He'll fall over soon in a corner or the bed of some new thing he's found." She tips a whiskey. "This is devastating for all of us, Detective. No one is sure what to do." She looks at me, direct, open, discerning, lipstick on her glass. She's tall, hair pulled back, wide gold necklace, nails long and polished. She has the mark of money, of someone who rides horses on fields of white fences. "I was in London when I heard that horrible, startling ringing in the middle of the night. All I could think of was when I first saw her dance. I was a dancer then too. But not like that, Detective. No. I was good, but I would never do that." Her eyes go away and come back. "She was magnificent."

"Andreas said you managed her."

"Lord, that girl could be difficult, as I'm sure you've heard. Famous for it. A prima donna extraordinaire. She'd call me now and then to fix something. A contract. To get her an audition."

"Were you close?"

She lets the question float.

"That's a hard one," she says, sipping and reaching over to brush something, perhaps ash, from my jacket. Her fingers stay for a moment, run down my lapel, and pull slowly away. "I don't mean to be elusive, but there are many and yet, no answers to that. You could love and admire Katrina, but I don't think you could get close. Does that make sense?" She leans toward me and lowers her voice. "We were intimate once; at least, I thought so. It was in New York years ago. It was the final night of *Romeo and Juliet*. She came from backstage and wanted to go for a walk. We went to Central Park, not deep in—it was late and dark, after all—but along the edge, you know, where the lights and shadows are. It was cold. We walked for hours. I was exhausted. I could only imagine what she was. We got back to the hotel and went to our rooms. An hour or so later—I was sleeping—a knock. It was her. Standing in the hallway in a white robe. She was restless. I let her in. She apologized and told me to go back to bed. She shut off the light and sat in a chair. A few minutes later, she stood and took off her robe and slipped naked under the covers next to me. I didn't know what to do." She shakes her head, turns away and back. "Look, I still blush at the memory." She sips again. "She pressed close to me. Her skin was cool, but then it warmed. She kissed me on the cheek, put her head on my shoulder, and went to sleep. I couldn't sleep at all, of course. Lord, I couldn't sleep. I must have, a little, though. Morning came, and she was gone. Nothing happened; I am not of that persuasion, but I understood how one could be. Katrina, of course, had a multitude of persuasions. But that night she just needed to feel another. Like a child with a bad dream. Does that make sense? I think it does. I would learn over the years that many others had similar stories about Katrina."

"Sounds like someone quite alone."

"Aren't we all, in some way? Katrina had no inhibition, you know—a girl not afraid of wanting to be held." She raises a finger, lifts away a tear. "The pills and the alcohol started as her talent diminished. Her mind could not accept what she called 'her body's rebellion.'" She looks at me. "Do you know what that's like? The moment you understand your mortality?"

"I do."

"I imagine, in your line of work, you must."

"When did you last see her?"

"Six months ago, in Spain. I was there on work, signing a promising dancer from Galicia, and Katrina flew in. She wanted advice on an advertising contract from Jimmy Choo to sell shoes. Dancing in high heels beneath the moon and across the Acropolis, or something like that. It was a good idea for a campaign. I offered advice. Before she left, she told me about Andreas wanting to do *Giselle*. I helped her with the contracts. It was arranged over phone calls and emails. And then I got the call in London a few days ago."

"Was she upset? Scared?"

"She was long estranged from Russia and her family. Her mother, especially. It bothered her. I don't know what happened there. You know how families can be. Her mother came to a performance once, in Geneva. Katrina left out the back door. Never said hello. I asked her why, and she shook her head but said nothing. I let it drop. There was more anger than regret in her eyes. I do remember that. Those angry blue eyes." The violinist plays a requiem. A dancer drapes toe shoes over the corner of Katrina's portrait; another hangs a scarf. A moment of silence falls, and then waiters move and glasses clink, and the hum of conversation returns. "Is this at all helpful, Detective? Or am I just babbling on. That's what one does, babbles after a death. Look at all of us babbling."

"It's very helpful. Did you ever see anyone threaten her? A man?"

"No."

"Her diaries . . ."

"Yes, she kept—"

"Have you found them, Detective?" asks Michael Paine, stepping beside Molly.

He reaches out and shakes my hand.

"No," I say.

"Do you two know each other?" asks Molly.

"Detective Carver was at my house the other day."

"Oh, yes, you saw Katrina the night she died," says Molly.

"She wanted me to write a book about her. She said she kept diaries. I asked for them, but she didn't have them with her. I think she wasn't sure she wanted to tell her story."

"Michael's writing a piece for *Vanity Fair*," says Molly.

"The Death of a Ballerina in the City of Angels."

"Right up their alley," I say.

"Oh, yes," he says, "I can see it already. Not the cover. No, she had faded too far for that, but a big spread inside. You know the way they do. Black-and-white photographs like in a masquerade. A shot of the morgue she was stolen from. Her as a child, of course. The prodigy from Russia. The rise and fall." He pauses. "Actually, it *could be* the cover."

"You've got it all worked out," I say.

"I don't mean to sound that way," he says. "Her end was sad. As I told you, she seemed agitated that night."

"Michael's interviewed me already, Detective." She turns to him. "I still feel ambivalent about it. It's so hard to get a life right."

"We are our complexities and contradictions," says Paine, smiling like a man in a hunt, drinking Perrier, his eyes, like mine, alert. But he has the charm of a mischievous dog and a confidence that he works hard to keep from becoming condescension. We look to the skyline and beyond, to the fires. I can feel Molly beside me—sense her, as if someone I knew from long ago had returned, and all the intervening years had vanished.

"Yes, Michael, we are complicated, but we can be wonderful," she says.

"It's why I write," he says. "Detective, I doubt we'll ever see those diaries."

"It'd be hard to tell a story without them," I say.

"If you come across them, I'd love a peek," he says.

I don't answer. He shakes my hand, nods to Molly, and drifts toward Andreas, who has taken a seat near the violinist.

"I've never understood writers," says Molly.

"He's done well. I was at his home in Los Feliz. He wanted to write a book about Lady Gaga, but it never came off."

"She probably couldn't sit still long enough. I guess Katrina is perfectly suited for *Vanity Fair*."

"Your world too."

"Not so much anymore," she says, looking to the distant glow. "I've never seen a sky like this."

"They can burn for days."

"You think someone killed her? Not the pills?"

"I think both."

"Every time I think of her body being stolen . . . well, I can't imagine, really. There's no peace for her."

"I hate that it happened."

"It can't be your fault."

"It's my case."

"You may never know, really."

"I don't think about that."

"I don't think I've been much help."

"Everything I hear helps."

She finishes her whiskey.

"Was it hard to give up dancing?"

"Oh, yes," she says. "I had many injuries. But I was never at the level one needs to be. Katrina taught me that. There are some who are just beyond us, Detective, and all we can do is watch in awe. But I stay close enough to it. I live on the vapors."

An old man takes Molly's hand and hugs her. He is crying and grasping a photograph of himself, Molly, and Katrina holding flowers on a stage. I turn away and feel Molly's hand on my arm, a whisper in my ear. She releases me. I walk and stand near the violinist at the roof's edge, streets alive below, fires in the hills. I turn to the south—plane lights in the sky, and beyond the flight path, blackness. A gust blows the scarf from Katrina's portrait. Dancers scurry to catch it, but it lifts, a ripple of color, and is gone. A heel clicks. A woman barely out of her teens steps beside me.

"She wasn't that special, you know," she says. "But now we've made her a saint."

"I thought she was one of the best," I say. "Isn't that why everyone's here?"

"They're here because they want to dance Giselle."

"The show's canceled," I say.

"There'll be other Giselles, Detective," she says, staring at the violinist. "See? All the money and choreographers. The air is full of opportunity. Ballerinas look like sparrows, but they can be quite mercenary."

"You a dancer?"

"Sabine Moritz."

"Andreas's company?"

"Two years. San Francisco before that."

"You have a French accent."

"*Oui.*"

"Should I know you?"

"Not at the moment. One day though."

"Like Katrina," I say.

"She lost her discipline."

"She had other things."

"A spectacular past and an addict's glamour."

"You sound like—"

"No," she says, laughing. "I didn't give her pills or kill her, or whatever. I was sad for her. A little envious, maybe. It's a cruel and jealous business."

"So I gather. Why do it?"

"Cruelty can lead to moments of unforgettable grace."

"You're not old enough to come up with that."

"You'd be surprised what a girl can pick up over the years," she says through the trace of a smile. "I will be a great ballerina one day."

"Why are you telling me this?"

"You should know the world you're in, Detective, that's all."

"Is it so different?"

"Maybe not. But it's prettier, at least on the outside."

The violinist plays. Sabine Moritz and I listen. Her hair is short, dark, and crimped, her neck slender and pearled. She seems so young to be so confident and certain. But I suspect that one day I may see her name lit up on a marquee, or in a headline, and be reminded of this night when she stood beside me, thin and sharp as angel hair. She closes her eyes and breathes in the music. I shut my eyes too. Minutes pass without a word. A siren below brings the world back. Sabine turns, nods goodbye, and walks toward the dancers.

I take the elevator down and walk a few blocks to Katrina's

building. The arched windows are dark and empty. Two men on the sidewalk are drumming plastic barrels, and another, all in white, is swaying and whirling like a talisman in a breeze. I stop in the Little Easy. Lenny's off tonight. I order a drink and go through my notes. Michael Paine may be right. We may never find the diaries. Or the body. Cold case. I hope not. I nod for another drink and watch silent, huddled families on TV. They have lost it all, not that far away, in a place of bright, burning armies. I keep thinking of Andreas Stein, and the way we break down over time, at first without notice and then with sudden clarity. I pay and walk west on Fifth through Pershing Square. I cross Olive to the Biltmore Hotel and into the lobby, past photographs, like the ones on Paine's wall, of old movie stars with their diamonds and cigarettes, and their confidence that it all might last a little longer, this dream they had found between the ocean and the desert's edge. I'd love to feel the slight buzz from a cigarette. I haven't had one in weeks, but I like patting my jacket, thinking I might find a stray. No. I get in the elevator, step out, and follow the numbers. I knock.

"I thought I might see you again, Detective."

"It's Sam," I say as Molly opens the door.

It clicks behind me. The curtains are drawn, the room dark. She takes my hand and leads me to the bed. I can hear her breathe. We stand together, still. I feel her, tall and slender and warm against me. Her robe drops. We kiss and lie on the bed. I undress. We don't hurry, and I think that we've only just met but no, I know her, although I don't, and I pretend, and she pretends, maybe of Katrina in her bed in New York, or a lover long ago in Spain, a dancer like her, young and lean, and I, closing my eyes, imagine Dylan Cross and that night in my apartment when she kissed me in her black dress and heels, and I tasted her wine and she said, '*Bye, Sam.*' What would it have been like? Molly makes me wonder. Perhaps it was her gaze on the rooftop, the conspiracy in her voice—not her accent, but her echo is like Dylan's, or close—and the way she moves, taught early that tall girls have their own grace. I don't know. So much is alive in this dark. Molly gathers and holds me, two strangers in a rented room, making love to different ghosts. She sits over me, caressing my face, and leans and kisses me and rises again, an outline, insubstantial, real, a breath, a slow drawing of air, then release, and she falls to me, and I run my fingers over her back, warm against the night air, and she slides beside me as this moment plays like recurring music, an unspoken memory through our lives. She kisses me.

"I'm glad," she says.

"You expected me?"

"We both expected you."

"Yes."

"The lives of others stay with us."

"For how long?"

"I suppose forever, or maybe one day they disappear as if we never knew them at all."

"What time do you remember most?"

"Dancing as a child across the living room."

"Started young, huh?"

"You have to," she says. "My mother's passion became mine. It happens like that, you know."

"I would have liked to see you dance."

"Well, then . . ."

She gets up and opens the curtains a crack, laughs, spins twice, and falls, a flash of white, back to bed and beside me again. We are silent for a long while.

"I never know what to do with death," she says. "I don't know how you do it. Your job, I mean."

"It's when they're most innocent, even the bad ones."

"Nothing can hurt them again."

"Never," I say.

"What do we do with this night?"

I don't answer. She presses closer. I hear footsteps and laughter in the hall. Drunken whispers, the scrape of a key card. Then nothing.

Molly is gone in the morning. No trace. No bags, no clothes, no scattered necklaces or rings. Just a note. *I won't forget.* I shower and put on a white robe, make complimentary coffee from the minibar, open the curtains, and stand at the window like a man with money, a man who owns things and is setting out on a day of consequence.

CHAPTER 17

"I got him."

"Who?"

"The guy."

"What guy?"

"The Jimmy Krause guy."

Lily Hernandez is hushed in stakeout-phone voice. It's her day off, and without asking, she's decided to help, telling me, "Time's passing, Carver. You gotta get somewhere on this, or it's gone. I'm making detective soon anyway. Let's do it." She's already run seven miles and worked the weights, and now she's in a Burbank bar, watching Jimmy Krause, the name Azadeh's CI passed along. Lily ran a check on him, pulled his driver's license, photo, and a rap sheet, which included fencing diamonds and running a chop shop.

"Get here," she says.

"How long's he been there?"

"Midway through a beer."

"Keep an eye on him."

"No shit, Carver."

"Why Burbank? Who hangs out in Burbank?"

"Bunch of Warner Brothers types and animators. Hurry."

I hop on the 101 and arrive forty-five minutes later. My eyes adjust to the dim light of the bar. Lily nods. A happy-hour crowd is drinking margaritas, and someone's having a birthday party in the corner. Two waitresses, two bartenders, spilled tequila, cut lemons; young white and Asian geeks huddled around a Mac, amazed at an anime character spinning in 3D and resembling a cross between Ant-Man and Catwoman. One of them says, "It's kinda like a transgender superhero." Another answers, "Catwoman's not a hero." The first guy responds, "Same genre, asshole." His buddy says, "Too hybrid and ambiguous for me, man. I mean, I don't know what it is. How do we build an origin story?"

Burbank at twilight. I slide in next to Lily at the bar.

"He's on his third beer," she says.

"Alone?"

"Yeah. What should we do?"

"Watch."

"Order something."

"What are you drinking?"

"Sprite."

"Jesus. Who drinks Sprite at happy hour?"

"This is technically work," she says.

"I'm having a beer."

"He doesn't look like a runner."

"Heavyset. Shaved head, bouncer type."

"Nice face, though," says Lily. "My guess, he used to pump

iron and take steroids. But he let it go. That's what happens to a lot of guys. I see them at the gym all the time. They let it go and get beefy. He's probably slower than the cellist. You could probably catch him, Carver."

"Screw you."

Lily winks and smiles.

"You see his rap sheet?" she says.

"Not much of a bad guy. But diamonds mean he travels in certain circles."

Lily's wearing jeans, beat-up Cons, and a tight yellow zip-up shirt. A cross on a gold chain, a gift from her dead father, Patrolman Federico Hernandez, killed years ago in a gang war, shines against her light-brown skin. She pushes back her short, black hair, turns, and looks at me as if to say this is how it should be, she and I sitting across from a mystery, wondering how it's going to go down. It reminds me of the first time we met, standing over Paul Jamieson, naked and rigid in a chair, a thread of lipstick, mascara on his lashes, and Dylan Cross's knife wound in his heart. Lily said to me that day, "The doer's a woman, no question. Only a woman could make him up that pretty. That's a special kind of hate to do to a man."

Jimmy Krause answers his phone. Puts it down a few seconds later, picks it up again, texts something, puts it down. Sips his beer. The happy-hour crowd is thinning. The door opens. A man in a black suit walks in, taps Krause on the shoulder, leans into him close. They walk out. I follow. Lily pays the bill. Krause and the man get in the back of an Escalade with tinted windows parked at the corner. They head south. Lily comes out, and we run for my Porsche and follow. We're two blocks behind but have them in sight. They head over the Ventura Freeway and keep south over the Los Angeles River and then onto North Highland, Franklin, and Hollywood Boulevard, heading west toward Beverly Hills.

"Maybe he's got a pocketful of diamonds," says Lily.

"Don't get ahead of things."

"I smell fumes. You smell fumes?"

"It's nothing."

"You've got to do something about this car, Carver. I get the whole vintage thing, but it needs work. Seriously."

The Escalade rolls through the gate to an Italianate mansion with a fountain in the courtyard and disappears behind high walls and ivy. The house lights glow soft and yellow. The gate closes. We pass and park across the street about a hundred yards away. Lily calls Dispatch with the address, to see who owns the place. I turn off my lights and roll down the window, breathing in hibiscus and wealth. The night hides us. It's quiet, clean. A light breeze from the ocean. The name comes back. Mickey Orlov.

"That's the producer, right?" says Lily.

"Big producer."

Lily Googles.

"Damn, Carver, this guy's done a ton of movies. Net worth— get this—two-point-three billion. Got a couple of studios, a few vineyards, owns a fucking castle in Croatia." The phone lights her face; she scrolls. "He was born in 1948 in a town outside Moscow, long-ass name I can't pronounce. He turned Mikhail into Mickey, and according to a story in *Fortune*, he was in the fricking KGB! Only in it a few years, mostly in Western Europe during the Cold War. Got out a long time ago and went into business. When the wall fell, he became an oligarch, although— get this—he doesn't like being called an oligarch. 'I'm just a businessman and a producer.' That's what he says. Modest, huh? Gimme a break, right?"

"What else?"

"Jesus, Carver, what *else*? Really? We're sitting outside the house of a one-time Russian spy turned movie producer, with a questionable character named Jimmy Krause inside, at a time you're investigating the death of a Russian ballerina and a Russian cellist. That's a lot of *else*." She scrolls, turns, and looks at me. "Wonder what he wants with a guy like Krause. Orlov doesn't need to buy stolen diamonds. He probably owns a diamond mine. What do we do?"

"Wait till Krause comes out. Follow him."

"I gotta pee."

"Hold it."

"I don't think you're ever a 'former spy.' Do you? Once you're in, you're in."

"Like a priest or a cop," I say.

"Exactly. You know too much about too many things. I'm thinking Orlov is playing every angle. He's loaded, connected. He must have known Katrina. Her parents too. Hang on." She types, scrolls. "I put in Mickey's and Katrina's names. Nothing. But this is in English. We're going to have to check Russian sites." More typing, scrolling. "Just popped his name into images with Putin. Look." She turns her phone toward me. "Fishing buddies."

"Let see what plays out," I say. "We'll stay on Krause."

"Could be in there a while."

"We wait."

Lily leans forward, presses her face to the windshield, sits back.

"You ever think about all the wonderful, strange shit going on we know nothing about?" she says.

"We eventually run into it."

She rolls down her window.

"Hear that?" she says.

"What?"

"Silence. That's what being loaded sounds like."

I call Ortiz and ask him to run deeper checks on Orlov and Krause. I pull up a *Los Angeles Times* profile on the producer, written a few years ago when his film *The Man from Marrakesh*, starring Clive Owen and Rachel Weisz, won the Academy Award for best picture. I remember it. Lust and intrigue in North Africa in the late 1930s, when spies with satchels and maps traveled by camel and slept in desert starlight. It must have been romantic in those times before the war, when the world's outposts, not connected as they are today, ran on the whispers of strangers. Orlov was reticent about his KGB days, saying only that he had served his government in "various capacities" and spoke German, French, Italian, and a bit of Polish. The story is careful, noting without indictment that Orlov was in Rome the day in 1981 when a Turkish assassin nearly killed the pope. He made a fortune in uranium and gold mines, which meant he had friends in the Kremlin, and in the nineties started a production company in Santa Monica, which he named *Solaris* after the great film by Andrei Tarkovsky, with whom he once shared a bottle of vodka and a bag of limes in Moscow. Orlov produced nearly two hundred movies, which won thirty-five Academy Awards, including three best pictures. He's prone to comic-book heroes and smaller biopics on artists like Van Gogh and Caravaggio, which fit his sensibilities. He paints still lifes and portraits that hang in a room across from his wine cellar. Few people are allowed entry. The *Times* writer was given only a glimpse from the doorway, noting that one painting featured a nude in candlelight, another, a rower alone on a river in winter. "I paint them for myself," he told the writer. "They are for me alone. My mirrors." Orlov owns homes in Paris, Monaco, and Barcelona; he skis in Sun Valley and dates actresses, but never for long. His real love, his friends say, was a girl he knew many years ago in St. Petersburg, a striking linguistics student with black hair, whose name he never mentions. The photograph of Orlov in the story shows him on a terrace in the hour before dusk: immaculate silver hair, blue shirt with rolled-up sleeves, arms crossed, hard, deep-set eyes staring right at the camera. The pose is softened by a shy smile, like that of a man whose mask has fallen off, exposing him for an instant. He's not like many in Hollywood, those content in their myths. But like the best producers and directors, he is driven by a practicality that beauty should earn its keep, and that money and power are not sins against art. Or so the story suggests.

"He's handsome for his age," says Lily. "Works out, I can tell. Probably has a trainer. All rich guys have trainers."

"I think he works out alone in the basement. Barbells and sweat. Old school."

"Could be. He's got an edge."

"Story says he used to box."

"What time is it?"

"Eleven fifty-three."

The gate opens. The Escalade turns right. We follow, reversing the route we took earlier, back to the bar in Burbank. Jimmy Krause gets out, walks toward the bar, reaches for the door, turns away. The Escalade disappears. Krause walks a few blocks to an apartment house. He sits on the front steps, smokes a cigarette, crushes it out, checks his phone. We stay in the car, watching.

"You see the fires when we were coming up?" says Lily. "The winds have died a little."

"Not burning as bad," I say.

"I love the colors of the sky when they burn," she says, "and the black after—you know, like nothing was ever there."

Krause pockets his phone and heads inside. A light goes on in a third-floor corner window.

"In for the night," says Lily. "We going to knock?"

"We question him too early and we lose him. We don't have enough on him or his connection to Orlov. We'll dig a little more."

"Orlov is going to come up clean. You know that, right? No guy like that is going to leave something you can find."

"They always leave something."

She smiles, shakes her head.

"You know, Carver, there are these weird moments when you're an optimist. How about my place? We'll have a beer on the porch and then sleep. I gotta run in the morning."

CHAPTER 18

"C'mon, Ortiz, let her work the case with me."

"She's not a detective," he says.

"She's almost," I say. "She can do it unofficially. Just to help with Jimmy Krause. I want her to watch him."

"You've fought me on not wanting a partner for years. I let you get away with it. Now, suddenly . . ."

"It's a complicated case."

"Okay, okay. I'll arrange it with her lieutenant. You're not sleeping with her, are you?"

I sip my espresso. We look at one another.

"Shit, Carver. I don't want to know."

"Best not to."

"You've got issues, man. A whole lot of fucking issues," he says. "Make sure you keep going to that shrink. It's required if you want to keep your shield. How was the last session?"

"My dreams suggest a Harry Potter–like escapism, but my id

represses them, which leaves me rather dark and fantastical on the spectrum. Not full-blown insane, but you know . . ."

"Screw you, Carver."

I laugh. Ortiz finishes his coffee.

"Where's the barista you like?" I say.

"It's Monday," he says, staring out the window at two uniforms passing on horses, which in LA is so ridiculous, it's not even quaint. He looks back to his empty cup, twirls the spoon. "She's off. I think she has a boyfriend. This guy came in the other day. Scroungy. What makes those types attractive, I can never figure out." He reaches for a napkin. "You check with your FBI friend on Orlov? They must have something from far back."

"She's looking into it. What about the Russian consulate?"

"Don't want to ask yet."

"Orlov would get a call."

"Pronto."

"What was the house like?"

"What do you think?"

"Yeah."

"Speaking of dreams, I had one last night about our ballerina," says Ortiz. "She was dancing in a fog or a mist or some shit, flickering like an insect here and there. I kept walking toward her, but she kept moving, and then the fog cleared, and I was standing on an empty stage. She was gone."

"Where are we on that?"

"Still nothing. What did you tell me about her neighbor? The costume designer guy."

"Antonio Garcia. Self-possessed, intelligent. Theatrical to the max. He's got a poster of Katrina on his wall, next to a vampire's cape. She looks down on the mannequins he dresses. He's working on a movie about Dean Martin and the fifties. Guy's meticulous. He and Katrina were close. He's still pretty shaken. He saw her as an artistic equal. 'A shared soul.' That's what he said. Adopted her cat." I finish my espresso. "I was there at least an hour. He was slamming tequila. Guy's got high tolerance."

"We know a few of those," says Ortiz, leaning in and then back, eyeing me.

"But get this. He goes on about her dancing, her costumes, finding her in the bed that day, alone and naked. He starts tearing up. But he never mentions her body being lost. Don't you think that's weird? That's the first thing everyone mentions, right? They want to know: How could it happen? A death is one thing, but a vanishing body stays in the mind, right? Like a lost kid."

"Didn't I just tell you about my dream?"

"Exactly. The unreconciled."

"What are you saying? This guy's a vampire and he's got her in a coffin in a basement."

"Don't be facetious."

"Fa-what?"

"You know what I mean. I'm not saying he's a psycho. I just find it odd that he never mentioned it. I'm going back to see him again."

"I thought he had an alibi. Paris."

"It checked out."

"So?"

"I think we're looking at two different crimes, two different motives."

Ortiz shifts in his chair, folds his hands on the table.

"You mean someone kills her, and someone entirely different, who had no hand in the homicide, steals the body," he says. "I don't think so. You steal a body before an autopsy, and there's no way to assign cause of death. No crime." Ortiz smooths his mustache. "Besides, the body was jacked like it was a special op, a military thing. Cars blow up outside the morgue. Two guys in ball caps pulled low hustle through the chaos. *Boom*, gone. From what you tell me, I don't think Antonio the dressmaker has that kind of résumé."

"Look at the video again. It's almost like the guys didn't exactly know where they were going once they got inside. Didn't have a blueprint. A pro would have known right where to go."

"They had a pretty good idea where they were going. They knew where shit was. It happened sixteen hours after she got to the morgue. That's on the fly, maybe, but still planning with a working knowledge of what's where. I don't know, Carver."

"Keep an open mind."

He stands and steps to the window. Checks his reflection, fixes his tie.

"Something better break on this soon," he says. "You see that piece in the *Times*?"

"Yeah."

"Is this 'indicative of the department'? That's what they wrote. Hate that shit."

"You know they're moving out to El Segundo. New headquarters. They won't be across the street anymore. Maybe they'll leave us alone."

"Who moves to El Segundo?"

Ortiz pays the bill and heads back to the office. I call Lily and tell her to sit on Jimmy Krause.

"No shit, Carver, I'm on this?" she says.

"Semiofficially."

"Cool. On my way to Burbank."

"Just watch," I say. "Be a shadow."

"I know how to surveil," she says. *Click.*

I walk down Spring to see Antonio Garcia. He's not around. I slip under the yellow tape and through the door into Katrina's loft. Quiet. The bed is unmade and half-stripped, as if she had awoken and hurried to a rehearsal. I kneel, look for her imprint, but she was too light. The morning I saw her, her black hair, a flare across the pillow, made her body even more incandescent. Like moonlight. I put my face to the mattress, breathe in. No scent of her. Her pills gone and bagged into evidence. An unopened vodka bottle sits on the counter. An unframed picture of her poised at a barre is thumbtacked to the wall. I sit in a hardback chair. Levon must have sat here when he played. I can see them. But they do not speak. I get up and grab the vodka and take the chair to the window. I sip and sit and watch the street; five floors up, faint voices beneath. I reach for my phone and call up the music to *Giselle* on Spotify. I close my eyes and listen. Woodwinds and violins. I drift for a moment. I take another sip, cap the bottle, wipe my prints. I put the bottle back, open drawers and cabinets, step into the small closet, and go through her two suitcases: scarves, balms, leggings, a black dress, a single toe shoe signed in blue marker by Baryshnikov. No little red books. I turn off the music, close the door, and slip back under the yellow tape, looking up at the hallway ceiling streaked with angels and dreams from the brain of a meth addict.

I walk home, flip open the laptop, and read about Mickey Orlov. A lot has been written. But except for the *Times* piece I read last night, not a lot directly from him. The stories are composites based on financial documents, court papers, production notes, the recollections of others. Most of the articles have no quotes from him at all, as if he is content to be more imagined than real, which, I suppose, he learned as a spy, if he ever was one.

A piece written years ago in the *Post* quotes a retired CIA spook as saying, "Orlov was certainly a Russian agent. He covered as a business tycoon, socialite, millionaire, and a bit of an artist. A communist renaissance man. He was a master at it." He grew rich as the Cold War ended. He applied for a visa and a green card and moved to America, donated millions over the years to Republican and Democrat candidates. The spook says to that, "Old enemies became new friends. We never could pin anything on him that would have prevented it. Besides, he had the right connections in Washington. Some thought he was a double agent."

It's night. I flick on the lamp, pour a scotch, make a turkey sandwich. I call Lily.

"Krause went to that same bar," she says. "He drank three beers and went home. Talked to no one. I'm sitting outside his place now."

"Give it another hour," I say, "and then get some rest."

"I gotta work out in the morning," she says. "Then I'll be back."

I pour another drink, step to the window. Esmeralda, small and bent, is sleeping in her rags and scarves in front of the Hotel Clark. I should go down and bring her tea. I'm tired. I put on Billie Holiday, her high, bruised voice, so close to ruin. We all are. I'm buzzed and warm. This solitary comfort I have long known. A shiver runs through me. I lean my head back, eyes heavy.

Someone's banging. Dark. I stumble down the hall and open the door.

"You look like mess, Sam. Get packed. We go soon."

Stefan steps in and hugs me. He is shaved, crisp, smells of cologne.

"What are you doing here? How'd you know where I live?"

"Really, Sam?"

"What's going on?"

"We're leaving on the trip. The person you need to see. Remember? The Russian. All arranged."

"I can't leave. I'm in the middle of a case."

"This *is* case. C'mon, Sam, get awake. We have to go." He pats me on the cheek, the night cool still on him. "Shower. Pack. Three days gone, max." He walks to the living room. "Drink?"

I pour him a scotch.

"Any bourbon?" he says.

"I'm a scotch man."

"Cool but not hip. That's you, Sam."

He looks around.

"Nice," he says. "A good cop apartment."

He studies the pictures on the walls: Kenyan holy man, icon from Bucharest, etchings from Egypt, charcoal street scene from Paris.

"The world in a tiny place," he says. "I like."

He sits at the piano. Dips his head, sets his hands on the keys. Strikes an F, makes a face.

"Needs tuning, Sam."

He plays.

"Romani ballad. My mother taught me before war," he says. "All of Sarajevo played songs then. Before. They didn't know. My mother played and told stories of knights and forests and girls, how do you say, *damzils* . . ."

"Damsels."

"Yes, damsels." He sips, plays with one hand. "Hurry. We can talk about damsels on the plane."

"Where are we going?"

"Surprise. But you need a coat. Do you have a suit? Good one?"

He holds up his glass. I pour him another. He turns back to the piano. I shower and pack. It's 2:00 a.m., I call Ortiz. I can see him startled, squinting, walking out of his bedroom to the kitchen, voice cracked and soft, so he doesn't wake his wife. I had told him before about Stefan stopping by the Little Easy with the prospect of a Russian who might know something.

"I don't know, Carver, leaving town now," says Ortiz.

"If Stefan says . . ."

"I know, but shit, we don't want an international incident, and the FBI doesn't think as highly of him as you do. They think all kinds of bad shit about him. This could go very sideways. It's not our turf."

"Ortiz," I say, "we're nowhere on this case. We need a break."

I hear him breathing, see him fiddling with his mustache in the dark.

"Okay, shit," he says. "Get back quick. I'll keep Lily on that guy."

"Jimmy Krause," I say.

"Don't fuck this up, Carver." *Click*.

I text Lily. Let her sleep. Stefan, his scotch on the piano, a cigarette slanting from his lips, is playing Beethoven's "Moonlight Sonata." His fingers float as if a too-hard touch would shatter a note. He's usually so brash and alive, but now, with his black hair shining, his face serene, he's at peace in the music. He draws closer to the piano, almost crying, but not in a broken way.

"How?" he says, looking at hands on the keys.

"How what?"

"Did he do it."

He stands, wipes his eyes, finishes his scotch.

"We go."

CHAPTER 19

We head north on the 101 in Stefan's restored 1967 Camaro. Deep blue with white stripes, the car is one of seven in his vintage fleet. He pops in an eight-track tape of the Jefferson Airplane. Grace Slick sings "White Rabbit." We roll down the windows, the cold wind blowing, roaring, carrying Grace's voice over the dark hills beyond the Griffith Observatory. I am tired, but I feel young, a boy of mischief. Stefan accelerates. The highway is almost empty. We streak into the valley. The stars harden, and the air warms. Stefan hands me a flask.

"Bourbon!" he yells.

"Why this ancient eight-track? You can stream all these songs, you know." I take the flask.

"I want car and sound to be just as it was then," he says. "Isn't it great? We're in another time, Sam. The sixties."

He sings with Grace. We race past Sherman Oaks, cut right before Encino, and roll into the Van Nuys airport. Stefan drives through an open gate and parks beside a Gulfstream. A pilot greets us. I hand my bag to a second man. Stefan and I walk up the steps toward a woman in a skirt and a hip-cut jacket. She hands Stefan a satchel and a drink. He and I sit facing each other. The woman, Alex, brings a bowl of pistachios, a joint, and bourbon for me. The pilot closes the cabin door. The engines whine. The last touch of earth falls beneath us. Wildfires burn in the west, smaller than a few days ago but still bright, like angry eyes looking toward heaven. They disappear as we bank east. Stefan kicks off his shoes, lights the joint. Alex sits across from us, twirling her hair and thumbing through a *Vogue*.

"Where are we going?"

"New York first," says Stefan. "Then to the old country. You're tired, Sam. Finish your drink and sleep."

He hands me headphones. I listen to falling rain and forest whispers. I look into the night, imagine how cold it is in the black beyond the wing. I think of my father, so many years gone. I am older than he ever was. He is down there, interned in darkness. I close my eyes and am subsumed by the night.

The plane banks. We drop beneath a low sheet of clouds and land in Islip, Long Island. The Atlantic is rough, gray green, the surf breaking hard on the beach. Alex hands me a coffee and a sliced orange. The plane door opens. Stefan's assistant, Chloe, a brisk woman with tied-back red hair, whom I met two years ago at Stefan's Malibu house, steps in juggling three smartphones, the financial papers, and a book on climate change. She is followed by Roberto, a soft-voiced young man from Argentina via the London School of Economics, whose role I have never discerned. He wears a blue suit and a muted tie. His black hair is parted to the side. He eyes me as if I were a stowaway, smiles, and says something to Stefan, who goes to the cockpit door and taps the pilot on the shoulder. Drizzle speckles the windshield. Gray light seeps through the cabin. Stefan returns to his seat. Roberto hurries to the cockpit and closes the door. The engines whir. Chloe buckles in beside me.

"Been a while, Sam," she says. "Glad you're on the trip. Roberto can be tedious on long jaunts, and Stefan, well, you know, man of many moods." She laughs and lets her hair down. It falls past her shoulders, fierce and untamed, like a storm. She scrolls on a smartphone. "Trump's on another Twitter binge. Market's been up and down all day. What a fucking country."

"Where are we going?"

"Brussels," she says. "Hurry-up meeting with a banker from Berlin, an investor from Vienna, and a casino owner from Montenegro. They're . . ."

"A deal," says Stefan, sitting across from us with an espresso in one hand, cognac in the other. "There are problems. The guy from Berlin is okay, but the Vienna man—his name is Viktor—is a bit of a schlub. You know this word, *schlub*? Anyway, it's complicated, but the plan is to move money, most of it legal, through Berlin and Vienna and then to Montenegro. The money will then go in other directions, and hopefully, more money will come back. Chloe can explain, if you want. By the way, Sam, I'm telling these men you're my silent adviser. They don't like cops—nothing personal, but you know. Viktor is already nervous. He dreams of financial police."

"What about—"

"Don't worry, Sam, it's all arranged. You will meet the person you need."

Chloe touches my arm, nods, yes.

We break through cloud cover. I see the last of the ocean. The sky blooms blue. Alex hands me an espresso and a scone. Chloe slides me the *Financial Times*. I read about Mark Zuckerberg and peddled data and how nothing of your own is ever your own anymore. We are pixels in the designs of others. I turn to the culture pages to a review on Paul Schrader's film *First Reformed*, about a self-doubting priest, a planet spoiled, and the faint hope of resurrection. I push the papers aside. Chloe, her head turned toward me, is sleeping. Her skin is polished and white. As a child, she must have burned easily. Sharp chin, full lips, no lines around her green-hazel eyes. She is still young—not as young as she looks, but natural and perfectly attuned to Stefan's erratic demands.

The plane is warm. Stefan is sleeping. I feel ripples of wind beneath us, slight dips and rises. The sky ahead is turning to dusk and, farther on, night, as if we had tricked time and were flying into a painting. Lights glow and multiply below. My ears pop, and I feel our descent. Alex brings hot towels.

We are awake but quiet as we touch down in Brussels. A van drives us to a small terminal. Our passports are stamped, and a gray-haired man in a cap and funeral suit leads us to a Mercedes and drives us to a hotel near the center. Europe. Pillars and carved angels, fluted gold, yellow, and magenta, apostles and whores, lovers kissing near fountains beneath the disappearing moon. It's good to be back. Stefan hands me a key card. "Sleep and shower," he says. "Maybe walk around the city. Meet us on the second floor for dinner. Seven. There's a restaurant at the end of a hall."

My room looks over a church. Early morning light, slick cobblestones. A man carrying bread, boys with knapsacks, a smoking policeman. I undress, shower, and climb into bed. I feel weightless, gone. I sleep until 5:00 p.m. The window is dark. I shave, text Ortiz, and put on my only good suit—a charcoal-gray Armani I bought a year ago with a couple of big overtime checks—a pale-blue shirt, and a tie. I step to the window and see my reflection. I feel as if I almost belong in this drama of Stefan's making.

I take the elevator to the second floor. I hear soft voices and step through the door. Chloe is in a short, purple dress, her hair bobby-pinned and bunned. Stefan wears a dark-blue suit, white shirt, no tie. He's talking to men in the corner—brandy and laughter, except for one, a nervous, stout man with thinning blond hair, who must be Viktor from Vienna. Stefan is at ease around men with money. I have seen him operate before. He moves about them like a blade, discerning, gaining confidences, twisting in a joke usually involving a priest or a hapless diplomat. Chloe leads them to a table. She and I—Roberto is not around—sit a few tables over, watching.

"Human nature, huh?" says Chloe. "You must know a lot about that, Sam. The way we feed off one another. Confidences and insecurities. Nothing brings them out like money." She nods. "Look at Viktor, fidgeting. The big man next to him is the Berlin banker, and the other one is the gangster—of course, Stefan calls him a *casino owner*—from Montenegro. I love his beard, don't you? Like a pelt." She smiles, checks a smartphone, and turns to her white wine and pheasant. I glance at Stefan, sitting in candlelight in a window over the street, looking over it as if the city had been passed to him by a sly old-world descendant.

Dinner ends, and the Berlin banker, Klaus, who looks like conductor Kurt Masur, and Viktor retreat to a corner and smoke a cigar. Stefan and the Montenegrin walk to a window. They are speaking Serbian. Chloe leans close to me and translates. They talk of the former Yugoslavia and Tito, the partisan-turned-dictator who once held it all together while riding horses and hunting deer on the presidential estate in Belgrade.

"It was always a false country," says the Montenegrin.

"It was our home," says Stefan. "We did many things well. We got along. Croat. Muslim. Serb."

"Yes, but you knew it wasn't to be. We were a stepchild of a country. Didn't really fit, did we? All those pieces."

"You got out okay."

"I don't complain," says the Montenegrin. "I stay on the coast. Quiet as—how do they say?—a clam. You have done well, too, although I don't exactly know what it is you do anymore. You are a mystery, my friend. Like your grandfather. How many years is Goran gone now? He was the fox of them all. Do you ever go back to see your mother's grave?"

"I do not want to see it. It's not in a cemetery. It's in a place below our house, near a stream. That time is long over."

"Be glad of it. I worry about the Russians though. You see what they're doing in America. The Russians eat but are always hungry. They tried to take me over in my own country, my own casino."

"This deal will help you," says Stefan.

"Viktor concerns me. He doesn't have the heart for this. Look at him. He looks like he got on the wrong train."

"He'll come around. Klaus is reassuring him."

"A German and an Austrian. That's not a good pairing."

They laugh, drinking wine and smoking cigarettes the Montenegrin rolls.

"Your fingers are still nimble, Silva," says Stefan, winking at him as if they are in a game. "They are like insects."

I look over the street, listening to Stefan and the men around me, thinking of Sunday train rides as a boy, from Newport to Hartford to New York and back, and how I felt rich racing along the coast, following the contours of boys before me and listening to my mother speak of writers and dead men in warehouses and how to make a highball or tip a doorman and, on one trip, which startled both of us, how to touch a woman. *Tender but never shy.* I take my wine and stand at a window in the corner. A man hurries toward a church. A bakery truck rattles past. A couple gets out of a taxi, laughing and falling drunk in the street, rolling and kissing near the gutter. It's nearly dawn. Stefan appears and puts his arm around me.

"You never look tired," I say.

"I'm a vampire. Night is my time."

"It's nearly light."

"A nice scene, don't you think?"

"Is the deal done?"

"Viktor was an ass, but yes."

"The guy from Montenegro looks happy."

"Silva is never happy. But this will make him content. For a while."

"Things worked out for you."

"Tonight. Not always. Look around. Isn't it perfect? This place, this city. Look at that street. Imagine where it leads." He presses his face closer to the glass. "Life is these moments, Sam. Not the ones you wait for. They never come."

We are quiet. The German, the Montenegrin, and Viktor leave. Chloe scrolls on her phone. A woman moves toward us in the window's reflection. Stefan and I turn. He puts his hand on my shoulder and whispers, "This is the one you need to see." He slides his hand away and wanders toward Chloe.

"I think you know me, Mr. Sam," she says.

"Zhanna Smirnov."

"That is a sometime name."

"You were with Levon the night he left the police station, after we questioned him. I saw you in the back of the car."

"Poor Levon. He was like child."

She is tan, silver-black hair cut above the shoulders, blue eyes looking at me, making calculations. She's wearing a black dress and pearls as if returning from a night out, perhaps from a castle in the hills, or a hidden corridor in a museum. Her bracelet is latticed gold; two diamonds peek from a ring. Her voice has a slight huskiness and flows with its own intentions. There must be czars in her bloodline. One can tell, or she's a damn good actress—a spy, too, maybe, like Mickey Orlov. She lifts a gold case from her sequined clutch, takes a cigarette, and lights it. She nods, and we sit by the window.

"How do you know Stefan?" I say.

"I don't know him. People I know do. But he is charming. I like."

"Money people."

She laughs.

"All kinds of people," she says. "And you?"

"He helped me on something a long time ago."

"It seems he is helping you again, no? You must watch those who help too much."

She blows an arrow of smoke and looks at me.

"Did you know Katrina Ivanovna?" I say.

"The whole world knew Katrina Ivanovna. Once."

"But . . ."

"I am her aunt. Her mother is my sister."

She registers my reaction.

"Not what you were thinking," she says.

"I don't know what to think."

"It's like Russian doll for you, no? Many pieces."

"That sounds about right."

"What do you look for, Mr. Sam?"

"How she died."

"I think overdose. She had many problems with drugs. They catch her finally."

"You believe that?"

"It's what I read. But where is body? Why did police lose her?"

"I'm sorry. We don't know who's behind it. That's why I'm here."

She glances to the window and back.

"Night is almost over," she says.

"Do—"

"You need to find something of Katrina's."

"The diaries."

"Little red books," she says. "Should be interesting for whoever finds."

"Why?"

"Many secrets in little books, maybe, maybe not."

"You were in Los Angeles when she died."

She blows smoke, crushes out her cigarette, looks at me hard.

"Katrina was not close to her mother. You know her mother? No. Maria Ivanovna. Very important in the right places in Russia. She is like—what is expression?—connected. Maria is connected. Oligarchs and money. She knows them. Moscow is happy and dangerous place for people with money. She understands them. They let her in. Maria always wanted to be in. Like Putin. But he was never out." She looks at her diamond ring and back at me. "Katrina stopped talking to her long ago. After she found out."

"Found out what?"

"You find, Mr. Sam. Maybe in little red books."

"But you know."

"It's hard to know what one knows these days."

"Why were you in Los Angeles?"

"Katrina called Maria one night. Crying. Maria said she was high. Talking like wild child. Like addict. Is that right, *addict*? Katrina was yelling into phone. Saying she would tell her story. The story of famous ballerina." She lights another cigarette. "Did you ever see her dance? She was beautiful. I am her aunt, so I can say this. But everyone knew it was true. But dancers cannot dance forever, can they Mr. Sam? Maria told her not to tell her story. Katrina wouldn't listen. She said she was going to meet a man who writes such books. I think this man wrote a book about Princess Diana. One of those writers. Maria called me and said go. 'Go see her. Stop her.'"

"Why you?"

"Katrina was close to me. I was dancer too. For a little while. Not like her. Nobody was like her." She closes her eyes, smiles, as if in a passing dream. "When I got to Los Angeles, I called her. She didn't answer. I went to her apartment, but she wasn't there or didn't answer. I went back to the hotel and waited. Then . . ."

"You heard she was dead."

"Yes, the next day, when police lost her body."

"Someone stole it."

"No matter, she is gone."

"Do you know Mickey Orlov?"

"Mickey, Mikhail. He is like cat. Many lives. Was spy, now a producer. Many in Russia are like him."

"He lives in Los Angeles."

"He's still Russian," she says, tapping her heart. "Inside."

"Did he know Katrina?"

"Mickey knows everybody. Katrina knew everybody. What you think? Maybe interesting relationship between Katrina and Mickey."

"What kind?"

"You find out, Mr. Sam."

A crack of orange runs across the horizon. Zhanna and I stare at the sky, saying nothing. She slides me a cigarette. It sits there. I touch it, hold it. Put it down. Pick it up. Smell the tobacco. I light it and feel that sudden detachment, that fleeting high, like the first drink, that I have always loved.

"You have quit?" Zhanna says.

"Until now."

Chloe and Stefan are gone. A waiter brings espressos, but the room is ours alone.

"Do you think it was an overdose?" I say.

"Yes, but maybe . . ."

"Two men came to her apartment. Levon said Katrina was upset by them. He said they were Russian."

"Many Russians in America these days. Too many, no? Mr. Trump likes Russians too much, I think."

"Who were those men who visited her?"

"In my country, when you speak on phone, the men with no faces hear."

"You think Katrina's phone was tapped?"

"This is normal, no?"

"Other people are looking for the diaries?"

"What you think?"

"KGB."

"No more KGB. Is now FSB. But same."

"What about Levon?"

"You know about Levon. You questioned him."

"Did he overdose?"

She breathes in, begins to speak, falls silent. Starts again.

"His parents knew Maria Ivanovna from long time back. They called maybe year ago to see if Katrina could help Levon. Music world is very cruel. Maria passed on to me, and I told Katrina to meet this boy. He played beautifully. So sad. He played for her. You know this. Katrina said his playing calmed her, and he kept coming to her apartment. Playing longer and longer. She dancing around him. Imagine. How do you say, lost souls?"

"Like Gogol."

"You read Russians, Mr. Sam?"

"A few over the years. Why were you with Levon that night at the police station?"

"When Katrina didn't answer my calls, I called Levon."

"Did he know about the diaries? What did he tell you?"

"He was frightened. I took him to hotel. He told me about the two men. I asked him about Katrina's red books. He said he knows nothing. I believe. He's a boy. I asked him to play. He played in my room for an hour, never looking up. Like monk, I think. We ate, and he left. I told him to stay with me. He said no. I told him again. But he left. I should have made him stay."

"Did he go to his parents?"

"I don't know."

"We can't get a hold of them. They're not home."

"I think you will never know them."

"Was he killed? A forced overdose."

"He was a scared boy who knew nothing, but maybe, someone thinks he did."

"Who?"

She slides her cigarette case into her clutch and stands, pushes her shoulders back. I can see the ballerina in her, distant. Is she here to lead me in the right or wrong direction? Like a Russian doll. Many pieces. She fixes her pearls, straightens her dress.

"Can I talk to Maria?"

"This will never happen."

"Can you and I talk again?"

"Maybe. I find you, Mr. Sam." She turns to leave, turns back. "You know the men with no faces listen to everyone."

She leaves. I stand at the window. She walks out of the hotel and gets into the back of a black car. The chauffeur closes the door. A light rain falls across the cobblestones. The car turns east. She is gone.

CHAPTER 20

"Change of plans, Sam."

"What?"

"A little detour," says Stefan.

"Where?"

"Africa."

"What are you talking about? I can't go to Africa. I have to get back."

"One day extra, max."

"Stefan . . ."

"Sam, we must go. Please."

I look out the Gulfstream window. Rain is turning to snow; yellow lights flash against trees at the edge of the runway. A small plane lands with silent ease. Baggage men laugh and hurry. Chloe is scrolling; Roberto is in the cockpit. I text Ortiz, tell him I met Zhanna but that I'll be a day late. I don't mention Africa. I text Lily. "Stay on Krause. Home soon." Stefan is eating Danish and sliced fruit. His deal is done, and he is pleased. He reads. Looks up.

"*The Bridge over River Drina*," he says. "Story of Balkans all in this book. I read it first long time ago."

"I don't know it."

"I let you have it when I finish."

"Stefan, I need to get back."

"Don't worry about things, Sam. You will be home soon."

We lift. Wind shakes the plane; snow squalls. Then, as before, we rise to blue, sun on the wing.

"Where?"

"South Sudan," says Stefan. I feel Chloe's glance. "Newest country in the world, Sam. Imagine. Hard place. Very hard place, like former Yugoslavia but much worse, yet also beautiful. Important place for you to know."

"Why?"

"You will see. Sleep now. Later you tell me about Zhanna."

I'm angry but captive. This is Stefan. I press him once more, shout expletives. He looks at me is if at an errant child.

"Trust me, Sam. We need to go."

I put on headphones and drift between jazz and sleep. I awake in Nairobi. A man boards, hands Stefan a bag, and hurries away. We fuel and take off for Juba. Chloe gives Stefan two folders. He reads. We fly over grasslands and thin streams. Thatched villages are covered in yellow-red dust, and men race below on motorcycles. I have never been to sub-Saharan Africa, but I have a framed photograph of a tribesman on a wall in my apartment. I saw it in a gallery years ago. It was cheap, but the tribesman, looking at a storm gathering on the horizon, had the bearing of a prophet. Chloe hands me a magazine and a few newspaper stories. I read about South Sudan's wars, atrocities, oil, women who are traded for cattle, and its president, a guerrilla-turned-statesman who wears a cowboy hat, carries a revolver, and speaks perfect English. I write this in my notebook. I write about the past thirty-six hours, Zhanna, and Stefan too—his "Moonlight Sonata," his deals, bits and scenes of him, but not all of him. Words cannot do that.

"So how was this Zhanna? Good-looking for an older lady."

"You're awake."

"I never sleep long on a plane," he says.

"She's not that old. How do you know her?"

"A man I know, knows another man. He knows her. She was a spy or is a spy. Who can tell with Russians? A dancer, too, I think, but long ago." Stefan yawns, looks out the window and back. "She was helpful?"

"She's Katrina's aunt."

"Must know something."

"More than she said."

"Like all women," says Stefan, winking at Chloe. "You will see her again."

"How do you know?"

"Some women go and come back, Sam. I think you will see her again."

"I don't know if I trust her."

"Like I said, it's hard to know with Russians. Businesspeople, spies, bankers all run together like, how do you say, very tight knot. Biggest place for secrets in world is Russia."

"Zhanna says Katrina knew Mickey Orlov."

"Maybe she danced for him."

"What do you think?"

"I think Mickey Orlov's a powerful man. Man you don't fuck with. He is part of the tight knot."

"You ever deal with him?"

"You're like a question machine, Sam."

"Just trying to know."

"You will. Zhanna, maybe, is a good person for you. But don't turn your back." He laughs. "Never turn your back on a Russian. Mr. Trump knows this. He turned his back; now he's in shit. Putin has the best face, don't you think, Sam? Shows nothing. Little eyes, staring. I love how Putin stares. Like animal."

"You ever meet him?"

"I saw him once in Moscow. I was there for a deal. Small one. I finished early and went to the Tretyakov Gallery. You know it? Beautiful, Sam, truly. It was a weekday in February. Not crowded. I heard noise down the hall, and big men in suits—you know the kind—rushing ahead of a little man. Putin. No kidding, Sam. Putin. They pushed us aside. Everything went quiet." Stefan is telling the story as if it happened a moment ago. "Putin stopped in front of *What is the Truth?* Do you know this painting? By Nikolay Nikolayevich Ge. Christ standing before Pilate. Pilate wants to know the truth, but he and Christ have different truths and so he will never understand. Putin stepped close to the painting. Examining it. Every inch. He stepped back and looked at it for a long time. Like a hypnotized man. Everyone was silent. A man whispered behind me, 'He can't figure out if he's Pilate or Christ.' We know what he became, yes, but then maybe we didn't. He stood for a little longer and disappeared behind the big men in suits."

"He say anything?"

"Not a word."

"What do you think?"

"I think no man knows the truth."

"What else?"

"Putin is small in real life."

Chloe brings us mango juice and peanuts. We look out to the sky and are quiet for a while. The land is shades of brown and dust. I think of Katrina and Lily. I touch a finger to the window, feel the cold. Stefan says tribes are fighting below. Battles here and there in a new country ruined even before it begins. He says war never goes all the way away. He starts to say something about his mother but stops, looks at Chloe and me, and turns back to the window. We are low, flying over a river, ladies washing colors along the banks.

We land. The air is hot. Dry. Soldiers in mismatched fatigues stand by rusted jeeps near customs. The hills beyond are green and small. A man rushes us with a sign: "Mr. Stefano."

"That must be us," says Stefan.

We hurry toward passport control, Chloe pushing ahead, directing young men to grab boxes and luggage stacked on the tarmac.

"Supplies," she says.

A captain in a beret thumbs our passports and looks us over until Stefan slips him cash. Stamps are thunked, and we pass through the gates, beyond night-black faces and soldiers, to the newest country in the world.

"Welcome to freedom," says a man in sunglasses, leaning on a motorcycle, with a Glock shoved in his trousers, and a girl, smoking a cigarillo, draped over his shoulder like a serpent.

Young men move, slow and effortless, barely mussing the air. We climb into a Range Rover. The driver looks to be twelve. He smiles and turns on music. The Bee Gees spill over us as we speed down a few miles of macadam to a dirt road.

"Whole country has only fifty-three miles of paved roads," says the driver. "But now we are independent. More roads will come. The Chinese build many roads. The Chinese are all over. This might *be* China." He laughs and continues, "Everyone is coming to South Sudan. But I must say—a man must be honest—it is bad and good times. We have too many tribes. Much killing. It will sort out one day. All things, my friends, sort out. Oh, listen . . ." He turns up the volume. "I love this song. 'Staying Alive'. Sounds like hyenas in the bush. I love Mr. Bee Gees."

We drive for two hours, passing boys with big guns at checkpoints. They hold ropes and sleep in the shade, sauntering toward us, asking for papers. Some want money, some cigarettes; Roberto hands one a flask of Johnny Walker. The grasslands are parched, and men with thin cattle roam past villages burned by marauders. A few warriors, their spears and Kalashnikovs resting against trees, splash and laugh in a watering hole. They bear tribal tattoos the color of eggplant and wave for us to swim. "Do not worry. No lions will come. The crocodiles have been eaten." They laugh and wrestle and stand naked in the sun, beads of water glistening. We watch them for a moment.

"They are like children," says the driver. "A new South Sudan is coming."

We race across flatlands, and after exhausting much of the Bee Gees's catalog, we round a curve through a stand of trees and roll toward a small lake. A band of men with guns stand smoking and drinking around a bed with billowing sheets, where a man wearing a medallion and a red beret sits bare chested, like a king.

"Mango?" he says. "Grapes? Lamb?"

He laughs. "Get over here, Stefan, or I will shoot you. You have been away too long. Do you like my bed? It fell off a truck in Juba, and my men brought it here. I think it is the bed of a diplomat. I wonder where he is sleeping now."

He laughs again, rising from the bed and hugging Stefan. His skin is splotched with scars.

"How is my hospital?" says Stefan.

"When you build a hospital, people are always sick. Have you noticed?" He laughs again. "Come, let's go see this thing you have made in the jungle. You are Stanley Livingstone. Do you know Stanley Livingstone? He was around here sometime long ago. He is in books I have read."

"How are things?"

"The Dinka and the Nuer fight. How long have we been fighting? I don't know. How long has the sun been in the sky? The UN sends people, but what can a few blue helmets do? We need guns, Stefan. You have built a hospital. But we need guns. Then you can have more people for your hospital." He smiles and finishes his mango. "Seriously, Stefan, you bring guns to other lands; this is what I have heard. Why not here?"

"I got out of the gun business. I am in finance now."

"This is true? You brought us guns in our war against the north. Our war for independence."

"Since then, I am finished with guns."

"Mmmm. I don't know if this is a wise move. The world will always need guns."

We walk along the lake. Stefan and Samuel—*King* Samuel, he jokes—lead the way past women carrying jugs on their heads, through a stretch of marsh to the north end of the lake, where we cut across open land to a collection of huts and a long wooden building with white curtains blowing in the shade. Villagers walk toward Stefan, some holding out their hands. One woman throws a flower at him; two others sing a native hymn. Children gather around us.

"They always sing when Stefan comes," says Samuel. "Always the same song. We need to teach them a new one."

Roberto and Chloe appear in the Range Rover with several of Samuel's men. They park and unload boxes and duffels that men in white lab coats carry into the building.

"You see," says Samuel, "your hospital is doing well, Stefan. No one has burned it down. It is very tidy. And clean. You can smell how clean it is. I love the smell of cotton balls and rubbing alcohol. Breathe in. See? Dr. Goodluck is very strict about dirt. Aren't you, Doctor?"

A man with a stethoscope and a clipboard appears. He is smoking. His glasses are thick. He hugs Stefan. "My friend, why have you been gone so long?"

Stefan puts his arm around him. We follow them up four wooden stairs into a ward rowed with beds covered by scrims of mosquito netting. Three nurses tend to the sick. We walk past them to a small operating room, an office, and two examining rooms, where boys sweep and wash instruments beneath a sign that reads, "Dirt brings sin and infection." We pass into a room at the back. A line of children and their mothers wait outside at the door, and a nurse, her white uniform bright against her black skin, sits on a stool with a box of syringes.

"Shot day," says the doctor.

He slides another stool toward the nurse. Stefan sits, and Samuel stands behind him. The nurse shushes everyone, and one by one, the families come. Children climb onto Stefan's lap; the nurse swabs and sticks them. Some cry, some shake, and when each climbs down, Chloe hands them a lollipop. The line lasts for two hours. Families arrive from far-off villages. They bring goats, carved trinkets, sweet potatoes. A priest holds up a rosary; a shaman appears with an antelope horn.

"They all come for Stefan," says Samuel. "You are king like me, Stefan. A white king in the jungle. Stanley Livingstone."

Samuel laughs and pats Stefan on the back. Stefan says nothing. He smiles and lifts another child as a mother kisses his hand. A tear rolls down his face. I have never seen a man so content. All his energy stilled. He starts to say something, but nothing comes. He gathers and calms the next child. They file up one by one. He whispers to them, light breaking through the door, shining on black faces—old, young, wrinkled, ancient, and new, scars aglimmer and palms, bright as river stones, reaching out, calling.

I look up and see her. Katrina.

In photographs on the wall. Surrounded by children, like Stefan now, she is white, like a dove flying through night. Stefan is with her in a few pictures, holding sick children, giving shots, fixing a roof. Two strange missionaries. The photographs are different from any I've seen of Katrina. She is relaxed, hair falling, big smile, far from stage and costume. It is her but not, a serene impostor. She draws you in, inviting, and the photographs, all in black and white, have the air of a past world. Stefan glances at me. He hands a girl to her mother and motions for me to follow. We walk to the shade of a tree and sit in rattan chairs. My anger seeps, my words low and tight.

"You said you barely knew her, saw her only once."

"At Harvey Weinstein's party when she danced," says Stefan. "That is when we met. But more came of it."

"Why did you lie to me?" I breathe in. I feel I might yell, but I don't. "Why are we here?"

"I wasn't ready to tell you then. I am now."

"Did you . . ."

"Let me talk, Sam."

Chloe and Dr. Goodluck walk toward us. Stefan waves them away. The children have gone, and Samuel sits on the clinic porch, smoking with his men.

"The night I saw her dance, I had to know her," he says. "We talked and drank vodka on the Weinsteins' lawn. She liked that I was half Serb. Came from people with souls like hers. She was taking pills then, I think, but not so many. She seemed . . . clear—is that right word? Most days. We started seeing one another. Not often. We both traveled a lot. It lasted a few months. It was a time she was beginning to question things about her past. Her family. She never said anything specific. But she was bothered. I knew she and her mother didn't get along."

He stops for a moment and looks at me.

"One night at my home," he says, "she saw pictures of this place. She said I must take her. We came and stayed for three days. She helped with the children. She sat in the sun. I could feel her loosen, you know, like on vacation. She sang morning songs with the women. She danced around a bonfire. She moved like a spirit burning up from the earth. You know how she could move, Sam. You've seen. They never saw that here. The tribal men danced with her. It was like in a dream. She said she wanted to never leave. Her career was over. She could not do what she once did, and it hurt to know that. She got a text while we were here. I don't know who from. Or what it said. It upset her." Stefan looks beyond the shade to women on the road, babies strapped to their backs. "She said we had to go. We flew to LA. She cried on the plane but wouldn't tell me why. I dropped her at her loft on Spring Street. We drank wine and made love. It was not the same. I left before it was light. I called a few times. She never answered. I came by. She was never home. I never saw her again."

"How long ago?"

"Maybe two years."

"How do I know that's the truth?"

"It is."

"Why didn't you tell me?"

"I was drunk on the night you told me she died. Before you came, I was remembering my mother and the war. I was talking crazy. I was no good. You saw me. I didn't know what to say. I couldn't believe it. But I knew I would help you."

"Are you telling me the truth about Zhanna? You don't know her?"

"I know people who know her. That's all. The first time I met her was with you the other night in Brussels. I didn't know she was Katrina's aunt."

"I'm supposed to believe that?"

"You're mad. I understand." A boy brings warm Cokes and a flask. He runs away. "Let's have some bourbon, Sam." We drink the Coke down a bit, and Stefan pours in the bourbon. A scent, a little rush. The taste calms. We sit in silence. Vultures perch in trees; smaller birds circle above. A breeze blows off the river, but not enough to cut the heat. Men with spears herd cattle past; boys kick a soccer ball made of tape, puffs of dust rising from bare feet. "I made calls after Katrina died," says Stefan. "It was clever who did it. To make it look like overdose for a girl who could overdose. Or maybe, really, she did overdose. Zhanna knows. I think she did not tell you all."

"What do you think?"

"Katrina was a child of secrets."

"I think you know."

"I don't, but I know it's true."

"Did you love her?"

"I think a little, yes."

"I could bring you in."

"I'm not the one you want, Sam."

Stefan pours more bourbon.

"Why am I here?" I say.

"Zhanna wouldn't come back to America so soon. Not after Katrina and Levon."

"Not Brussels. Here. We didn't have to come here. You could have told me. You knew that eventually I'd find out. I'm pissed, Stefan. Brussels was good, yes. Zhanna is probably key to something. Thank you. But this. The FBI is suspicious of you. They've wanted you for a long time. They probably know I'm with you. You lied to me, and now I'm flying around Africa."

"You needed to see, Sam. People are not one thing. We are many people in one. I wanted you to see this other person in Katrina. You saw the pictures. That is not the same girl you found. It is not the same ballerina on pills. It is another her. The one who couldn't survive. Does that make sense? I wanted you to know that about her. It seemed the best place to tell you. Why not come and see? A day late back to LA. Big deal."

"What about the other *you*? Who is he?"

"This is part of him."

"Penance? Absolution for your other life?"

"Sam, you are like a Serb." He smiles. "Yes, maybe penance."

"I don't think I'll ever know you."

"We are the same, Sam."

"No."

Stefan empties the flask. We sit, saying nothing. It is dusk. Lights come on in the clinic. I can see Dr. Goodluck working at his desk, the nurse counting syringes. Mosquito nets hang over beds of sleeping children. Samuel and his men are gone. The clearing is quiet, but night sounds rustle beyond the tree line. Fires rise here and there. The moon will soon be over the river; the stars are as if from a storybook, endless. Chloe walks over with a satchel. She hands out cigarettes, and we smoke—I, who have quit and will quit again—and sit quietly with the other people in us, those the land awakens. The Range Rover pulls up. Roberto waves. Our boy-man driver slaps on cologne. The Bee Gees play all the way to the airport.

CHAPTER 21

"You disappeared," says Lily.

"I told you where I was."

"Yeah, for a day. It's been four. Nothing."

"I texted."

"One text. One."

Lily is midway through a set of curls. I drop my bag and head for the porch. She follows. She gives me a quick, joyless hug, sits beside me, sweating. I unfold the short version of my Brussels and South Sudan trip. Her anger cools. She wants to hear more about red-dust villages and tribesmen on motorcycles and children dancing around night fires beneath the stars.

"When I was a child, I had a picture book about lions and jungles," she says. "It was paradise, you know, like Eden. I'd sit in bed at night staring at the pictures, seeing if I could find God hiding with the animals."

She lingers on God and the funny things children think. She slides closer to me, leans back, and tells me about Jimmy Krause.

He keeps a pattern, stays close to Burbank. No friends. He went for a head shave at a barbershop. He watches a lot of TV, walks to the grocery store, eats canned stuff and half gallons of ice cream. He pets passing dogs and keeps a night-light on in his bedroom. Twice, he met a well-dressed big guy with polished shoes at the Burbank bar and at a parking lot in Santa Monica.

"They met near the beach, both of them facing the water— Krause slid over to his passenger side—talking out windows, watching the waves. And the guy? Get this," says Lily, as if she'd spotted a twenty blowing across a sidewalk, "the guy is Armando Torres. You know who that is? Orlov's head of security at the studio. Former army captain. Tours in Iraq. Now, he's in LA looking through tinted wraparounds and driving an Escalade. Beats shooting hajis, I guess."

"Hajis?"

"Jesus, Carver. Hajis are what our guys over there called Iraqis."

"That's racist."

"It was goddamn war."

"What are you thinking about Krause?"

"He's working off-the-books stuff for Torres. Which means he's doing them for Orlov."

"You think—"

"No," she says. "Not his MO. He's more of a fixer, bouncer type. I'm thinking he was the contact for the two Russian guys who showed up at Katrina's loft and at the Cubano café in Echo Park to see Levon. Two Russians would need a local. Someone to get them where they need to go. These Russians disappeared, right?"

"Vapors. But why would Orlov bring Krause to his estate? He'd want to keep his distance. Krause is a small-time fence and car thief. Orlov's a billionaire spy. Why get tangled with a guy like Krause?"

"Maybe Krause has history with Torres. They both did time in Iraq. *Band of Brothers* kind of shit. Who knows? Besides, Krause might be smarter than we think. Don't look at me like that. People surprise you. You, if anyone, should know that. I'm liking Krause in this."

"Too many maybes."

"It's something, Carver. A connection. Just like your Zhanna Smirnov."

"Zhanna's more Orlov's league."

She stands, stretches, tightens her laces.

"I'm going for a run. Coming?"

"I'm tired. Long flights. You go. I have to call Ortiz anyway."

"See ya, wouldn't want to be ya," she says, laughing.

"How far you going?"

"Five. You gonna be here?"

"Yes."

The door slams. I watch her run up the gentle slope toward the church, making a right, heading west toward the 101 and the skyline, which she likes at dusk, when the air cools and the colors simmer and girls are skipping rope in the plaza near the trumpet man and the painted virgin. Lily would be a good partner if I wanted one, and maybe I do. I don't know yet, but I do like sitting on this porch, knowing she's out there and coming back. I pat myself for a cigarette. Pretend I have one. In my mind, I light it and throw away the match. I call Ortiz. He's calm as I tell him about Brussels and Zhanna and then the detour to South Sudan. He stays quiet, letting me spool it out. He's sitting on his lawn, probably on his second beer, and his wife, Consucla, is inside watching *Survivor* or *Dancing with the Stars*. My story done, he says nothing for a while.

"You there?" I say.

"You ever think, Carver, what it all comes to? All these perps. Put one down; another pops up. Can't keep faces straight anymore. The species depresses me." He sips. "It's still and dark in my backyard. I can count my breaths, you know, feel them hit the air. I like it out here. You've been here, so you know. I read this story in the paper the other day." He sips. "They think they found this whole ancient hidden city beneath some farmland in Kansas. Can you believe that shit? Some conquistadors looking for gold hundreds of years ago come upon an unexpected city." He sips. "Amazing, the shit we don't know. Right under our feet. Whole fucking lost cities."

"You want to go find one?"

"I'd like to." He laughs.

"You have all those old maps."

"Love 'em. They're our claims on the earth. They tell you what's where, but they also tell you what was once imagined. You know what though?"

"What?"

"We don't have a map to her body. That bother you? A dead ballerina out there we don't know fuck about. Where she is. Who took her. Second woman we've lost." He sips. "Dylan Cross is out there too. Alive, no doubt. I don't know if I ever told you, but I drove to that little church she designed out near Joshua Tree. It was after she got away. It was a cold day. The wind was blowing hard over the desert, and there was this perfect little church, sitting on the horizon by itself. I got out of the car to go in. It was locked. I walked around and watched the light play on the stained glass. I thought about staying there for a long time. Just me and the church and the desert wind. You ever go out there?"

"More than a few times," I say. "I keep imagining that's where she'll turn up, sitting alone in a pew. Waiting for me. I dream about it. I don't know if she can hide forever. Some people aren't built to stay gone." The moon is high off Lily's porch. Kids are laughing in the street. "Don't worry, Ortiz. We'll find Katrina, and Dylan Cross too."

"We have to find Katrina now, Carver. Put this thing down. I think it's time you pull in Krause. Get him to talk. Lily may be right about him being an errand boy in this whole thing. Sounds like she's into this, huh? Being a detective."

"She's good, smart."

"She could kick both our asses," says Ortiz.

"There's that."

He sips and laughs.

"Tell me more about this Zhanna chick. Sounds like she's something out of one of those books written by that English guy with the French name."

"Le Carré."

"Yeah, him."

"If she told all she knew, we'd find everything."

"I'm getting calls from the FBI. They're getting calls from the CIA."

"I'm going to see Azadeh tomorrow," I say.

"The married lesbian?"

"That's her."

"I met her once. A little too know-it-all, maybe, but she's sharp." He sips. "I'm tired."

"I'm guessing you're reaching for the third beer."

"How can you tell?"

"The way you get philosophical. Put your energy on low."

"Maybe. My wife calls it drunk. I'm going to bed."

I nod off and wake when Lily gets home, sweating. She's been gone a while. She unties her running shoes, rolls a cold beer across her forehead. Sits with me. She tells me she watched *Touch of Evil* on AMC while I was gone. "Orson Welles was great, but Charlton Heston and Marlene Dietrich are no Mexicans. All that dark makeup. Terrible. Couldn't get away with that shit today. Twitter'd be all over that. *Hashtag racist.* It was good, though. I like black-and-white. You ever see it? You've seen all the old stuff." She hands me a beer. "I like the opening scene," she says. "The camera moving from low to high, following a guy, you know, the guy who plants the bomb, from running through an alley to a shadow on the wall. Mysterious shit." She leans against me. I feel her through my shirt, how warm she is, and I think I'm not going home tonight. I'll sit here with my maybe partner, falling in and out of sleep, watching the sky change beyond the church on the corner.

"Hey, Carver."

"What?"

"I was keeping something from you earlier. The thing I hinted at before my run. I was waiting on a guy to confirm it."

She smiles, clicks on a light, hands me a picture.

"I took a detour. Met with this guy a few days ago who does security for Krause's building. You wouldn't think it. I mean, the building's okay, but you wouldn't think it'd have security—but they have cameras. No shit. I asked the guy to pull some stuff. Quiet, you know. Anything recent with Krause in it. Didn't think he'd get back to me, but he calls while I'm running. Look at this."

I put my beer down, sit up, lift the picture close. Krause

passing through a lobby with two very big men dressed as if they fell off a train in Kiev. They're both smoking, in a lobby of a Burbank building. Definitely not locals. One of them is wearing a ball cap, his face mostly hidden; the other has a thick, pale face of stone, black eyes looking into the camera. Lily presses closer.

"The Russians," I say.

"That's what I'm thinking. The guys who went to Katrina's."

"We don't know that."

"Look, Carver, they fit the description. That CI you met put Krause in this."

"Could be just two guys. Two of Krause's bouncer friends. Need more."

"C'mon, Carver, look. These guys couldn't find the 405. They're not from here."

"When's the footage from?"

"The week Katrina and Levon were killed."

I stare at the picture. Three men frozen in gray, caught for a split second in time and then gone, fluid, moving through the world.

"We're only going to get one shot at Krause," I say, looking at the picture and then to Lily.

"Then we better not fuck it up."

CHAPTER 22

Dawn. Echo Park. A few homeless guys stand in their blankets, rumpled and biblical in the mist. The lake is calm. Geese float, still as decoys. A man slices mangoes and pineapples on a cart, but it's too early. Only joggers out at this hour, and a guy with a sketchbook, and some lost soul with a guitar, sitting on a bench, singing to empty swan boats. I open the *Times*. I like the feel of it—not always what it says, but the paper, its scent and black words, reminding me of my father when he'd get in from his morning run, sitting at the kitchen table, snapping through the *Boston Globe* and the *New York Times*, reading about tragedies distant and close. This hour, this fading twilight, this half-world— this is Los Angeles, stirring, gray, sun slanting across downtown toward the ocean, mountains taking shape, party boys fumbling latchkeys, cars running red lights on Glendale, ragged palms blowing on Sunset, Latinas hurrying for buses, Asians racing with fish on ice, cops changing shifts, garbage trucks clanging, all of it just starting, the clouds breaking to light, the day coming at you with peril and promise.

"Jesus, Carver, I said the south end."

"Thought you said north."

"Here."

Azadeh hands me a coffee.

"You bring scones?"

"Screw you, Carver."

"Why so early?"

"I got a court thing."

"I like it here in the morning."

"Kinda like South Sudan," she says.

"Ah, you've been checking up on me. It was a little vacation."

"They track Stefan, you know. Everywhere. Who he's with. Who gets a ride on his plane. Brussels. South Sudan. Quite the vacation, Carver. Zhanna Smirnov. You got the deluxe package. Bet there were plenty of scones." She sips her coffee, looks at the geese. "We—you—have another problem too. When my CI gave you Jimmy Krause, I didn't know he had a connection to Mickey Orlov. He wasn't on the radar. I found out the same night you did, when Krause got driven to Orlov's mansion."

"But . . ."

"Let me finish," she says. "FBI, CIA, and NSA have had surveillance on Orlov for at least two years. We think he's one of the smart guys behind the election hacking. You can thank him for Trump." She shakes her head. "It's perfect cover, you know: former Russian spy stays clean—or appears to—for decades, has all the right friends. Becomes a billionaire gold miner and movie producer. But he never stops being who he is. Like one of those terrorist sleeper cells. The Russians figured it out. Facebook, fake news. They knew where to hit."

"Why not bring Orlov in?"

"Can't prove it. Not enough to stick, anyway. The better play is to watch him. Where he leads. Guy's smooth though. No traces. Always that extra layer of separation. Anyway, we're staking out and following things, and guess who pops up?"

"Jimmy Krause."

"And you. And your new partner, Lily Hernandez."

"We're not partners," I say.

"Look like partners."

"It's complicated. Tell me more about Orlov."

"I just told. That's the gist."

"So he controls the whole thing?"

"Didn't say that. But he's a big part of it."

"What about Zhanna?"

"You tell me," she says. "You met her."

"She's Katrina's aunt."

Two geese, wings beating the air, feet slapping the lake, lift to flight. Azadeh reaches for her vape.

"What else?"

"Was or is a spy. Gave me that impression, but how the hell do I know? She's connected like her sister, Maria, Katrina's mother. There's jealously there. Something happened between Maria and Katrina. Don't know what, but it was bad. Zhanna got close to Katrina. She became the go-between. I got the sense Maria's the bigger deal in Russia. Better friends. Could be completely wrong though. These people are like grabbing at air."

"Welcome to my world," she says.

"Zhanna suggested there's a connection between Katrina and Orlov. She wouldn't give it up. 'You find, Mr. Sam.' Great accent. It's a voice you'd follow."

"Don't get romantic, Carver. You've got two murders and a lost body."

"Just saying."

We drink our coffee. The sun is warming things.

"Your hair's straighter," I say.

"I blow-dry it longer when I have court."

"Why?"

"Juries like blow-dried. It's proven. They do studies on shit like that."

"I prefer natural."

"Maybe that's why you look like shit today."

"I traveled halfway around the world."

"Shave, Carver."

Azadeh hands me the vape. I take a hit, feel the rush.

"So?"

"Watch yourself," she says. "Orlov is a national security interest, which means—"

"Don't get in the way."

"See, you *are* smart." She winks.

"I'm going to bring Jimmy Krause in," I say. "We don't have a lot but we're going to rattle him."

"What do you have?"

"I'll let you know after we talk to him."

"You better call me if anything points to Krause and Orlov."

"You probably already know."

"Could be."

"Could all be unrelated too."

"Bitch of a case you've got."

"Says the woman chasing Russian hackers. Why all these Russians in our lives?"

"Cold War reboot."

"You know anything about Orlov and Katrina? You holding back?"

"Could be deep Russian shit buried in Moscow. Aliases and reinventions. All kinds of mirrors that don't reflect back what's in front of them. Speaking of which . . ."

"Don't get on me about Stefan. I'm already pissed at him. He dated Katrina for a while, about two years ago."

Azadeh nods. "I'd be more than pissed," she says. "I'd be goddamned suspicious. Don't get played, Carver. I know you have this bruised-past-guy thing with him. He whispers tips and all that shit to you. But we don't think he ever went clean. Guys like that never get out of what brought them to where they are, no matter how many clinics in Africa they build." She hits the vape. "Think about it. All of a sudden, he delivers you Zhanna, tells you he dated Katrina—"

"I'm sufficiently warned. But he's a good source."

"Jesus, Carver."

She reaches into her bag, puts on lipstick. Her hands are quick, her eyes too. I like that about her, the deliberate way she approaches herself and the world—not without compassion, but with a wry acceptance that one shouldn't be surprised by disappointments never anticipated or imagined. Perhaps her exiled Iranian father taught her that.

The mist has burned off the lake. The joggers have multiplied.

Anglers are casting in the shallows. A couple of actors running lines from a sci-fi script pass; the man mentions the cruelties of the galaxy, but the woman says no, there is a planet in the fourth quadrant where goodness reigns. Azadeh rolls her eyes. She brushes her hair and heads to court.

I finish my coffee, and since I'm close, drive up the hill to Carroll Avenue in Angelino Heights. There's a family in the house now. Toys on the porch, trimmed bushes, clipped green lawn. It must have been hard for her to leave. All the work she put into the wood floors, banister, kitchen, turret, and caves of the old Victorian. I wonder what she thought while staring out of those windows. What the skyline seemed to her. What she was going to build. The dreams she had. Dylan Cross almost told me the night she broke into my apartment, tied me up, and tried to explain why she killed two men and left another chained to a wall in this house. She wanted to tell me about architecture, the mathematical and the divine. How cities are born to die and rise again in cycles; from ruins, new places are born. She started to tell me but she disappeared, leaving behind this house, which was sold to others.

CHAPTER 23

"Thing is, Jimmy," says Lily, sliding next to Krause at the bar, "you're in a jam."

"She's right," I say, slipping in on his other side. "Serious predicament."

We flash our badges. He looks at her, at me, back at her. Stares ahead, sips his beer. It's after happy hour. The place is quiet. Elton John is playing softly from the speakers. A waitress pockets her tips and heads into the Burbank night. Krause checks his phone. He starts to make a call but puts it down.

"I saw you the other day around my apartment building," he says to Lily. "Thought you were moving in. Thought I might ask you out. I'm neighborly like that." He smiles. "You're in good shape, I noticed. Used to be myself." He grabs his left shoulder. "Blew out a rotator cuff. Hard getting back to it. What do you bench?"

"Enough."

"Secret, huh? I get that."

"What do you weigh, Jimmy," says Lily. "I'm guessing two-twenty."

"Give or take."

"Six foot three, shaved head—I like that cologne, by the way. But you're starting to lose the cut. Pecs going, biceps shrinking. That's why the big shirt, right? Loose fit. Cover things up. I sympathize. Happens to a lot of guys."

"I'm beginning to think I don't like you," he says.

"Nobody does at first," she says, nodding toward me. "Even him. But then he did. It's like that with me." She signals the bartender for three beers. "But tell me, Jimmy, what is it with Burbank, anyway?"

"Peaceful up here," he says, taking measured breaths, holding his anger in. He would run if he could, but he's wedged between us. "I like peace. Like now, I'm sitting here enjoying this beer and then I'm gonna leave. Walk out that door into a peaceful night. Know why? You got nothing. I'm clean. Did my time a while ago for a few things. I'm what you call *reformed*. Zen-like in my thinking. You guys bringing me in?" He looks to us both. "Thought not. So sit and have a beer if you want. I got nothing for you."

"I can see that logic, Jimmy," I say. "But I don't think you know the shit you're in."

Lily drops the security-camera photo on the bar. He squints, looks at it. He reaches into his pocket and pulls out a pair of glasses. "Need these for reading," he says, lifting the picture, studying it, putting it down, picking it up again. He takes off his glasses, rubs his face. "I'm calling my lawyer," he says.

"Could go that route," says Lily.

"Then we'd have to take you in," I say. "You'd be upping the suspicion level."

"Dramatically," says Lily.

"We wouldn't be taking you in for us," I say. "We're LAPD. You fucked up higher up."

"What are you talking about?"

"FBI. Homeland Security," says Lily. "You could end up in a small, dark room for a long time. Orange jumpsuit. National security threat. I don't think they waterboard anymore, but who knows, right?" She leans closer to Krause. "This isn't about a chop shop or fencing diamonds, Jimmy."

"What the fuck you talking about? They're just two guys."

"Two Russian guys involved in hacking our election," I say.

"These guys?" he says, pointing at the picture and laughing. "Give me a break."

"FBI thinks so."

"They're gone. Outta the country. They didn't even have fucking laptops with them. *These* guys hacked us? I don't think so."

"They're not out of the country," says Lily, playing the bluff.

"Drove them to the airport myself."

"Did you see them get on the plane?" I say.

"Jimmy," says Lily, "you look confused."

He takes a long draw on his beer. Runs a hand over his shaved head.

"Saw you were up at Mickey Orlov's the other night," says Lily. "Nice company, movie producer. They casting you for something? You shopping a screenplay?"

Krause's eyes go to the door and back. He looks at us.

"I don't know Mickey Orlov. A friend of mine works for him.

I did a little security work for the studio when I got back from Iraq. Temp thing."

"So you know Armando Torres?" I say.

"Same unit," he says. "What's this about?"

"We just want to know who these two guys in the picture are," says Lily. "These two, right here."

"I'm calling my lawyer."

"Go ahead," I say. "We have a car outside. We'll all go downtown together. Once you do that, though, everyone knows. I'm wondering if you want everyone to know, given the company you keep. It's a situation."

"A predicament," says Lily.

Krause sits back, sighs. He puts his glasses on and picks up the picture.

"I don't want in this," he says. "You keep me outta whatever this is."

"We just want to know who these two guys are."

He glances at the door again, checks his phone.

"It's like this. Armando calls one day looking for someone to ferry two guys around town. That's all he says. Two guys from out of the country who want to see Hollywood. Good money. Two thousand bucks a day. Pick them up at the hotel in the morning, drop off when they're done." He sips his beer. "I took them to the usual spots. Venice Beach, Rodeo Drive—you know the drill. They don't talk much. Talk Russian to one another. Something like Russian, anyway. Quiet but nice, you know. Shit dressers." He holds up the picture. "Who dresses like that?"

"Fashion is different all over the world," says Lily.

"Whatever."

"You take them anywhere else?" I say.

"I don't know. I drove them all over the place."

"Think," says Lily.

"Took 'em to La Brea Tar Pits. LACMA. They weren't museum guys though. I should have known but I was trying to show them a good time. It's killing me you say they're Russian hackers. I'm laughing inside. Where else? Took 'em to lunch out near Echo Park. Some Cubano place. They had the address. Someone told 'em best sandwiches in LA. I waited in the car. Don't know how they ordered. Barely spoke English. Probably pointed. They brought me out fries. Oh, yeah, and twice I took 'em downtown."

"Where?"

"Café on the corner of Spring and Fourth."

"Why there?" says Lily.

"I don't know. They gave me the address. Said they were having a drink with a friend from back home."

"They gave you an address for two places, right?"

"Yeah, the café and the Cubano place."

"You didn't go in either one," says Lily.

"Listen, man, I'm carting these guys around all day, like *all fucking day*. They want a little free time. That's fine with me. I like a breather myself."

"What'd you do when they went into the café on Spring?"

"Parked the car. Walked over to Grand Central Market. Had a coffee, read a book. I like it over there now. Everything's fixed up. Expensive though. Four and a quarter for a coffee. Ridiculous, right? It's the hipsters. Changing the demographics and pushing up prices."

"You didn't meet anyone?"

"Just me and my book."

"Both times?"

"Yeah, both times."

"What are you reading, Jimmy?" says Lily.

"I read all kinds of shit."

"Give me a break," she says.

"What?"

"You read cereal boxes."

"Hey," says Krause, glancing over to me, "your partner's a bitch." He looks to Lily. "That week, I was reading about coyotes."

"The smuggling kind," says Lily.

"The four-legged kind. Amazing species, you know. They almost disappeared a century ago. But they came back. Resistant as hell. They're this creature between mythology and reality. My bet is that if anything survives the apocalypse, it'll be coyotes."

"I've seen them downtown late at night," I say.

"My point exactly," he says. "You push them out of one place, they find someplace new. Highly adaptable."

"Okay," says Lily. "You can read. I'm impressed. So, after you drink your coffee and read your coyote book, what next?"

"Get the car and pick them up."

"Each time," I say.

"At the café," says Lily.

"Yeah, each time at the café. Jesus! You guys are an aggravating tag team."

The door opens. Krause looks. A man in a suit lets the night air in. He sits across from us, orders a scotch rocks, looks around, and opens a magazine on the bar.

"Expecting someone, Jimmy?" says Lily.

"No. I'm almost done with my beer. Then home. I told you guys; I don't know anything about hacking. I drove two fucks around for a week, took them to the airport."

"Was Armando Torres happy?" says Lily. "I'm asking cause, well, since you're a big reader, must read the *Times*, right? Keep up on the news. You know anything about a dead ballerina?"

"OD case. You guys lost the body. That one?"

"Exactly," I say. "The café where you dropped your guys off is on the corner next to her loft. You take two big Russian guys to that corner on two days in the same week that the ballerina gets visits from two big Russian guys. What are the odds?"

"And she ends up dead," says Lily.

"Then two big Russian guys meet a friend of hers at the Cubano place, and guess what?"

"He ends up dead too," says Lily. "You starting to see a pattern?"

"Were these guys carrying anything when you picked them up at the café?" I say.

"Like what?"

"Little red books."

"I didn't see any little red books."

"You sure?"

"Absolute."

Krause finishes his beer. Sets the glass down. Slow. He looks at the picture, shakes his head, wants to smile but can't, rubs a hand over his mouth, thinking he's been in deep before, in Iraq, then back home fencing diamonds, getting arrested, doing time, wondering how a kid from Ohio ends up with a rap sheet in

Burbank. Lily's quiet, letting Krause take it in, wondering whether he can find a narrow tunnel out. He looks to the door, blows out air, slides his reading glasses into his pocket. I believe him. He didn't know what the Russians were up to. But he knows he's put this thing inside Orlov's mansion, which, if he makes the call—but my guess is, he'll try to disappear—Armando Torres will not be happy about. Seconds pass. I like the intimacy of these moments. The calculations between strangers. You wait and study, letting the man next to you wear himself out over a choice that he'll never know is the right one or not. There's no rushing it; it unfolds in its own time. Lily sips her beer. She's smart, playing off me, going at Krause, then backing off. A good partner, if I wanted one. I take out my notebook and scribble: bottles, bartender, Elton John singing "Mona Lisas and Mad Hatters," Krause drumming his fingers, Lily's stillness in the warm, alluring yellow light, Mickey Mouse sketches on the wall, the bartender scrubbing glasses, the guy with the scotch across the bar, blond, slender, midthirties, who—

Two shots.

Krause goes down.

Lily falls.

I reach for my gun. The guy pops off three more rounds over my head. I duck. He bolts out the door. I check Krause: bullet to the forehead, dead. I scramble to Lily. Blood on her neck. A grazing wound—alive but unconscious. The bartender is staggering, rag in hand, pointing to the door, mumbling. I run to the sidewalk. The shooter is gone. Not even a car, just a bottomless quiet and a thin wind out of the canyon. I call dispatch, run back inside to check Lily. She's got a bump over her eye. Must have hit the bar when she fell. I pat her neck wound with a cloth napkin—a few stitches probably—and rub ice over her brow. She stirs, in a haze. She tries to get up. I tell her no. Her eyes go heavy, and she drifts off again. Krause is on his back, looking up, a nickel-size wound centered in his empty stare. Sirens. Red lights in the window. The bartender is crouching in a booth, crying into a phone. I check my gun. I didn't fire. I play it back in my head, kneeling beside Lily, holding her hand, watching the bar fill with faces, syringes, vials, and kits. Radio squawks and footsteps far and close, voices echoing across broken glass.

CHAPTER 24

"She okay?"

"Bullet grazed her. She'll be fine. Hit her head on the bar. She was out for a minute. They're keeping her overnight."

Ortiz sits with me outside Lily's hospital room. A janitor is running a mop. It's nearly midnight.

"Krause?" says Ortiz.

"Perfect shot. A pro. I saw him come in. Blond, trim guy in a suit. Looked like a young studio exec. Krause had been glancing at the door the whole night. Like he was waiting for someone. But the guy didn't register. He ordered a scotch rocks and read a magazine. Quiet. Krause didn't seem agitated."

"This guy have an accent?"

"I couldn't hear. He was across the bar."

"Bartender say anything?"

"His back was to me. I only saw him grab the bottle and pour."

"Did Krause know our two big Russians?"

"Yes, but not what they were up to. It was a chauffeur job. Armando Torres hired him. They go back to Iraq together."

"Torres means . . ."

"Mickey Orlov."

"Maybe, maybe not. But it's looking that way. We're in dicey shit here, Carver. We're at the bottom looking up. FBI. CIA. They want Orlov for this election-hacking shit. They don't want it sidetracked with the murder of a ballerina and her cello player." Ortiz looks down the hall and back to me. "I can't figure out the why of it. Why would Orlov take out a ballerina? Maybe he was screwing her. Things didn't work out; he got jealous. Doesn't seem like him, though, right? I mean, Orlov's all about control. Isn't that what you said? Maybe it's a connection or shit from back in the old country. But Katrina Ivanovna was not a spy or a hacker."

"We don't know."

"She was a troubled pill popper on her way down. She wasn't cracking DNC hard drives or posting fake shit out on Facebook. Not her profile."

"That's the thing with a spy."

"C'mon, Carver. What's your gut?"

"Orlov."

"Or she had a thing with Torres that went bad."

"No. It's about Orlov."

"Then get me a why."

The janitor turns the corner with his mop. Voices float over the nurses' station. The hallway is empty.

"She was good," I say.

"Who?"

"Lily. Real good."

"Partner good?"

"She almost got killed with me."

"She can get killed anywhere, Carver." He stands, stretches, pats me on the shoulder. "I'm going home. Get some sleep yourself. You've got blood on your shirt. Broken glass in your shoe."

"I never got off a round."

"Guy was a pro."

"I should have—"

"No, Carver. Way I see it, no way. Too fast. He knew what was coming; you didn't."

Ortiz walks down the hall. He stops at the nurses' station, leaves his card. He's gone. I go to Lily's room and stand at the foot of her bed. She lies in white linen, an IV tube in her arm, a bandage on her neck, sleeping. I go around the bed and put my ear to her mouth, listen to her rhythm, soft and warm. I kiss her forehead. I stand over her like a strange angel flown in on the wind. I am not. I pull a chair to the window. The city is serene. It's 3:00 a.m. Lights and dark. Reimagined and mingling with the sky—it has changed much since I moved here. New architecture, taller buildings, glass reflecting glass as if the city were a maze folded into a mirage. Not in the night though. In the night the skyline is crystalline and sharp, and the eye is drawn toward the miraculous. Looking down, I can see the dead. They flicker and roam. I've thought this since I was a boy. I didn't want to accept that my father was gone, so I put him back into the world, among the buildings and along the coast of Newport. In churches, gyms, and bars. I'll do it to for my mother, too, when she is gone. She'll find my father, and they will go their way, appearing every now and then, slivers of light in an alley, flashes in a doorway, remembrances of each of them tucked in my inlaid box of souvenirs with Katrina's locket and Levon's scrap of sheet music.

I wonder about boyhood—the things it won't relinquish, the phantoms we carry into age. I sit by the window. I cannot sleep. *Zhanna Smirnov, you have not told me all. Where are you? Mickey Orlov. So close and so far from it all. Azadeh. Stefan. Ortiz, just getting home, sliding into bed beside your wife, thinking maybe of your barista and the maps folded in your drawers. Jimmy Krause, stripped and cold in the morgue. Please, don't disappear.* I reach into my pocket and pull out his reading glasses. One lens shattered from his fall, a speck of blood on the other. I put them on. The world goes away and comes back. I return them to my pocket. They will go into my box. A nurse comes in, checks a monitor, holds Lily's wrist, runs a finger through her hair. I have done that, too, on our late nights on her porch, when the breezes come through Boyle Heights, and she can run no more. It's 5:00 a.m. I reach for my phone.

"Maggie."

"Sam. You're up early."

"How are you and Mom?"

"She's still sleeping, if you can believe it. Rarely sleeps through the night anymore. She's the same though."

"You're in the kitchen with a coffee."

"Yes. You know that. The sun is in the sink."

"I like it, then."

"Is anything wrong, Sam?"

"No. I just wanted to call."

"You sound different. You're whispering."

"I feel like quiet."

"I guess that's it. The sacred is in the quiet. Father Quinn used to say that. Remember him? You were just a boy then. He was a handsome fellow. Deep voice. He was the only priest your father ever liked. When you were young, your mom and father and you came for a visit, and your father went to confession with Father Quinn. He never went to confession. But he did that day. I asked him why, and he said, 'I like the sound of that priest's voice.' I told your father, 'That won't get you redemption.' He laughed and said, 'Maggie, I'm not looking for that.'"

"I remember Father Quinn," I say. "You still holding up okay?"

"I am, Sam. You know that nurse I told you about? The one who works up at the hospital? She lives a few streets over. She's been a godsend. She checks on your mother, helps me bathe her. Your mother puts up a fit about a bath. But Sara—that's her name, the nurse—is so patient. We sit and talk in the kitchen after we put your mom to bed. Sara even had a few beers with me. She's pretty too. You would like her."

"The hospital send her?"

"A few hours a couple of times a week. She stops by before or after her shift. Sweet girl. Hang on, Sam."

A minute or so passes. Dawn is edging toward the San Gabriels.

"Okay, Sam, I'm back. You're mother's stirring. I better go. You sure you're okay? You don't usually call this early."

"I happened to be up."

"I'm glad you called. It's a good way to start the day. I'll tell your mother. Bye, Sam."

"Bye, Maggie."

I am losing my mother. Maggie is older too. There is no one left after me. It will all fall to obscurity—my family, my name, the words and stories I carry—like a cold case in a forgotten file. This transitory moment is all we have. A few breaths hushed by eons. But it is something, I suppose—a faint trace of splendor and sorrow, like the spirit of my restless father, or a fossil etched in a rock.

I turn my head toward the window and close my eyes. Things are stirring here too. Footsteps, voices in the hall. Lily's room is coming to light. I feel myself fall toward sleep, slow, almost warm, sounds floating farther away. And then I feel a soft weight, an impression. I open my eyes. Lily is sitting in my lap, curled against me, her hair in my stubble, an amber stain of antiseptic on her bandage. Her eyes are closed. She is sleeping. I stroke her hair and wish that the day, which has already begun, would not come so quickly and we could be here, alone, suspended above the city. She wakes.

"Carver."

"Yes."

"Krause?"

"Dead."

"I got shot."

"A graze. You'll be fine. You hit your head on the bar. You were out for a bit."

"It hurts."

"You want the nurse?"

"I feel fuzzy and sore."

"I'll get the nurse."

"No. Catch the shooter?"

"Got away."

"A lot of people are outrunning you these days, Carver. You gotta get faster."

She tilts her head up, tries to smile.

"You would have caught him," I say.

"No question."

She pulls herself closer and sleeps.

CHAPTER 25

I take a right into the Solaris Studio lot. Orlov conceived it well: long driveway, palms, magnolias, bougainvillea, gardeners, golf carts, and whitewashed bungalows in the 1920s style—a re-created past rising two miles from the ocean in Santa Monica. It doesn't have that gentrified Hollywood artifice. It feels as if built in the time it conjures. Orlov must have been a good spy. Deception so fine, you don't notice the trick of it. I half expect Fitzgerald or Faulkner to come wandering around the corner with a script and bottle. Or maybe Valentino. Lillian Gish. Buster Keaton. The old crew. When it was all new, and they were bits of gray, magical light. I pull to the guardhouse, show my shield. The guard runs a finger down a clipboard.

"You're not on the list," he says.

"I'm here to see Armando Torres."

"But . . ."

"You don't want to get in the way of a police investigation, do you? Could be bad for you. Conspiracy, who knows what else.

You don't let me in, I get suspicious. I get suspicious and, well . . . Call him and tell him I'm coming."

He says nothing, staring at me through tinted wraparounds. He did time in Iraq or Afghanistan. You can tell. The distant stone gaze. Looking into you and past you as if he were still manning a checkpoint in Ramadi or Kandahar. But now he's holding a clipboard, wearing a pressed gray-blue suit with badges on the sleeves—another uniform, but one without lethal power, and far from Babylon. He steps into the guardhouse, lifts a phone.

"Okay," he says, bending to my window with a look meant to harm. "Go down to lot C and park. Someone will meet you."

I find a space. A costume rack rolls past. Carpenters are resting beneath a palm, watching a girl in jeans and a tank top navigate tangled leashes and a parade of dogs. A helicopter lifts and skims away. George Clooney walks by with Emma Stone. No, but close. You never know. They disappear down an alley. A young man in a black suit hurries toward me and points to a billboard of Ryan Gosling suspended in a galaxy, the scion of a doomed planet in *Star Battle: A Love Story*.

"Just finished postproduction," says a young man, his red hair shining. "Coming soon. Do you like Ryan? Everybody likes Ryan. He tests so well. Good numbers. But you never know, right? A bad film here and there and, well, you know, no more upgrades or top-shelf swag."

"Never thought about it."

"It's a preoccupation. I'm Tyler. You're here for Armando, right?"

"Yes."

"Come."

"What do you do?"

"I gather people. It's a confusing place. These little alleys and avenues. I mean, they're all marked. Mr. Orlov is very precise. But, you know, it's big."

"Looks like it's from another time."

"It is quaint, isn't it? Our little make-believe land." He laughs, rushes on. "Watch out for anything that might be moving. Things have a tendency to dart out of nowhere."

He races me down Casablanca Way. We make a few lefts and rights and arrive at a courtyard. A fountain bubbles beneath a sycamore. The buildings are low with clear, open windows. Voices. A clarinet. The scratchy sound of a TV. Tyler leads me to a man sitting in the shade, smoking a vape, binders and coffees spread before him on a wrought iron table. Small, muscular, and compact, he rises with the speed of a fist—another former soldier with war still in him.

"Thank you, Tyler."

"Yes, Mr. Torres. Anything else?"

"No."

"Pleasure," says Tyler, nodding to me and vanishing into a building.

"Sit, Detective." He pours coffee, slides it to me. "I hate being inside," he says. "The whole point of LA is the weather, so why is everyone inside? I come out here in the mornings with these." He lifts a binder. "Security. Not just on this lot, but all over. Location shoots, press junkets, anywhere there's a star. Stars love security. Everyone wants a bodyguard. They're like accessories." He laughs. "Men in black suits and—"

"Tinted wraparounds."

"Imposing, don't you think? That's the point. Control without force. Always control without force, if you can. We wore them in

Iraq. The hajis thought they had special powers. Thought they were X-ray, and we could see through clothes to the naked bodies of their women. Drove them nuts. We were omniscient behind them. For a little while. Christ. What a clusterfuck it all was."

"How long were you there?"

"Three tours. Got out as a captain. Took a year off and traveled around Europe. Lived lean, but it was good. Then I found my way here."

"Not bad. Did you know Orlov before?"

"No." He laughs. "Friend of a friend got me the job. Security's an incestuous business. Like the army and cops. You know that." He sucks on the vape, blows smoke. He reaches for his coffee, motions for me to drink. He is latticed by the shadow of a sycamore branch. He's early forties, black hair, shaved tight on the sides. Military, yes, but his face has a boyish delicateness. His dark eyes find mine and stay there. Like a sniper. He doesn't mind silence, drawing me in, leaving me to float on the passing seconds, which I am comfortable doing.

"What can you tell me about Jimmy Krause?" I say.

"It's a shame. I saw it on the news this morning. Poor Jimmy. He'd been troubled for a long time. He was in my unit in Iraq. A gunner. Never got over it. A lot of guys didn't." He looks into his coffee, back to me. "He contacted me a few years ago. We met and talked about the *Odyssey*. That was his thing. He was a big reader. He loved the *Odyssey*. War is one thing, but the journey home is hell. He told me about his arrests and jail time. I tried to help, but with his record, I couldn't bring him on here. Pretty strict about that. I got him a temp thing over on lot D for a long weekend, but that was it. I made some calls, but he'd disappear. I wouldn't hear from him for a while. Then he'd resurface."

"He said he worked for you not long ago. Driving two Russian men around LA."

"Jimmy never worked for me."

"He said you hired him."

"He was mistaken."

"He was up at Orlov's mansion less than a week ago."

Torres pours cream in his coffee, hits his vape. Looks at me, unruffled.

"I invited him up. Mr. Orlov has a couple of bungalows near a pool on the north end of his property. He lets me use them for get-togethers with army buddies. We drink and swim, glorify the past. Typical shit. I invited Jimmy up. Thought it might do him good. I sent a car to pick him up in Burbank. Jimmy had a tendency to drink." He pauses, watches women in sequined gowns and men in tuxes pass. "They're shooting a remake of something." He thumbs his binder pages. "Jimmy was getting delusional, you know—PTSD, whatever they call it now. I heard one shrink on TV describe it as an 'injury to the soul.' Jimmy never really made it back from the desert. He couldn't make it work stateside. All that 'thank you for your service' bullshit. No one cared. Jimmy kept saying he was worried. He had enemies. People following him. That kind of shit."

Torres stands.

"C'mon, Detective, let's do a couple of laps. I've got a little shrapnel in my knee. I need to loosen it."

We walk on a brick path around the courtyard.

"How?" I say.

"IED. Side of the road. Boom. Killed three of my guys. The power of those things is amazing. Fire and smoke. Everybody down, knocked off kilter. Fuzzy. Then the world starts coming back to you, like it's approaching from a distance and filling itself back in. Not everyone comes back. That day, three never got up when the smoke cleared. My leg was pretty torn up, but they fixed it except for these little pieces."

"Hurt?"

"Now? No. They move around, and then I need to move around to get them back where they should be."

"*The Things They Carried.*"

"Jimmy gave that book to me on our second tour. You know, though, and I'm no writer, but I think writing about war must be easy. It's there in front of you. Real-time drama spinning around you. You know? *Boom. Boom, boom.* You just have to take it in, right? The colors, sounds, blood. Take it in and put it down like you saw it."

"Sounds like a man contemplating a memoir."

"I don't know about that, but all that shit stays with you."

"Jimmy read a lot. Did he write?"

"Not that I know of. He could quote long passages from books. Come up with all kinds of shit. He never came across as smart, you know. Always seemed to be the dumb one. But he could surprise you. One time, our unit camped west of Baghdad. We sat in starlight like an ancient herd." Torres smiles but not long. "Jimmy starts quoting from Stephen Crane's *Red Badge of Courage.* I don't remember exactly what he said, but it made me feel that the soldiers in the Civil War were just like us, hoping not to die and be buried in someplace not home." He catches himself and looks at me. "I'm going on too long about shit that doesn't matter anymore. Let's cut to it, Detective."

"Jimmy was certain you hired him. We have security-camera pictures of him with the two guys he said were Russians. He told us he took them twice to a café at Fourth and Spring, next door to Katrina Ivanovna's loft. You know her, right? The ballerina who died. She had two big Russian guys visit her that same week. Then Krause told us he drops those same guys off at a Cubano place in Echo Park, and, get this, they talk to Katrina's cellist, who also ends up dead. Then Jimmy goes to Orlov's place, and a few days later, last night, Jimmy catches it. Very professional hit."

Torres stops in the shade near the fountain. He looks at me for a long time.

"I have nothing for you, Detective. Jimmy was troubled. He owed people money. Ripped off a lot of people. He had enemies. I don't know who killed him. I did try to get him work. But I know I didn't hire him. I certainly know he didn't cart Russians around for me. I don't know about any cellist. But I did read about the ballerina. Wasn't it an overdose?"

"We think she had help."

"You get her body back?"

"No. What about Orlov?"

"Mr. Orlov? What's your point?"

"Did he know Katrina Ivanovna?"

"I have no idea."

"I want to talk to him."

A pause, a draw on the vape.

"He's in Italy. He likes to be on location when a shoot starts."

"When is he back?"

"I don't know his schedule."

"It's not in those binders?"

"Okay, Detective, I think we're done. I'll inform Mr. Orlov that you want to speak with him. If he agrees, I'll arrange it with his lawyers."

"It's not about agreeing," I say.

He shakes my hand. Tyler appears. Torres leaves the brick path and sunlight. He slips back into the shade of the sycamore and sits at the wrought iron table, pouring coffee and opening a binder. He glances at me, his face betraying nothing—a boy sniper with a long desert gaze. I breathe in the morning cool. Tyler hurries me down Casablanca Way, and I think I'd like to have been an actor—not these days, but back when you could disappear into a studio and never venture beyond its walls. You could live mysteries written for you and know the endings before you started. It would have been a good life, getting rich on pretending, receiving invitations from homes in the hills and canyons, and up the coast in Malibu.

"As I was saying," says Tyler, "the new Brad Pitt and Jessica Chastain film—well, we're just all excited."

We stop at my car.

"Have a nice day, Detective."

He turns and is gone.

CHAPTER 26

Lily is quiet on the drive home from the hospital. I help her inside. Bill Evans is playing on the porch radio. I make coffee and change her bandage—five stitches—and hold a cold compress over the bump on her forehead. She looks at me. I know what she wants. I hand her the crime scene photographs. Krause on his back, blood around his head like a dark halo. Broken glass, spilled beer, scattered coins. Everything illuminated. She points to the right side of Krause, imagining herself unconscious on the floor.

"I would have been there, right?"

"Yes," I say.

"And you?"

"I checked Krause. Dead right away. Checked you. Saw the bullet graze and the knock on the head."

"You held me," she says.

"I ran out to the sidewalk. The shooter was gone. I came

back in and sat with you and waited for the ambulance. You were fading in and out. You kept saying how handsome I was."

"Dream on, Carver," she says, smiling and taking the compress from me. "No one hits their head *that* hard.

"I have to go. You rest."

"I need to run."

"Not today."

"You're thinking it's—"

"We'll talk tomorrow."

Bill Evans is midway into "Autumn Leaves," meandering through and around notes, lifting, impossible to catch. Lily looks across the small garden and into the street. A man on a bike pedals past with a shoeshine box, rags twirling in the breeze. Two girls skip rope. Voices from a TV are coming from a window; an old man is picking oranges from a tree in a yard with a high fence. A dog barks far away. Lily says she knows all these sounds: bicycle chain, flapping rags, *slap-slap* of the jump rope, and the faint snap when the orange stem breaks from the branch and the fruit is taken by Mr. Lorenzo, who once had an affair with a woman from the water department but lives alone since his wife left him. Lily sits back and listens.

"The day my dad got shot was so quiet," she says. "After they told us, our house went still. Everything stopped. We sat into the night until morning. No one said a word. My mother didn't turn on any lights. We didn't eat. We kept thinking that they went to the wrong house. That he would come through the door and reach for a beer, and dinner would come, and the dishes would be done, and the house would be like it was all the other days." She wipes her eyes. "That's what went through my mind when I got shot, Carver. Not having days anymore. You don't even think about them, because you think they're all the same, but they're not, you know? Each is a little different, and you only see that when they're gone." She shakes her head. "I'm nuts, huh?"

"I was the same when my father died. It's too big a thing for a kid."

"It takes up all of you," she says. "For a long time, there's nothing else."

"It finds its place."

"The rest of you comes back around it, you know, like this island inside," she says. "I guess there's nothing original about death except the name that's gone."

"They're going to send you to a psychiatrist," I say. "They do it for anyone who's been shot or had a trauma."

"I know."

"Ortiz made me see one after the Dylan Cross thing."

"Advice?"

"Endure it."

"Hope it doesn't fuck me up," she says.

"It didn't feel like anything was going to go down, did it?"

"No. We had Krause too. He was caving."

"I don't think he knew what the two Russians were about," I say.

"I don't either. But he was breaking and scared. Bringing us closer . . ."

"Rest."

I get up to leave.

"You think the shooter wanted to kill me?" she says.

"No. He drew a perfect bead on Krause. He could have done

the same to you if he'd wanted. You weren't a target. He didn't want to kill a cop. He grazed you before you could react, and he fired three over my head to keep me down. Krause and you were on the floor beside me. He knew I'd have to check each of you. Then crawl over you."

"Obstacles."

"Yes."

"Pro."

"I have to go," I say.

"Coming back?"

"Maybe."

"Bring tacos."

I turn.

"Hey, Carver."

"Yes."

"How'd the shooter know we were cops?"

I meet Ortiz in a café in the Arts District. Two espresso cups and a couple of files set before him. He's rested, eyes clear, smoothing his mustache, thumbing through a book of black-and-white LGBTQ postcards, and another that has neon words written in night skies in different languages. *Chaos. Love. Money. Bliss. Genocide. Silk.*

"They go on and on like this," he says. "Page after page of words."

"Messages?"

"No. More like who we are as a species. What defines us."

"Look at this one: 'Sorrow.'"

"Different skies?"

"Each one over a separate country. They're all night skies. The words are all neon. What happens when day comes? The words disappear, right? Can't see neon in daylight. Loses its power. That's what this artist guy is saying. The words can change. They can fade or disappear. We can become something else."

"You buying this book?"

"Fuck no. Cool café, though, right? It's connected to the gallery. Look at all this art shit."

"What about your barista over at Demitasse? She'll miss you."

"I'm trying new things. That's still my go-to place. But the city's changing, Carver."

He finishes his second espresso and waves for a waiter to bring two more.

"How's Lily?"

"Shaken but fine. She wanted to go for a run."

"Good to get back to who you are as quick as you can."

"What's this?" I say, nodding to the files.

"The beauty of technology."

He opens a file, slides it toward me.

"Phone records, texts, emails, all kinds of shit. All the stuff that sits out there in the ether."

The waiter brings espressos.

"Read through them," says Ortiz. "I'm going to finish this neon book."

"I thought we had everything from our tech people."

"They scoured more from her phone and laptop on a second go-round."

Katrina Ivanovna didn't text much in the days before she died. Back-and-forths to Levon and Andreas Stein; a few to Michael Paine (which the first check found) to arrange the meeting at the NoMad for a possible book; two to Antonio Garcia to check on

Nishka, the cat; one to her sometimes manager, Molly Ames, saying how excited, alone, and scared she felt about *Giselle*, and how maybe, as everyone said, it was all past her. No emojis. No exclamation points. She texted herself the name Mickey Orlov with a string of links to newspaper and magazine stories about him, most in English and Russian. She texted another line that simply read, "Mikhail Orlov???????" He's in her phone—nothing substantial, a searched-for name, an unsolved equation. What would a judge do with that? Not enough for a warrant. No diaries. No significant clues—just typed strands from a life ticking, oblivious, toward its end. She left behind broken grammar, twists of unexpected poetry, like etchings left millennia ago on cave walls.

Katrina's texts to Levon were mostly about setting times for him to come to her loft and play, except for two: a joke about how Levon brooded like Rachmaninoff, and another telling him not to worry about the two big men who knocked on her door when he was there. "They are nothing." It was written at 10:39 a.m. on the day she died. What was I doing then? Boarding a flight back from Europe. I was in Heathrow, in a bar, with a scotch, watching planes come and go, the clouds low and tinged with light. I remember the feeling of not wanting to come home, not knowing that my trajectory had already been set toward a ballerina in her final hours, in a Spring Street loft. How big and small the world. Degrees that once kept us strangers suddenly rearrange and bring us together. Cop and vic. A story eternal.

Her texts to Andreas Stein are about the second act of *Giselle* and how she is borne aloft and floats for an instant "shaped to beauty," and how a blister on her left foot must be tended but the pain ignored. To Molly, she writes, "Is my vanity making me foolish?

The body no longer goes like it used to." I wonder what Molly made of that. I can still see Molly's naked pirouette in the room at the Biltmore, the way she fell into bed and kissed me, whispering in a voice from the South about long-ago dancers and backlit stages.

To Antonio Garcia, "Thank you for Nishka. Rehearsals went long. You're a dear." But as I turn the page, I see another text Ortiz has marked in yellow: "I hope Paris was good to you. Left you a box. If something happens, do as discussed."

I look to Ortiz. He holds a finger up.

"Read on," he says.

I open a second folder, marked "Antonio Garcia."

I turn to Ortiz.

"You got a warrant?"

"Read," he says.

I scan page after page of links to stories, and images of costume designs: "Greek aesthetic," "Elizabethan fashion," "grunge look," "punk style," "silk," "lamé," "vampire black," and "*Mad Men* hats." Those links change to articles about death rituals, funeral pyres, human sacrifice, mummification, and sky burials, which, I recall from a Tibetan monk I knew in my Berkeley days, is a ceremony in which the dead are cut into pieces and fed to birds high in the Himalayas. "The body that once ate becomes food," said the monk. "Nothing wasted on the spirit's journey to a new life." The links go on for pages, from the death masks of Egyptian pharaohs to the dead who are burned along the Ganges, their ashes swept into the river in endless cycles. Garcia is fascinated by death—not the soul or the afterlife, but by what becomes of the body. He has spent much time dressing it, so meticulous with his pins and fabrics, so precise in drawing its angles and degrees, understanding its lines, bones, flesh, and cartilage. The body is more sacred to him than the soul. The body is temporal, though, degrading in the seconds and minutes after death—imperceptibly at first, but falling prey to elements and molecular designs, like an unprotected land.

"How'd you get a warrant on Garcia?"

"He's a suspect," says Ortiz. "We've got nothing, so everyone's a suspect. Plus, I found a sympathetic judge. Plus, what you told me about Garcia not mentioning Katrina being stolen from the morgue. I thought about that. Odd, right? This guy so wrapped up in her life. Feeding her cat. Got a poster of her on his wall. Why wouldn't he ask about where her body had gone?"

"Because . . ."

"He knows. Not a mystery to him. You get where I'm going, Carver?"

"He might have stolen it."

"Why all these links to death rituals and burnings and shit? Why this ghoulish interest right at the time she dies?"

He waves to the waiter for two more espressos.

"Coincidence," I say. "He's researching costumes for a movie."

"Could be," says Ortiz, smiling and sliding me another sheet of paper."

"What are these?"

"Texts to and from Garcia to one Wallace Blackman. Wally has an interesting résumé. He once drove for the Medical Examiner's Office. Picked up stiffs. Didn't do it long. Couple of years, maybe. Worked at night, took film classes in the day. Guess what he is now? And no, I'm not making this shit up. A makeup and special-effects guy for a B-grade horror film studio. Some

YouTube channel that took off and got bought. It's in the Valley. And—this is the good part—a year ago, he worked on a movie *The Night Bride*, with guess who? Garcia."

"We know where Blackman is?" I say.

"No. But he's trouble. Real fuckup when he was a kid. Delinquent. Stole cars. All kinds of shit. His dad was an assistant fire chief. Real prick. But wired, you know. A lot of cop friends. Little Wally never did time. I guess they must have thought he grew out of it. The old man used his contacts and got him the ME job."

"Where's the old man now?"

"Dead, I hope. Like I said, real prick. Faked disabilities, bilked the city out of all kinds of money. False overtime—you name it."

"Cops have been known to do that too."

"Yeah, but the fire guys have made it an art form. You ever see them strolling around Smart and Final loading up their carts with steaks and organic mushrooms? All tanned. Shit, man, cops have nothing on firemen when it comes to bilking."

Ortiz sits back, pleased.

"Krause is the connection to Orlov," I say. "Torres denies he put Krause in touch with the big Russians."

"You didn't expect him to give it up on the first date," says Ortiz. "We'll get there."

"It doesn't feel right—about him, I mean. Orlov's too smart to let a guy like Krause in."

"And still . . ."

The waiter arrives. Tall, black, rainbow eyeliner, manicured nails. He moves with a grace both intimate and aloof. "This one here," he says, pointing to Ortiz, "is drinking all our coffee." He winks and slides espressos before us. "Not too much sugar, now," he says, straightening his white apron and gliding toward another table.

"So you're buying into my theory that killer and kidnapper are not connected, or at least, not the same."

"It's not kidnapper," says Ortiz. "It's body snatcher. But, yeah, it's looking that way. Plus, we know Katrina left something for Garcia. He never told you about that, did he? So . . ."

"Her diaries."

"I'm thinking."

"Why him? Why not Paine? Paine was the one she wanted to write her book."

"Things were happening fast. The Russians come, spook her. She doesn't know Paine that well. Not at all, really. She trusts Garcia with her cat. Didn't you say he told you he and Katrina had a bond? Artistic soul mates or some shit. Makes sense she'd go to him. Plus, she tells Garcia in the text, 'as discussed.'"

"I wonder what language."

"What do you mean?"

"The diaries. She's Russian. They're probably in Russian."

"She knew English. Look at all those texts."

"A diary is who you are. A foreign language is not nuanced enough. You think in your native tongue. Or . . ."

"Or what?"

"Nabokov was Russian, but he wrote his best works in English. He had only just learned the language. Maybe she's like that."

"Carver, don't start. These tangents you go on. This obscure shit."

"Nabokov's not obscure. He won the Nobel Prize."

"Okay, good for Nabokov or whatever. If the diaries are in Russian, maybe Garcia doesn't know what he's sitting on."

"Or he's getting them translated."

"That'd be a bad move for little Antonio, given all the Russian assassins running around. Speaking of which, where's Orlov?"

"Torres says he's on a film shoot in Italy. You hear anything from the FBI? Others?"

"Nothing. Even the Russian consulate's gone quiet. Guy was bugging me every day about Katrina. Now, silence. That hit on Krause last night, though, I mean, you gotta figure."

"Everyone's rattled."

"Dead ballerina ends up in the middle of a new Cold War."

"Still can't prove it."

"We need the diaries."

Ortiz finishes his espresso, closes his book of neon words, collects his files.

"How's Lily, really?"

"Shaken. Who wouldn't be? Always amazes me how fast something like that goes down. Five shots pulled off, and boom, the guy's out the door into the night. She keeps playing it back, trying to fill in pieces of it. You never can."

"I like her, Carver. A real directness about her. No bullshit. You know about her father, right? Cop killed by gangbangers back in the day. A hero. That's the myth the department created." Ortiz thumbs through his wallet, lays money on the table. "He was dirty. Nothing big. Lifted a little drug and fencing money off the gangs. Standard procedure. Tried to take a little too much, I guess. Department needed a hero back then though. So they made one."

"Lily know?"

"I don't know. Some cops who knew him back then might

have whispered something when she got her badge. Maybe she heard shit in the Academy, on the street. Whispers like that keep traveling."

"I hope she doesn't know."

"Me too."

Ortiz shakes his head. He looks around the café and back to me.

"If you ever find a sacred thing, Carver, let me know. I mean pure sacred. Like communion. I think I see it sometimes at dawn—you know, a sacred thing out there—but it fades in the light."

"Is that what your neon words say?"

He reaches for the book and opens it to the last page.

"Look," he says. "Nothing there. No neon. Just a night sky. All the other skies have neon words. But not the last one."

CHAPTER 27

Antonio Garcia is not home.

I wait, knock again, put my ear to the door. Nothing. I cross the hall to Katrina's loft. I decide not to go in. It has yielded little anyway; the home of a wanderer is not where secrets are kept. The hall is quiet. Late-morning sounds drift in from a city at work: voices, horns, boom boxes, jackhammers, a siren, always a siren. I walk to the end of the hall and stand at the window.

A man races past on a bike. A Lyft makes a drop-off; a woman rushes by with flowers; a cop tickets a jaywalker; a couple carries a headboard into an apartment building across the street. Probably New Yorkers. A lot of New Yorkers moving to LA these days. They walk around as if it were theirs, but it's not. They'll learn the trick of it in time, as I did—how the city teases and plays and lets you think whatever you want, but underneath, like Katrina's loft, yields little. That's what I like about it. It's not a lie. It's your own delusion. It's homeless on sidewalks, and hustler boys in the hills. It's laborers and Latina housekeepers and billboards of lust, dystopia, apes, robots, Chewbaccas, Kim and Kanye, and Lady Gaga's latest thing. It's clear skies, no mosquitoes, and laser-sculpted people with money, hedgerows, and sins. You can make it what you want for a while, like *Westworld*, or a lover who gives you a key but then one day changes the locks. It's a thing now. LA. It started a few years ago with artists, tech money, architectural blueprints, cultural essays, countless chefs, battles over income and justice, philanthropic visions. The skyline turned crowded and newly pricked, rising above vintage pastel bungalows that now sell for two million plus and are gutted and remade for the conceits of a new century. I drive into the San Gabriels sometimes on weekends and look back over the city, the glass bright, the ocean shining, Palos Verdes jutting from the south, Point Dume to the north, silent and stretched out, nothing moving except an occasional hawk lifting, circling, gliding, skimming close, and then gone.

"Always a dreamer, huh, Sam?"

"Taking in the sidewalk scenery."

"No, Sam, you dream like little boy. You go places. Where do you go?"

I turn. Slide my notebook into my pocket. Stefan walks toward me, changing from shadow to person in the sunlight. We stand at the window. Stefan traces on the glass. His hair falls over his forehead. He pushes it back. His face is pale and unshaven, his eyes sleepy and narrow. No hint of cologne.

"I was here a few times when we went out," he says. "Katrina never made it a home. I told her this was wrong. She needed a place. But I don't think she knew how to make a home."

"Why are you here?"

"I need—"

"I'm still pissed at you."

"Am I a suspect?"

"I don't know."

"This is deep-shit stuff, Sam." He grins, shakes his head. "C'mon, Sam, let's get a drink. We are better when we drink."

We walk down the hall. Stefan nods to Garcia's door.

"Not in," he says.

"No."

"He may be gone a while."

"What do you mean?"

He lifts a finger to his lips. We take the elevator down and walk toward Fifth street, saying nothing, turning the corner, and stepping into the Little Easy, where Lenny is wiping the bar and listening to Betty Davis and her funk guitar, playing low in the speakers. Lenny looks at me, cuts his eyes left to a blond woman in a tapered blue dress, a scarf loose around her neck, her glasses black and sleek. I don't recognize her at first. She stands, steps toward me, kisses me on the cheek.

"Mr. Sam," she says.

"Zhanna?"

"You like? New look for me, no? I am blond. Like Madonna."

I step back, take her in, look at Stefan.

"Sit, Sam," he says, and goes to the bar.

We sit in two French-style brocaded chairs, the kind found in flooded and forgotten Louisiana mansions. A portrait of a woman who looks like Napoleon's wife, Josephine, looks down, keeping with the Little Easy's ragged, bygone charm. A small candle burns between us. Zhanna lights a cigarette. Lenny starts to say something, but I wave him quiet. No one else is in the place. Stefan sets two scotches on the table and returns to the bar.

"So, Mr. Sam. I am not supposed to be here. My disguise. Don't tell your FBI friend. What's her name? Azadeh, yes? The Iranian."

"Iranian-American."

Zhanna sips.

"I heard about the shooting," she says. "This Krause man is dead. Very professional assassin kill him."

"Do you know who?"

"No. Not me. The man you are looking for knows who."

"Why are you here?"

"I think the story is coming out now, Mr. Sam. The story we talked about in Brussels."

"The diaries?"

"We have."

"Where did you find them?"

"This funny little costume man. The cat feeder."

"How did you know?"

"I told you about men in my country who read phones. You remember this? Faceless men all the time reading phones. No secrets anymore. You have faceless people too. So we both know about the costume man. But I know before you."

"Where is he?"

"He had to go someplace," she says, blowing smoke, smiling. "He will be back, I think. Short trip. Very interesting, strange man. Talking all the time. Like little puffing train."

"He's a suspect."

"You must find him, then."

"I could take you in," I say.

"Mr. Sam, please, let's be smart people."

"What's in the diaries?"

"Such a direct man you are. I like it."

She lowers her voice.

"All what I knew but did not want to know about Katrina," she says. "Her life was hard, Mr. Sam. People with such talent—it is like a sin, you know; it always must be forgiven. Too hard to live with. There are beautiful times too. She had them. I'm glad for this. But she didn't understand. She wanted something she could not have. Something impossible."

"What?"

"You will see."

"Is Stefan involved?"

"Only for loving her or, at least, lusting her. It is as he told you. They were together and then apart."

"Is Mickey Orlov mentioned?"

She crushes out her cigarette, sips her whiskey, and sits back. She is cold and lovely, this remade Zhanna. She looks years younger, her voice alluring, ageless. Stefan brings two more scotches and returns to the bar. So unlike him to be the second man, but Zhanna and her world are bigger than his, and Stefan, in his sly way, gauges the odds and acquiesces, as he did when he was a war orphan in the mountains of Bosnia.

"He did care for her, Mr. Sam," she says, nodding toward Stefan. "Katrina told me so, but I didn't know how much until I read the diaries. She wrote of him. *S*, she called him. She loved him, too, but not to be. By then, you know, the pills and all those things made her someone else. Not the girl I knew. I tried, Mr. Sam, to bring her back. I could not."

"It's hard to do."

"Yes. But now she is gone."

She lights another cigarette.

"Why can't all Americans love Russia like Mr. Trump?" she says, raising her eyebrows, smiling. "The world would be safer, no? The Cold War never ended. Americans thought it did. You had your Osama bin Laden and new bad men. But Russians, men like Mr. Putin, never let it end. He is a man of pride. Too much, maybe. Americans did not understand this. Russia must win. Like Olympics long time ago. Americans are foolish. You think you are better, and don't see what makes you weak. Mr. Putin sees. Your Facebook and Twitter. He knows all about you. Like mind reader. Is that right, *mind reader*?"

"Yes."

"But Mr. Putin is not the smartest one. He is a good spy but not great spy."

"Like Mickey Orlov."

"Great spy. Built new life here. Movie producer. Rich man. Flying around world. He's like man with twirling plates. You look at plates and don't see the man. I knew him long ago. Now your FBI, CIA all peeking into Mickey Orlov. Yes? I think so. But to prove is a hard thing."

"You admire him."

"I think, yes. But hate too."

"Who are you, Zhanna?"

She laughs. "I am a woman with many friends."

"And disguises."

"Like actor."

"You were a dancer."

"Many years ago. In Russia, to be dancer was like to be saint. Once, Mr. Sam, I danced in snow on a night outside Kremlin. You might not think this, but it's true. It was for celebration of state. It was cold. But I danced and did not feel the cold. Katrina was there. She was just a girl. She wrote in her diary that on that night she wanted to be ballerina. I did not know that." She stops, looks toward the door and back at me. "I don't know how this case will be solved, Mr. Sam. It is in too many worlds."

She reaches down, pulls up a large envelope, and slides it across the table.

"Read, Mr. Sam. You will know."

"The diary."

"A copy. Not everything, but what you need. Translated."

"Why are you doing this?"

"Maybe we'll meet again in another disguise, and I'll tell you a long story." She finishes her scotch, rises. "Be careful," she says. "Faceless men are everywhere." She nods for Stefan, and they leave in a slant of light.

"Not your average customer," says Lenny, setting up a scotch on the bar. "Is there a movie shoot going on downtown? I usually know all the shoots. Like keeping up on that kind of thing." He puts the bottle back on the shelf, turns, and leans close to me. "What's in the envelope, Sam?"

CHAPTER 28

JANUARY 20: *Where is he? He promised. Always he is late. What to do? Sit. Scratch my skin. Like you, Nishka. One pill. All I need. One pill and vodka. It hurts. The body. It never ached when I was prima child. In Moscow. Paris. St. Petersburg. New York. They loved me. I was like toy. Where is he? I need to buy tights, toe shoes, bandages, cream. You need food, Nishka. But we sit, waiting. My mother was good at waiting. Very patient. I am not. But ballet taught me to make body one with time, to make air part of skin. I still do this. Not so pretty now, but most cannot tell. They see my name and see me how I was. Like old rock star with broken voice. You still want to hear. No? I am still pretty. I am not that old. But ballerinas live in cat years. Like you, Nishka. Pity. Where is he? My Oxy man. I am still not used to LA. This loft. I miss winter. The hard cold of Russia. Coming out of rehearsals, wrapped in fur. Snow falling. Like dream. My apartment above the river. My barre that looked over the czar city below. "You are like dove, my child." I still*

hear her. My mother. She is deceitful, like crow. My head hurts.
My toes. I met Nicole Kidman in restaurant last night in Hol-
lywood. She came over to my table. She saw me in Swan Lake
years ago. I was wonderful, she said. I blushed. I said, "I am not
wonderful anymore." Her face went very sad. Like her movie
face. She hugged me and walked away. Where is my Oxy man?
When will he come?

I put the pages down, pour another drink, and stand at the
window. Night. I see Katrina. You never get to see most people,
even those closest to you. But I see her. Hear her. Echoes of a life
of cruelty and privilege. The bruises, blisters, and broken places we
don't see onstage. We see only the sublime. But that disappears in
increments. What must that be like? I suppose we are all witnesses
—and conspirators—to our own diminishment. I sit at the piano.
I close my eyes and play and see her in this room, dancing over the
street, spinning. I feel the way Levon must have felt setting loose a
firefly. I stop. I go back to the chair and sit with the diary pages. They
are marked only by month and day, no year. I turn backward and
forward through her life.

MAY 14: *I am thirteen today. They brought me cake at re-*
hearsal. Suly told me, "Only sliver, Katrina." He is good
teacher. Mommy says best choreographer in Russia. But I am
girl and I eat cake. It is my birthday. I met a boy outside the
train station. He followed but was shy when I turned. He ran
away. Boys are funny when they are not mean. Mommy tells
me to stay away. I have to dance. Only dance. We fly to Paris
tomorrow. Daddy is not coming. He has work and likes his
dacha. Nureyev died in France. Of AIDS, Mommy said. He

was my favorite of all. Suly has tape of him dancing. It makes me cry. Will I ever be that good?

DECEMBER 4: *I've decided I like men and women. I sleep with both. Depending on mood. I'm told I'm getting a reputation. So what. I did not like my performance in* Romeo and Juliet *tonight. Mommy did not like it either. I do not care what Mommy thinks anymore. I love New York. It is old but new, like pieces changing in same picture. But I never dance the way I want the city to see me. Suly says I have to work harder. He gives me pills. The pain goes away. Sometimes it is blurry, sometimes I can fly. I looked at my body in the mirror. Naked. I saw age. Suly says age is like evil whispers sneaking into you. He says a lot of things like that. I should write more of them down. My weight is just right, and my lines still are good. Maybe too puffy near chin. I was thinking. I'll never have a child. My body won't give one. I feel lonely. I was glad Molly walked in Central Park with me. She is good with advice. I'm going down the hall to her room now. It is 3:00 a.m. I hope she lets me in. I want to sleep with her. Not in that way. But just not to be alone.*

JULY 10: *Ahhhh. Summer. The sea is green. The waiter boy is bringing drinks. Nobody knows who I am on this island. My tendon is healing. I am girl in paradise.*

AUGUST 7: *Andreas Stein called. He wants to do* Giselle *in LA. Am I interested? Am I okay? Am I too much on pills? He has checked on me. Talked to people. Read stories. Mostly lies. They love lies, those people. Taking one thing and making it all of you. Why? Do they not remember? The same ones who christen you send you to hell. Mommy says this. She should know with all her Putin friends. Daddy in his dacha ignores it all. Ignores me too. For a long time. I don't know why. I like Andreas. Always to the point. I remember the night years ago we walked through Paris. We had done it. Our* La Bayadere *was a great success. It was good to do it in Paris, where Nureyev died. I felt him. I told Andreas this as we walked along the Seine. Isn't that romantic? To say that. "Walked along the Seine." Like something beautiful. We ate fresh bread and drank wine in the dawn and watched the flower ladies come. Andreas kissed me on forehead. I leaned under his arm. I felt worth. How long ago that was? I tell Andreas I would think about* Giselle.

The things we hold, what we set free. I stand and go to the window. I don't want to hurry. I want the pages to seep into me. We are a bit alike, Katrina and I. Her diary, my notebooks, the asides and the deeper things scribbled in bursts of thought. Moments that return to us. My mother kept a diary for a while in the years after my father died. She stopped at some point. I don't know when. I remember seeing her small bound books as a boy. Tied with string and full of secrets, even though a son doesn't imagine that his mother has secrets. She does. I would like to read them one day when she is gone. She doesn't know me anymore. I hope I am in her pages. I never peeked, but I must be there with my father, who was dead when they were written. I'm sure he fills lines, just as he did when he'd step with his hurts and scrapes through the doorway of our small house on Malbone Road. My phone buzzes.

"So?" says Lily.

"Still reading," I say.

"What time is it?"

"Little past eleven."

"You're not bringing tacos, I guess."

"Tomorrow. How you feeling?"

"Headache, but better. The moon is big tonight."

"You okay?"

"Yeah, just never been shot. I opened that bottle of merlot you were saving. I poured a glass and watched an old movie. *Key Largo.* It was all right. I'm on the porch. The moon is so big, Carver. Go out and see it. It's a special moon. It's like white and see-through." She yawns. "Call me when you get to the part about the killer."

"What?"

"He'll be in there. You know what's weird, Carver? I feel bad about Jimmy Krause. Guy didn't even know what's what. Cruel goddamn world."

"You just figuring that out?"

"No, just being reminded."

"Get some sleep."

"Hey, Carver."

"What?"

"Wish you were here."

I slide my phone on the counter, walk the room, look at the pages. I boil water, feel the steam on my face, make tea. I wonder if Dylan Cross kept a diary: what she wrote about after she was raped, the years that passed, her buildings, designs, decision to kill. On the page, vengeance must look clean, logical, and redemptive. I wonder where she is. I see her in this room, looking out over the street in the moments before dawn. Her kiss. I taste her still. I sit, pull the lamp closer, turn a page.

MAY 14: *I am thirty-three today. No cake. I am on a yacht somewhere off Greece. The islands scatter like stones. The water is calm. Like blue-green lake. Suly is with me. He is old. His eyes are going. He says we are "like two beaten-up gunfighters in old American movie." An oligarch has given him the yacht for the weekend. I don't like oligarchs. They pretend what they took is theirs. Many such men admire Suly. They do him little nice things. We are alone on the yacht with the crew. Suly sleeps and drinks. I read and listen to Beyoncé and watch DVDs Suly brought of my dancing, from child to now. I don't like to watch, but sometimes I see me like you see somebody else. That is when you are greatest. When you don't recognize who you are. I danced at the front of the yacht today. I felt the sun, and for a moment, I was part of the air. The crew clapped, and we ate fish caught from the sea below us.*

OCTOBER 12: *A boy came to the hotel with roses. Dozens of them in vases. It was early. He had night's chill on him. He was cheery. He said they were from admirer. A man who did not want to be known. There is no obligation except to enjoy them. That's what the boy said. He set them by the window, over the river. I tipped him and curled back into bed. I am taking too many pills. But how to stop? I try. But the urge. Like applause at final curtain. You must have. Nothing so pure, nothing so vanishing. Levon will play for me when I get to LA. He is such a child, so big but a child. But he plays as if he is making each note in the exact moment I hear it. Like things being born. He is easy to be with, and he likes me. I see him looking through his half-closed eyes when he plays his cello and I dance. Two strange creatures in a loft. He is like drug. I need him. The roses are pretty. The room smells like garden. St. Petersburg. So many years since I've seen you. I meet Mommy tomorrow. I don't want to. But she has news. This is what she says.*

OCTOBER 14: *My life is lie.*

OCTOBER 15: *I always felt it was a lie. But now Mommy tells me. She is queen of lies. My father is not father. Mikhail Or-lov is father. He and Mommy were lovers when he was young spy and she linguistics student. They had flat in Moscow. They went to movies. They drank vodka in hidden clubs and got tickets to Bolshoi. "Like normal," Mommy says. What is normal? This lie she has kept. She says I need to know. She can keep secret no longer. My father who is not my father knows. Poor Anton. He has known all along. "That's why he's always at the dacha," Mommy says. "He is good, but weak man. The state knew this. That is why he was only KGB analyst. Mikhail was strong. State knew this too. He was man they wanted. They did not want me with him and . . ." Mommy never cries. Not when I slipped and fell in* Cinder-ella, *and the critics were mean. Not when her brother died. Not at freedom. But she cried when she told me of Mikhail. The state released him into world. Mommy says this like he is bird and state is God. "Yes," she says, "back then this was so." He went to East Germany then to Paris, Brussels, and*

Madrid. To spy on world. I was inside her then. He didn't know. Mommy kept me and married Anton, who is like Joseph in Bible. A good man with another man's child. I cry. To know this. Mikhail doesn't know he is my father. But he is spy. He might know all secrets. Or maybe does not want to know. Mommy says no. He does not know. She saw him one time in St. Petersburg. I was five. She didn't tell him. She said she wanted to but then saw in his eyes that he was not same Mikhail. He hugged her. They had coffee. But Mikhail had other life. Mommy too. "Such love we had once," Mommy says. Mommy is worried. It is dangerous in Moscow. The oligarchs and Putin people are angry. Sanctions won't go away. Russia inside is bad. No trust. People poisoned. "One day," Mommy says, "someone is there, next day not." Like Moscow dogs in winter. Mommy thinks maybe she is on wrong side. She still has Gazprom job. Knows many people. Mommy is smart with people. She is like snake charmer. Suly told me this, but he didn't have to. I already knew. But people are changing. Then Mommy says, like mommy I know: "And famous ballerina daughter not so famous anymore, or famous for wrong thing." She says this like when I was young and did a clumsy petit battement. Mommy tells me about Mikhail because if something happens, I will need friend. I ask what will happen. Mommy doesn't say. She looks away. She says he might not want to know me. To expect this. But there is nobody else. She is hoping, that is all. Mikhail used to love ballet. This is what she says. He must have seen me then. Before. When I was something to see. I wonder what he thought. Did he think I might be his? Did some quiet thing move in him? Mommy wanted Mikhail but only got me. She *made me great ballerina. But that is all. I know this now. Maybe Mikhail will give me money and tell me to go away. How can he be father to daughter already grown? Maybe, I invite him to* Giselle. *See me in my last performance. The girl he made. I am angry. Confused.*

Before Mommy left, she gave me folder and stood by window staring at the gray, black, and gold of St. Petersburg. I opened the folder and read. Pages and pages. Mikhail Orlov, my father, is man behind the American election stealing. The papers tell of network. Facebook. Fake news. Racism. White fear. Immigration. Anger. The papers say all this and more, and how Mikhail reached into America and played it like magician. Putin knew. He and Mikhail talked all the time. They met in Milan. They met many places Putin traveled. But no one ever saw Mikhail. Mommy says he is like space between dark and light, gone before one becomes the other. Trump is fool. This is what papers say. They are written like communiqués *from former times. The words I read had no feeling. Mommy says this is common. We smoked cigarettes and looked at river. The cold is coming. The leaves are almost gone. Wet and fallen. I cried. Not because Mikhail is great spy. I don't care about such things. The Americans do the same. It is game. But Mommy says be careful. Spies are everywhere. They follow me too. This person I've become. There is folder on me somewhere. Mommy says this. Mommy says things might turn bad for Mikhail. Americans watch him. Moscow watches him. They all might know—even though I didn't know!!!!—that I am his daughter. Mommy says this could be trouble. The file is protection. "To have but only use like parachute." Mommy looked at me to know I understood.*

I did. But who could understand such a thing? I took two pills. Mommy stayed, pretending, I think, that she loved me. I awoke at night. She was gone. I am writing a new story for diary. One day, I will turn it into memoir about what happened to great ballerina. Maybe it will be movie. Who will play me? Who could ever? Ha. Mommy told me to keep file on Mikhail. Hide it well. No one must know.

OCTOBER 16: *Zhanna came to room early. I feel like girl in fairy tale, roses all around and witches. Ha ha. Zhanna is the good witch. I love her, like I loved Suly. She knows more people than Mommy, but Zhanna is more quiet. A better sphinx. This is what Suly said. I wish he was here. I miss him. I will visit his grave before I leave. I didn't tell Zhanna about Mommy, Mikhail, and folder. I thought to but didn't. I don't know why. I tell Zhanna everything. Sometimes I think she knows things before I say them, even sins. Is that what they are? I wonder what you call things that weren't there but then are. I don't know what to think. Zhanna and I had tea and biscuits. Zhanna loves biscuits. She is like child when she eats them. I laughed at her, and she smiled. She is younger than Mommy. She stood and kissed me on forehead. Zhanna told me: "Katrina, you take too many pills, drink too much vodka. This is true, you know. It must stop. You must try. Do this* Giselle. *Be her one last time. You can do this. You must stop destroying yourself. It is not a time to be foolish." It made me mad. She was right. But I can't stop. I don't want to. That is lie. I do want to. But what would be left? Old ballerina. I am forty-two. That is not old. Is it? But my body is eighty. My heart ancient. I dreamed the other night when I first stepped onto stage. A girl. Thin as an arrow. The lights went down. I could see the faces, a sea of faces before me. All watching me fly, like daughter of air.*

OCTOBER 18: *Tomorrow. Fly to LA to meet father.*

The last line. I sit with the pages on my lap. There must be more, but Zhanna is clever, giving me just enough. How did Katrina say it? Like a good witch in a fairy tale. I collect the pages and lay them on the table. I reach for the phone to call Azadeh. I stop. I don't call Ortiz either. Or Lily. I pull the chair closer to the window and look down Hill Street to the neons in the diamond district. I want Katrina to myself a little longer. Let her linger, child to woman. Every vic takes you back in time; down roads of damaged things. It's simple, I know, but that's what it is, finding the spot that leads you back to where you first met the vic, dead in a bed in a loft, pale and slender, no marks on her. I pick up the last page and read the line. Declarative. Matter-of-fact. No hint of what's to come, as if she had known Orlov all her life. Father. I put aside the page and imagine her boarding the plane with her diary, pills, and *communiqués*. It's 4:00 a.m. My hours are terrible, but I like the stillness, the pages before me. I look down. Esmeralda is camped on her piece of sidewalk in front of the Hotel Clark. I make fresh tea and take the last of the scotch down to her. She's lost in rags, scarves, and boxes. I hear her breathing—a wheeze, rattle. I sit next to her. She peels back a scarf and looks at me.

"You're a bothersome man," she says.

"I have tea."

"How about ten dollars?"

"And scotch."

"Pour a little in."

She takes the mug, warms her hands.

"I seen them monsters in your place over there. They're gone now. Back to eternity. That's where monsters live. Eternity. I don't want to go there." She drinks, her voice like a murmur in a foxhole. "I don't let 'em see me. They pass right by. I look out. Don't look at 'em. That's the best way with 'em. Let 'em be."

"You okay?"

"Been cold."

"You want another blanket?"

"I want ten dollars."

"Have some more tea."

"Man, you cheap."

She laughs.

"My daddy was cheap," she says. "He's in eternity. You got a case? You're always poking around when you got one. Sometimes I remember; sometimes I don't. Someone's always dead, though, when you come by. One day you'll come buy with some good news. Like you won the lottery or something. Then maybe you'll give me ten dollars. Who's dead?"

"A ballerina."

"A what?"

"Ballerina. Dancer, you know."

"I know what a ballerina is. You think I'm a fool? Speak up. Who did it?"

"Her father."

"Just like a father to do some terrible shit. God's the worst of all. Sent his son down to be crucified. What kind of shit is that? All fathers since have followed that path. Fucking up the lives of children. One, two, five, nine, twenty-three, sixty-six. They're there again. In your building. See 'em?"

"No."

"Up there near that lighted window. See, he's moving around the corner now. Ahhh, he's gone. Four, ninety-nine, thirty-six, two. They go away when I count." She holds up her mug for more scotch. "You arrest the father?"

"Not yet. Still can't prove it all the way."

"But you got a feeling?"

"Yes."

"That don't mean shit."

She hands me the mug, disappears beneath her scarf.

CHAPTER 29

"What now?" says Lily.

"We go to Orlov," says Ortiz.

"Might be too soon," I say.

"No," says Ortiz. "He's in the diary. She came to see him. Gotta go see that spy. Rattle his cage."

"We're only going to get one chance with him," I say. "Guy like that doesn't rattle."

"Everyone rattles," says Lily.

"What about the FBI?" I say. "They're going to want the diary. Azadeh's been good to me. I don't want to burn her."

"Shit," says Ortiz. "Azadeh might already have it. We don't know what kind of game this Zhanna is running. We don't even have the whole diary. We don't know what's missing. I tell you one thing though: Zhanna's the one I'd want on my team. Pretty sneaky broad. Disguises. Pops up all over the place."

"I don't think we're called broads anymore, Captain," says Lily.

"Sorry, figure of speech," says Ortiz.

"Like in the old movies."

"Yeah," he says. "You feeling better? You look good."

"I need to get back in."

"Nice place you got here," says Ortiz. "I had family who lived in this neighborhood. Long time ago."

Lily says, "Everybody who came to LA started in Boyle Heights."

"Back in the day," says Ortiz. "When everyone went to church and prayed to Our Lady of Sorrows. How many prayers, right? We came here once to visit my dad's brother. Someone was having a first communion. The sidewalk was full of white dresses. I'll never forget that long line marching into church. Not like then now. Not anywhere, really."

"How long have you been a cop, Captain?"

"Thirty plus. My old man, his old man."

"Same here."

"It's like a weed, right? Once it gets in a family. I wanted to be an explorer when I was a kid."

"Carver told me about your map collection."

"I'll show you one day. But by the time I got old enough, everything had been discovered. Maybe some places deep in the rain forest, but then, I figured that with my luck, I'd get down there and be three weeks in the bush, thinking I'm on virgin land, and there'd be some outpost left by Spanish missionaries turned into an Airbnb. Then I'd die of malaria or dysentery. Plus, no money in it."

"You were born a century late," I say.

"Victim of time," he says.

"I like being a cop," says Lily. "I'm going to make detective, Captain."

"You got the eye. How fast are you, anyway? This Iron Woman stuff."

"It's called Ironman, but women compete. I do a five-ten mile."

"Damn. You gotta swim, too, right?"

"And bike."

"Why?"

"It takes you to a place. You can feel all of yourself."

"You know, Carver likes being a cop," says Ortiz.

"Won't show it though."

"He's cagey that way," says Ortiz, smoothing his mustache and smiling.

Lily pours more coffee. A breeze blows across the porch. It's cold and cloudy, rain to the west. We pass around pages from the diary. Lily wonders what it feels like to be onstage, to dance. She understands the precision, pushing the body, long workouts, sweat. "I get that in my own training," she says. "The mind making the body obey. But Katrina was making art, you know. There's a difference. I've been watching YouTube videos of her. A body telling a story with no words. It's beautiful, like she has no bones, you know, like you could bend her into whatever dream you wanted."

"Must suck to lose that," says Ortiz. "To hit the downslope." He holds up a page. "Look what she says here; she's forty-two, but her body's eighty. Toll taken."

"She wasn't handling it," I say.

"You know," says Ortiz, "in the end this could be a suicide or accidental overdose."

"We don't have—"

"The body. No shit, Carver. You always got to bring that up."

"Well . . ."

"Where'd you get these croissants, Lily?" says Ortiz. "They're good."

"Guy a few streets over."

"Good coffee too."

"Cuban guy around the corner."

"Mmmmm."

We drink and eat. Lily turns the radio to late-morning bossa.

"You ever wonder," says Ortiz, "about what it must be like to be Orlov? I mean, shit, you've been on both sides of a dangerous game—decades of it, you know, all the secrets you're walking around with—and now you just heisted an American election, and look, you just also happen to be a movie producer and a gold miner. A billionaire. You gotta admire the guy on one level. Who has the capacity for that?"

"He's from another time," I say.

"Maybe," says Lily. "He's a master reinventor."

"Wonder if he ever knew Katrina was his daughter," says Ortiz. "I mean, knew way back."

"Diaries don't say so," says Lily. "They say her mother never told him."

"Yeah, but you ask me, Orlov knows a lot of shit no one ever told him. Where'd you say he is, Carver?"

"Italy. Film shoot. He might be back."

"I know he's back," says Ortiz, smiling. "Got a friend at the FAA. His studio jet landed last night."

"So you can be useful," I say. "Waited long enough to tell us."

"Lily," says Ortiz, "if you ever do become this asshole's partner, you have my sympathy."

"I'm an acquired taste," I say.

"That's one way of looking at it," says Lily.

She and Ortiz laugh. Stan Getz plays "The Girl from Ipanema." Lily winks. She's feeling better, the thing of it fading, but it'll always be there—the scar, the heat of it. I wonder whether Zhanna's out there watching. Seeing how we'll play this. She's got Antonio Garcia too. Or had him. Little Antonio is in deep. Orlov and the Russians have won, short-term. America has turned into what they wanted. What did Lincoln say: "A house divided against itself cannot stand?" Or was that from the Bible? It's hard to watch TV, contemplate it all, the rushing busyness of it, tweets and clamor, empty air turned into fear and paranoia, and the kind of meanness that stays in the heart. We have slipped beyond caricature. Our spoiled orange king-baby has drawn us in. We don't know truth from lie, or we don't want to. We're a rolling, sad circus. Orlov knows. He is one of us. He makes movies we see ourselves in. He has slipped into our tissue. That's giving him too much credit. We were breaking before. He and Putin just widened the cracks.

"I gotta go," says Ortiz, looking at me. "Don't tell Azadeh yet. Let's talk to Orlov tomorrow and see what we can get on Katrina. Once it goes to Azadeh, we lose him." He turns to Lily, hugs her. "Glad you're mending. Thanks for coffee and croissants."

"Maybe we should get to Orlov now," I say.

"I talked to his lawyers this morning," says Ortiz. "I told them we want a meet. Let's play it this way."

Lily and I sit on the porch. The radio says the brush fires north are still burning but not as fiercely. Three firemen have died so far, trapped when the wind kicked and the blaze doubled back. Nine hundred homes destroyed. I had forgotten about the fires. They linger in and out of the consciousness, one burning into another, catching the night sky. Mudslides will come with the rains. The earth spoils, and the cycles will get tighter, the radio says, citing a United Nations report that gives us ten years to fix the atmosphere or gradually burn ourselves up.

"Like sun through a magnifying glass," says Lily.

She straddles me, kisses me. Leads me to bed. We leave the porch doors open and lie looking at the gray sky. It's not yet noon, and a killer is loose, but this feels like a dark, pleasant, wasted day. I pull Lily closer, and for the first time in a long while, I don't think or imagine. I let the seconds run through me, accepting their mystery. Lily sits over me. She peels off her Band-Aid. I reach up and feel the stitches, hard and brittle. The scar will be small, I say. Yes, she says. She leans down and kisses me and slides beside me again. Our eyes go back to the sky. The rain in the west has moved our way. We watch it blow and dance on the railing, feel the cool air run over us, and hear children laughing up by the church. It rains hard. Lily gets up and stands naked at the door, feeling drops splash on her, laughing, and returning to bed, wet and cold, pulling the sheet over us and whispering to me to stay the night and be lazy, to leave my gun on the dresser and pretend.

CHAPTER 30

The gate swings open. I drive through and park by a fountain. A peasant girl with a vase—the kind of centuries-old, perfectly scaled statue that one sees in small towns in Europe, calling no attention to itself amid the honeysuckle and jasmine. The villa is pale yellow with green shutters and a Mediterranean tile roof. Vines run along the corners, and two small angels peek down from above the front door, inviting yet watchful. The sounds of the city have fallen away. I feel as if I have wandered into the Italian countryside. One senses that from time to time in LA, those moments when air and earth awaken the ancient. It is the feeling J. P. Getty had when he built his villa beyond the Palisades. But this is different. The home's beauty is in its simplicity, the way it rises in rustic grace.

Armando Torres appears, dressed in chauffeur black, wearing wraparounds and betraying nothing, not even the disgust I know he burns with after Ortiz bypassed him and arranged the meeting through Orlov's lawyers. He nods and leads me to the front door, across the mosaic foyer, through the living room with billowing linen curtains, and out back to a pool and gardens. A man is swimming. On the other side of the pool, a woman in a blue one-piece lies on a chaise longue in the sun, a few books and a pitcher beside her. Torres points to the table and retreats. I sit beneath an umbrella. A man in a white blazer pours coffee and lemonade, glancing at me, then away. He disappears. I watch the swimmer doing laps. He glides at a fast pace with no splash. The lawn stretches to an ivy-covered wall at the west end of the property. I wonder how difficult or easy it is, depending on one's wealth, to build a world inside another. It takes a certain architecture, I suppose, a discipline. The woman on the chaise longue stands; she looks like Juliette Binoche. I think she is. I remember *The English Patient*, and her shadow dancing on the wall of an abandoned villa very much like this one, and how she read to a dying man and cut off her hair but was still beautiful in the way only a few can be. She looks at me, says nothing, and walks into the house. I am alone. I listen to the man in the water. Ten minutes. Twenty minutes. I take out my notebook. I smile. I could write here in the mornings, drink coffee, think of plots, turn them into movies, and swim in the afternoons with Juliette Binoche.

Mickey Orlov rises from the pool. He walks up the steps in the shallow end. He's in his seventies and taller than I expected, thick in the shoulders, with long-muscled arms. He wraps himself in a white robe and turns toward me, water dripping off his silver hair, his face stony and tan. I can't tell whether he's had work. Everyone in this town has, I suppose, but like his home, he has an unadorned elegance about him. This is a man who could slip into places and convince you that he belongs. I stand and shake his hand.

"Was that . . ."

"Yes," he says, "Juliette's in town. We're making a little film and we want her to stay a bit longer, but she has to be on another shoot somewhere else. It's all timing, you know. Never the project, but the timing."

He pours us lemonade.

"I suppose it seems strange," he says.

"What?"

"To have Juliette Binoche in one's backyard."

"It's your world."

"It is. But it still amazes, Detective. I've never taken it for granted. I hope I haven't, anyway. When I came here a long time ago, before my first film, I met Kirk Douglas at a party in Malibu." He runs a hand through his hair and laughs. "The classic name-dropping story, but I was younger then. Not immune. Kirk was standing alone on the beach. It was dusk. He was drinking a martini. His profile—you know that famously etched face—was cast against the sky. For me it epitomized Los Angeles. How beauty can overwhelm. I found it ironic too. The first movie I had seen Kirk in was *The Bad and the Beautiful*. He played a movie producer, and that's what I was going to be. He's still alive, you know, Kirk." Orlov drinks his lemonade. The man in the white blazer appears, pours coffees, vanishes. "I love film, Detective. I always have. My studio is named for Andrei Tarkovsky's film *Solaris*. Do you know it?"

"Science fiction."

"A psychological mystery in a space station. Tarkovsky had big ideas. He wanted to explore emotional crises in the blackness of the cosmos, where things, both inside and outside us, can float away."

"Pulled by other forces."

"Exactly, Detective. Exactly."

He nods toward the villa. Torres is standing in the window, arms crossed, wraparounds snug.

"I'm afraid you've made an enemy, Detective," says Orlov, smiling. "Armando likes to be my gate. You and your boss went around him."

"I don't see your lawyers."

"We don't need lawyers, do we?"

"I tend to do better without them."

"I like your sense of humor, Detective. I miss the wonderful noir that came out of Hollywood. Chandler. Hammett. Bogart. Those kinds of movies aren't as clever today. I've made a few. One was good. Quite good, actually, but still, there was something. A missed slyness. That's why they worked, you know. They were sly and fast, and the dialogue snapped. It was smart. They don't write smart so much today, or it's so smart it's unintelligible."

"I wanted to talk to you about Katrina Ivanovna."

"My daughter."

He sits back, lets the words settle.

"You look startled, Detective. That's why you're here, correct?"

"Yes, we've learned—"

"I only just learned too. A few months ago." He smooths his robe, crosses his legs. "I had never met her before. I had known her, of course, as a ballerina. One of the best. In her day." He pulls a pack of cigarettes from his robe pocket, offers me one. I accept. He strikes a match. I lean toward it. "She appeared unannounced at Solaris. My secretary came into my office and said, 'There's a Katrina Ivanovna at the gate. Do you know her? She has no appointment.' Just like that. I had no idea why. I was intrigued. She came up. She was a mess. Too thin, not made up. The eyes of pills. I know those eyes very well. This business is full of those eyes. She sat and stared right at me. 'You are my father.' I'll never forget that look or those words. Tell me, Detective, what does one make of that? 'You are my father.' Out of thin air." He blows smoke. "She told me about Maria, her mother. She and I were lovers once, back when we and the world were very different. Maria had told Katrina. I never knew."

"You were a spy traveling the world."

His eyes narrow; his jaw tightens. Just a bit.

"I was a government worker stationed at various embassies," he says. "Maria became a linguistics professor. Our jobs took us apart."

"Maria is something much different today."

"I don't know. I've lost touch with all that. I loved her, Detective, long ago. You're too young to know about the Cold War. Decisions made. Lives given up. You sacrificed back then. On both sides of the Atlantic."

"You sound nostalgic."

"I don't deny it. But lives go on."

"I thought spies—government workers, that is—were good at knowing things. You really didn't know you had a daughter?"

"I did not."

"You don't have an accent."

"As I've said, and as you know, I haven't lived in Russia in many years. Accents aren't like fingerprints, Detective. They can disappear. Maria taught me that when I was young."

"You had no idea she was pregnant?"

"You keep pressing this point. I had no knowledge of a child." He quiets and looks to the pool and back. "A young woman appears out of nowhere and says she's your daughter. I remember her face when she said it. Hope, anger, the sadness of somebody lost. I didn't know what to feel. I stepped closer to her. We looked at each other in silence for a long time. It was as if we were animals trying to detect a scent. Isn't that strange? I told her what a beautiful dancer she was. I think I said she was a genius. She was, you know. I saw her dance twice in Europe. Nobody moved like Katrina. You felt it. Everyone in the audience did. She was our ideal. That yearning in us when, for a moment, the human becomes divine. Have you ever had that feeling? I'm sure you have. I had no sense she was my daughter. I knew only that she was magic on the stage." He crushes out his cigarette and lights another. "We'll never know, will we, Detective," he says, staring at me as hard as anyone ever has, "if she was my daughter?"

"It's in her diaries."

"I supposed you had read them. Why else would you be here? I have never seen them myself. Katrina told me she kept them." He leans closer. "I suspect, Detective, that you have not seen all the diaries. What is that word? Oh, yes, I would bet you have read only the abridged version."

"Why do you say that?"

"A feeling." He leans back. "May I ask you something, Detective?"

"Please."

"Do you think she suffered? I suppose everyone asks you that. But I hope she didn't suffer."

"She looked as if she was sleeping. We don't know how she died."

"Yes, I read. Quite an embarrassment for you to lose her."

"There's no way to change that."

"No autopsy."

"I can't say."

"No use holding a hand you don't have, Detective."

"Let's leave it at that, then."

"She was quite troubled," says Orlov. "Too many pills, too much drinking. I could see it in her that first day we met and the days after."

"How many times did you see her?"

"Three or four. She was back in LA for *Giselle*. She had such hopes for it. I think it was the penance she wanted. She thought if she could dance beautifully one more time, she could be redeemed. I understood that. Who doesn't want absolution? We talked about it. She was so sarcastic. She could be quite cruel to herself. She said Maria did that. The second time I saw her, we had lunch right here. She reached across this table and held my hand. She didn't let go. Like a child."

"Imagine."

"I do. The last time I saw her was two days before she died. It was here. I wanted to believe she was my daughter. I wanted certainty. Not diaries and stories from Russia. I asked if she would take a DNA test. I told her we could go together." He takes a breath. "It changed then, Detective. It was a threat to her pretend world or the world she believed to be true. Perhaps I wanted to believe too. She burst into such rage. She looked at me with hate, as if I had betrayed her. The change in her was instantaneous. She started yelling. She said she knew things. She said she could destroy me. I tried to calm her. I held her, but she pushed away and ran out the door."

He pours lemonade, looks across the pool, down the lawn to the ivy wall. "That's the last time I saw her. It was a rejection. That's what she thought. She thought I was rejecting her because I wanted proof. The drugs didn't help. She was delusional. Paranoid, I'd say. But mine was a simple request."

"Most people would want proof."

"She didn't see it that way. So volatile even in the short time I knew her. Too many addictions, Detective. She didn't want to hurt, and she was running out of ways not to. What I asked hurt her." He looks to me. "I don't know if she was my daughter. I suppose I won't."

"We can do a DNA test."

"Her body's gone."

"We have evidence we collected from her loft. We could pull a sample from it."

Orlov's eyes quicken. He looks at me, away and back, crosses his legs. He must have anticipated my suggestion. He was a spy or, as he put it, "a government worker." From what I read about him, he was always ahead of everyone. Why does he seem agitated now? Not much, just a glimmer. He tucks it away.

"I suppose we could arrange that."

"When?"

"I'll have to check my schedule, Detective. I fly to France in a few days. Perhaps when I return. We can arrange it with my lawyers."

"Do you want to know?"

"I did. I'm not so sure now, to be honest."

"What do you suppose she meant by 'destroy you'?"

"I have no idea. But you must know a lot about me. You've read."

"Many lives for a government employee."

"Maybe someone from one of them wants to do harm."

"I read you were the cleverest of all."

"No clever man would believe that about himself."

"Do you know a man named Jimmy Krause?"

"No. Armando told me you asked about him. I think he told you this Mr. Krause served with him in Iraq. I never met him."

"Krause drove around two Russians. He took them to Katrina's in the days before she died."

"As I said, Detective, I don't know a Mr. Krause."

"He's dead."

"Yes. Armando told me."

"Do you know the two Russians?"

He laughs. He wants me gone.

"I know many Russians, Detective. But the two you're referring to, I have no idea."

He looks to the house. The door opens. Armando Torres is on his way down the path.

"I have an appointment, Detective."

"Juliette?"

"She's probably gone by now. Out to lunch somewhere."

He stands. Shakes my hand.

"Armando, please show the detective out."

Torres steps beside me, nods toward the path.

"We should get the DNA test done quickly," I say.

"I'll arrange it," says Orlov.

"I hope we meet again."

"Perhaps."

CHAPTER 31

The gate opens. Armando Torres stands watching and then walks to the villa and disappears in the rearview. I drive toward West Hollywood. My phone rings. Azadeh.

"Meet me." *Click.*

I cut down to Wilshire and head toward the barbecue place Azadeh likes off South Serrano in Koreatown. It's where we meet when things can't wait. I pull into the parking lot and see that her car is already there. The lunch crowd is thinning. Azadeh sits in a back booth near the kitchen, talking to the owner, a fat man in a stained white apron drinking a beer. His *seng bulgogi* and *tteokbokki* have become legend since both the *Los Angeles Times* and the *New York Times* reviewed him in the space of a month. That was years ago, but a chef can ride on that cred for a long while. He winks at me and hurries through swinging doors into the heat of the kitchen.

"Shit, Carver."

"I know."

"We've been watching Orlov. You didn't think we'd see you pull up to the villa. What the f—"

"I—"

"Don't say anything. You screwed me. I need to be mad. Sit there."

"You ordering?"

"Don't speak."

Two phones buzz and glow before her. She doesn't reach for them. I take out my notebook and write "perhaps." The last word Orlov said to me. Open-ended with the scent of possibility, it's also a word that connotes obscure inexactness. I wonder what Maria, Orlov's long-ago lover, the linguist, would have made of *perhaps*. That was, in the end, when he went his way and she hers—all she got: two syllables with no clear intention. I write "diary" and "daughter" and "Where is she?" Azadeh twirls her long dark hair into a bun. She looks tired, no makeup, rattled. I imagine her hours earlier, leaving her South Pasadena craftsman at dawn, stopping at the coffee shop on the corner in those last moments before the noises—landscapers, yoga women, and school buses— steal away the quiet and send her, cup in hand, to her Prius and toward crimes waiting in the cool of a new day. The coffee shop is her ritual, one she keeps even from Elsa. But I know it. I've seen her over the years when I've been sleepless and out driving.

Azadeh looks at me.

"I thought we had an understanding," she says. "I told you Orlov was off limits, that we were looking at him for the election thing. It's much bigger than you, Carver. You know that, don't you?"

"I never mentioned anything about the election to him. Nothing about spying. I only talked about Katrina."

"You don't have anything. Not solid."

"We've got Jimmy Krause, a friend of Orlov's chief of security, shot by a pro. We've got Krause driving two Russians to Katrina's loft before she dies. The Russians vanish. When we talked to Krause, he was starting to break."

"And who the hell gave you Krause? Remember? My CI— that's how you got him. Then you get Krause killed."

"We've got a drug-addicted ballerina who wants to write a memoir that could implicate Orlov in something. I don't know what, but it certainly gives him motive."

"Not enough to bring him in, and you know it. What else have you got?"

"What else do I need?"

"Don't be coy, Carver. You're no good at it."

"I've got nothing else."

"Why did you meet with him, then? You must have more than you're telling me."

"What do you have?"

"I'm not playing this game, Carver. You're pissing people off and you're jeopardizing a national-security investigation."

"What about a woman's death?"

"Tragic. Is that what you want me to say? Gifted ballerina dies. The world weeps. But the world doesn't weep. She wasn't gifted anymore. She was a has-been."

"You don't believe that."

"I believe you're getting in the way of something more important than a dancer's death."

Azadeh doesn't have the diaries. If she did, the FBI would have moved on Orlov. What is Zhanna's play? I don't know enough about her except that she was Katrina's confidant and refuge from Maria. Zhanna's an operative. But for whom? Katrina called her a sphinx. Are the diaries real? Or the work of some would-be novelist typing away down a Russian intelligence hallway? I haven't seen the originals, only translations by someone not fluent in English syntax and grammar. Orlov said I have the abridged version. He was smug about it, but how would he know? He's a spook, so he would know, but I don't think so. He allowed me to see him—sent away his lawyers and made Armando Torres wait inside the villa—to gauge what I knew. The diary pages I have aren't in chronological order, and much is missing, but for my case, they're another piece of evidence leading to Orlov. Or am I being duped?

"What's he like?" says Azadeh.

"Confident, gentlemanly," I say. "He's a swimmer. Barely makes a ripple. Juliette Binoche was sunning herself poolside."

"Sounds like a scene from one of his films. I've been watching his movies, Carver. You know what they're all about? Loss. Everyone one of them. Comedy, drama, thriller, fantasy—doesn't matter. They're about loss and things taken. Sometimes it's subtle. Other times it hits you in the face, but every movie is about diminishment and what happens when our desires can no longer feed our soul." She sips water, pushes a napkin aside. "It's an impressive body of work when you consider the source. A man who constantly reinvents himself loses who he is along the way. He becomes the lie. The great delusion. He tells the world through make-believe. It's like the Cold War days when hidden meanings were tucked in books and letters, numbers on postcards."

"Film School 101."

"Screw you. We do analysis at the FBI. We don't fly off through the city on whims, chasing nebulous leads, getting people killed."

"Ouch."

"You deserve it."

"I know what you mean though. I got that from him too. He came at me in full. You should have seen him step out of his swimming pool. It was like a director called *action*. It was for my benefit. To see his vigor, strength. He's built for an old guy. Relaxed. Suave. They must teach them that. You know, betray-nothing kind of shit. Juliette was a nice touch. It almost seemed cliché but it wasn't. It was what he's created. There was a sad nostalgia about him though."

Azadeh looks at the menu. The kitchen doors swing open— flame and steam and busy hands, the air sharp with spices, scallions, and kimchi.

"Why can't you bring him in?" I say.

"Too many layers." She reaches across the table, takes my hand. "You're not telling me everything, are you?"

"I may have a few things you don't have."

"No. You have something bigger. You wouldn't have gone to him without it. You owe me, Carver."

She pulls her hand away. I take a sip of water, close my notebook.

"I'll give you one thing now and another later," I say. "I can't tell you all of it now. I want him for Katrina's murder. You can have him after. I just want him charged, in the books. You take him after; that's your business. Don't be disappointed or pissed. You'd do the same. We're each working a case."

"But mine's national security."

"I know. But he's not stealing another election for at least two years. I think it'll be a wrap by then."

"A wrap. Really, Carver?"

"I'm tired, and it fits."

"So tell me."

"Zhanna."

"You met her in Brussels. We talked about that."

"I saw her again."

"Where?"

"My bar."

"No way. She couldn't have gotten into the country without us knowing."

"Way."

"You're not shitting me?"

"I am not. She was in disguise. Looked like Madonna. I didn't recognize her until she spoke."

"What'd she say?"

"She thinks Orlov had Katrina killed. She suggested that Katrina is his daughter."

"From Maria? Ah, yes." Azadeh sits back, then leans toward me, lowers her voice. "I suspected that. I did. Reading his files from the agency and other places—a lot of paperwork on this guy if you look. There are bits here and there about his relationship with a linguistics student. They were lovers. Her name is mentioned only once. Maria S. That's it. We went through old microfilm, university yearbooks, all kinds of stuff. We found one picture of

Maria S. from back then. We did an age analysis. It's the same Maria who today is connected to the oligarchs and Gazprom. Does Zhanna have proof about Katrina?"

"Not definitive."

"Did Orlov know?"

"He says Katrina came to him with the story a few months ago. Things went well. They met a few times. He asked her to have a DNA test. She got angry. She wanted to be believed, not tested. She stormed out. Days later, she was dead. I think Orlov wanted to her to be his daughter. He wanted it to be true."

"Why?"

"The way he talked about her. A sense he had. I don't know, maybe a connection to that time with Maria."

"So why kill her?"

"She threatened him with something."

"What?"

"That's the what I can't tell you now. I don't even know if it's true myself."

"Carver?"

"I can't. Give me a couple of days. I told Orlov we had hair strands and other things from Katrina's loft that we could do a DNA test with. It was the only time he wavered. Lost his cool. He regained quickly, but the prospect rattled him. He's leaving for Paris in a few days. I'm going over to the villa before then with a DNA team to ask him for samples. Tell him we want to prove it one way or the other."

"What do you think?"

"I don't know. Might be a mystery he doesn't want solved. If he does, and we prove the link, I can arrest him. I at least have enough to get charges."

"If he doesn't?"

"I don't know yet."

"His lawyers won't let that happen. This is a master spy, Carver. I'm thinking he's a few steps ahead."

"Either way, once I confront him on the DNA, I'll give you what I have."

"What you have come from Zhanna? Originally, I mean. She's the source."

"Yes."

"Don't get played, Carver. This is way beyond you and the death of a ballerina."

"What do you know about Zhanna?"

"You have your secrets. I have mine."

CHAPTER 32

I head downtown. Eight cranes swing over the city, raising buildings in spaces I never noticed were empty. I stop at Demitasse. Ortiz is three espressos in, wired, and sneaking quick glances at Mariella, the barista.

"It's become an obsession," I say.

"Mere fantasy."

"You won't . . ."

"Aw, hell no. But I like that she's here. Look. She's pretty, don't you think?"

"Jesus."

"Don't act like that," he says. "We need escapes. Shit that keeps us sane. Little stories we keep inside. She's my story. No harm."

"What do you imagine in this story?"

"It's not sexual, which, I guess, is kinda strange. Mostly, it's just us driving down roads and talking, and me dropping her off at work."

"How exciting," I say.

"Don't be a prick."

"What do you talk about?"

"It's imagination, Carver. I don't really know what we're talking about. We're just talking. I hear us talking."

"Inside your head?"

"Daydream shit."

I lean closer to him.

"Azadeh's pissed," I say.

"I got a call from her boss. Everyone up the chain is pissed. Screw 'em. It's our case now. We've got the diary. I have a DNA team arranged. We've got Katrina's toothbrush and hair strands. Should be no problem." Ortiz looks out the window and waves to a passing uniform talking to an assistant DA. "Orlov's lawyers called. They want ground rules or some shit. They're going to try and delay. You think he'll bolt? He's going to Paris, right?"

"He says in a couple of days."

"I called Lily. She's better. Wants in. I sent her over to Orlov's to watch the villa. At a distance, don't worry."

"She's still a little banged up."

"It's time, Carver. She can't sit around thinking about it. Getting back to work is the best thing. She's a bird dog, I'll give her that. Must be all that Ironman stuff."

Ortiz waves for two espressos. Mariella winks. She is lovely, the way her hair falls; her brown skin against a white shirt; her small hands moving over cups and spoons.

"Most guys run up a bar bill," I say. "But you've got a coffee tab. I've got to be honest, though, these espressos are too bitter for me."

"Bullshit. They're fine. Okay, maybe a little acidic. But I like the bite. Put an extra sugar in."

"You're weird, Ortiz."

"*I'm* weird? You crack me up, Carver. You're the weirdest son of a bitch I know."

"I'm off. I'll meet with the DNA guys, and then I'm going to do more reading on Orlov. I need a little sleep too."

"Not too long."

"At least I know where to find you."

He rubs a hand over his face, rolls his neck.

"I'm starting to think about things," he says. "Not big things. I've already come to peace with those. But the little shit, you know? The cliché stuff. The stuff you're not supposed to think is important but it is. Like now, you sitting here, Mariella steaming milk. The sounds. The shit that makes life. I'm starting to notice it. Like maybe things have slowed down, you know. I'm taking notice."

"Of unimportant shit."

"It's all important. That's my point."

"You getting ready to retire and not telling me?"

"I don't know," he says. "Could be."

"You wouldn't last two seconds at home thinking about the shit that makes up life."

"Maybe not. You think you'll always be doing this?"

"For the foreseeable. You're just having a bad day."

"Probably. Or maybe too many bodies, you know. Too many faces. Hundreds over the years. Gone." He raises and opens his hand as if he were a magician releasing an invisible bird. "Only a few stick out. Isn't that something? Only a few. I don't even complain about the paperwork and office politics anymore. That shit's just part of it, like bone." He smiles, looks at Mariella's reflection in the window. "It's existential."

"Ooh, Ortiz is going deep."

"I've been reading," he says.

"I think it's too much espresso."

He sighs and checks his phone. I reach over and grab his hand. I stare at him for a moment. "You're good at this, Ortiz. You're just going through it again. What did you call it last time?"

"Period of doubt."

"They pass."

"Lasting longer each time though. Which reminds me, you keeping your appointments with the department shrink?"

"Have one next week."

He laughs.

"If the people of this city knew the weird shit in the heads of the cops protecting them, they'd fucking flee."

"I think they suspect," I say.

"You better get going."

I drop a ten on the table and leave him to Mariella. I keep my car parked on Main and walk past the Independent toward Third Street, up past the Bradbury and through Grand Central Market to Hill Street and home. I call Lily.

"You good?"

"Fine," she says. "Nothing moving here. I'm a couple hundred yards away with binoculars."

"Stakeout."

"I needed to get back, Carver."

"He might take off."

"I'll see him."

"Follow but don't stop."

"I know the drill. Hey, Carver."

"Yes?"

"You ever wonder what it'd be like to have money? A lot of

money, you know, the villa-no-other-houses-around-you kind of money?"

"Didn't I tell you? I'm loaded."

"If you were, we'd be having a different conversation."

She's quiet for a moment.

"Hey, Carver."

"Yes?"

"We'll get him."

I put on Nick Cave and sit at the piano with a coffee. I play along with "Into My Arms" and then shut Nick off and play alone. I close my eyes and gather unruly notes, but every now and then, I hit a stretch of the sublime. I backtrack, rework it, try to keep it, but it slips away. The coffee's cold. I add scotch. Just a little. I pull my shortwave radio from the bookcase. It's small with a silver antenna and rows of numbers and frequencies. I bought it at a yard sale years ago in Alhambra. The guy who owned it once lived in Lebanon. He died, and it made its way to his brother's home, where it was marked for eight dollars and buried in a box with vases and empty frames. I like its crackle and the distant voices that come in clear and then fade in bits. I catch a soccer game from who knows where. I hear the crowd, the air of the foreign. Then static. I turn the dial and get the BBC, which makes me think of the time before mine—the time of Orlov—when the world came to you through a voice. My phone buzzes.

"Sam."

"Maggie. Is everything all right?"

"Yes. We're fine. I just put your mother down."

"You sound tired."

"A little."

"Should I come? I have a case, but I could get there in a week or so."

"No. But yes, maybe later. In a few weeks." I hear her breathing. She says nothing for a moment. "It's disquieting, Sam, to be like this. To be with one person all day who doesn't know you and can't care for themselves. I woke up today and didn't know what day it was. They all run together, you know? Your mother always thinks it's Sunday. She keeps telling me to get dressed for church. I haven't gone to church in fifty years, but she thinks we're children. When she thinks at all. I wonder what she sees when she looks at me. If I exist in some dimension or if I'm just fuzz in her brain. I don't like to complain, Sam, but it's tiring."

"What can I do? Is it time . . ."

"Not time for that yet. I don't want to put her in one of those. I guess we'll have to one day. I hate the thought of it. I'm just having a weak moment. I'm opening a beer now, Sam. I'm sitting in the kitchen. Picture it. How many times have we sat here over the years?" I hear her sip. "Tell me about a case, Sam."

"Are you still reading your mysteries?"

"Yes. But tell me something true."

I tell her about Katrina and Orlov and spies and Stefan and flights to Sudan. "Are you making this up, Sam?"

"No, Maggie."

"Well, it sounds quite fantastical. I remember the Cold War. The Russians were our archenemy. I suppose they still are."

"I think so, Maggie."

"Tell me about Africa? I always wanted to go and stand on a savanna and let the wind blow over me. It was a dream of mine. I imagine it came from a book I must have read as a girl."

"It was dry and sad, but there was a clinic along a river, and children playing soccer."

"I never had children, Sam."

"You have me."

"What's it like to see a dead body, one that's been killed?"

"The ballerina had no marks, Maggie. Her skin was so white it was almost clear. People like to say that the dead—the ones with no marks—look as if they're sleeping. They don't. There's something about them, something unsettled."

"That makes sense. I read in the *Boston Globe* today about all the starving children in Yemen. I wonder if they'll look like you said when they die. I sent money to a relief organization. How can we let children starve?"

"Are you okay, Maggie, really?"

"Oh, yes. I'm just having a moment of weakness. I look at your mother and want to pull what I knew of her out. To find the girl inside I knew. She's gone. She doesn't know she's gone. But I do. The burden is with the ones who still remember. Do you think of her much, Sam?"

"All the time, Maggie, all the time. And you too."

"I know you do. I just wanted to hear."

"How's that beer, Maggie?"

"Didn't I tell you? I've switched to IPA. The taste is stronger. I like it."

"You're becoming a hipster."

"I was a hippie once, you know. I marched on the Pentagon."

"The rebel."

"You have to be. Look what happens when you're not."

"Tr—"

"I do not say his name."

"How's the window?"

"The man came and fixed it a few days ago."

"The radiators?"

"Bled and working fine. Sara helped with that."

"Sara?"

"The nurse I told you about. The one who comes over from the hospital sometimes to help with your mother."

"Yes, I remember."

"I want you to meet her next time you come. She's very good with your mother. She helps me bathe her. She's quite patient. We had pizza the other night. Sara and I put your mom to bed, and we ate pizza and drank beer until midnight. She's good at cards. I showed her a picture of you. She thinks you're handsome."

"I'll meet her when I come."

"I feel better now, Sam. Thanks for the talk."

"I love you, Maggie."

"Your mother would be proud of you. I better go up and check on her. She stirs sometimes."

"Bye, Maggie."

"Bye, Sam."

CHAPTER 33

The phone rings at 2:12 a.m.

"Get here," says Lily.

I race west on the 10 and north on the 405 toward Brentwood and Bel Air. Nobody's out. The night is crystal. Palms in moonlight. I drive up a slight rise and pull in behind Lily. I park and get into her car.

"You were supposed to stay farther away," I say. "You're right across the street."

She hands me binoculars and points to Orlov's villa. The gates are open. All the lights are on. Silhouettes move in windows. Three black SUVs are parked in front, near the fountain of the peasant girl. On the lawn, just beyond the jasmine and bougainvillea, a movie, Orson Welles's *The Third Man*, with Joseph Cotten wandering the black-and-white streets of postwar Vienna, is playing on a screen about half the size of a billboard. Chairs are set up on the grass but they're empty. No one is watching, except a woman sitting in the middle of a row. Small crews are filming around her.

"What's going on?"

"Looks like they're making a movie," says Lily. "Shit started happening about two hours ago. The gate opened, and the SUVs rolled in. Bunch of guys and a woman got out. I think it's the same woman who's watching the movie. She talked to Orlov on the lawn for a while; then they went into the house and came back out. The movie on the screen started, and she sat down. The camera crew arrived. Then a bus came, and people in tuxedos and evening gowns got out and walked around back. But the woman and the crew stayed. The movie kept playing. I think the guy behind one of the cameras is Orlov."

"I can't tell, but I think you're right."

"This is surreal, even for LA. What's the plan?"

"Gate's open," I say. "Let's go in."

"Hey, Carver, I think other people—FBI or who knows who—are casing the place too. You feel it? Lot of eyes. A few cars went up the road earlier, parked, and then left. More cars came. They left too, but I don't know. We're not alone."

"Probably not. Let's go in. You okay?"

"Don't get me shot, and I'll be fine. We need backup?"

"No. Let's just see what's going on first."

We drive through the gate and park by the SUVs. Armando Torres appears in the headlights. Lily clicks them off. He walks toward us and waves us out. He's dressed in his usual chauffeur chic, but his tie is loose, and he's holding a martini glass and smoking a cigarette.

"I'm an extra," he says.

"What's going on?"

"I don't like you, Detective. If it was up to me, I'd toss you out. Who's this?"

"Lily Hernandez."

"You gotta pee, Lily Hernandez? You've been sitting out front a long time. What kind of binoculars you using?"

He doesn't wait for an answer. He leads us across the lawn toward the screen. I see the extras, in tuxes and evening gowns, at a party in back by the pool. No music, no sounds, just pantomime and silver trays. It's reminiscent of Jay Gatsby and his parties in West Egg—rich and pretty people beyond the ash heaps and smoke of New York before the crash. They move like jeweled ghosts as cameras glide among them. Lily and I stop at the last row of chairs facing the movie screen. Joseph Cotten and darting eyes and spiral staircases and men following shadows in a Europe ruined by war. The sound is off. The woman watching alone in the middle row is Juliette Binoche. A camera is perched a few feet beside her, another behind. A hand touches my arm.

"Shh, come, Detective," whispers Orlov.

He leads Lily and me to a bank of monitors off to the side. Juliette Binoche appears on three small editing screens. She's wearing a dress and pearls; her hair is combed behind her ears. She's crying, looking up at the movie, gray light playing against her face. She seems a long-ago lover from a scrapbook. I imagine her wandering into a cinema from a rainy street in Paris or Belgrade or Berlin. Orlov leans close to the monitors. He traces a finger against her profile. He gently pulls me down, so my face is level with his. "Do you see it?" he says. "The ache. Look at her face. She is remembering. The movie has brought her to a time. It has unfrozen what was once before. Do you see it? Juliette can do that. She can put the past into an expression. It's exquisite, don't you think, Detective? The pain of memory."

He rises. The big screen goes dark. Joseph Cotten and Vienna disappear. The villa's lights click off. Juliette vanishes from the three monitors. The only radiance is the silent party in the distance by the pool. Orlov is not so formal. He wears jeans and a black cashmere sweater. He strikes a match and lights a cigarette, hands me one. We stand in the night. Juliette Binoche stays in her seat in the middle row. Alone.

"I've produced a lot of films, Detective, but I've never directed one," he says. "This is *my* film. I've been making it for years. My passion project." He smiles and nods to the big, empty screen. "Orson Welles worked on films for years, you know. He was either too obsessed or too distracted. Somewhere between is where his genius lay. That's true with many artists. I work on this whenever I can, accumulating bits and pieces. I fear it's becoming a too-scattered mosaic."

"What's it about?"

"A woman's life. She sits in the theater watching the movie on the screen, and another inside her head. One is real; one is not. But sometimes it's hard to tell. They spool together and apart. That is the battle of life, no?" He blows smoke. "Do you know who the woman is, Detective?"

"Maria."

"You are right. Katrina's mother. I thought you might guess that. Juliette is such a close resemblance. She is how Maria would have aged."

"And Katrina?"

"I don't know if she'll be in this movie." He looks to Lily. "Who's your friend?"

"Lily Hernandez," says Lily.

"That's musical. Lily Hernandez," says Orlov. He glances to me. "So tell me, Detective, why have you wandered uninvited onto my property?"

"You know why."

"I already told you . . ."

"Will you take a DNA test? That's why I'm here."

"Now?"

"Tomorrow."

He looks at Lily. Looks at me. He looks over the dark lawn to the outline of Juliette Binoche.

"Come in the morning, Detective, and we'll get this over with. It's a misguided supposition you're working on. If I'm her father, I'm her murderer too. I don't understand it. But you have your logic. I'll have my lawyers here."

"We just want to check—rule out—everything."

"Yes, I know how it works," he says. "You know, in another time, you could not . . ."

"Could not what?"

"Let's leave it at that," he says walking toward Juliette. He turns back around.

"I often wonder," he says, "if I'll ever finish my movie. I don't know what memories to give her and what not. I don't know if we remember the same thing in the same way. I would hope that some of it is the same; that for a brief moment long ago, two people saw themselves and the world so clearly."

"It doesn't happen often."

"I suppose not," he says. "You're a romantic, aren't you, Detective?"

"A little, maybe."

"I think more than that."

Orlov scans the lawn, twirls a hand in the air. "Much is going on tonight. Within and beyond these walls. Can you feel it? I can."

"How long will they stay?" I say, pointing toward the silent party at the pool.

"Until dawn, I should think. They are part of her memory."

I start to speak.

"Yes, I know, Detective. It's a time for new disguises, like in the movies."

"Did you . . ."

"Don't finish that thought," he says with clipped anger. "You don't want to be straying too far out of your jurisdiction, do you?"

He turns and walks toward Juliette. She hasn't moved. He sits beside her. Joseph Cotten appears again on the screen, and they watch, like a couple on a date.

"You were going to ask him about the election hacking," says Lily.

"Yes."

"You see how pissed he got. His eyes. Instantaneous."

"Then it went away."

"She's a good choice," says Lily.

"Who?"

"Juliette Binoche. No one cries like her."

"You're the romantic," I say.

"No, I just know a good weeper when I see one."

"Let's go."

"I love this town," says Lily.

"This isn't our world."

"For a little while, it is."

We get into the car and drive through the gate. It closes behind us.

"Where?" says Lily.

"Across the street, where you were earlier."

"I like stakeout overtime. It adds up."

"This is the only in and out?"

"Yeah, there's a wall around the whole thing."

We sit in the car, passing the binoculars, watching Orlov's stylish dream through the gates. Lily is good, on the mend. Ortiz was right. She had to get back to who she is. I reach over and touch the scar on her neck. "The stitches came out yesterday," she says. She presses my hand there for a moment. The scar is small, a slight bump. It will fade. I take my hand away and look at her and imagine the movie I would make. It is after four. Cold, clear, a night of stars. It's quiet from the arroyos to the ocean. LA slumbers, and I can feel its almost imperceptible pulse.

"It was calculated, you know," says Lily.

"I know."

"He wanted us to see that part of him. Why?"

"Another deception."

"The movie was real."

"I believe the movie. But he let us in. He knew we were here, and he let us into his great unfinished project."

"You'd think a guy with all that money would just finish the damn thing."

"He doesn't want to finish. If he finishes it, he loses it."

"Maria must have been some woman," says Lily. "What percent odds do you give that he's Katrina's father?"

"One hundred."

"Guess we'll find out in a few hours."

Lily yawns and says, "Bitch of a stakeout up here. No coffee shops around. Just money and space."

Dawn burns in slowly, creeping through Lily's back window, warming us. Orlov's gate hasn't opened. The movie screen is blank. Juliette Binoche has disappeared from the middle row. The villa's lights are out. A few windows are open; a curtain blows back and forth in one. And on the circular drive near the peasant-girl statue, a couple from the pool party, their chic from the night before rumpled and tawdry in the new day, kiss and wander across the lawn, leaving dark footprints in the dew.

"It's a little after six," says Lily.

"We'll get the DNA guys out here at eight."

"Bet they don't show up before ten."

I pass her the binoculars. She lifts them.

"I like the night better than the day," she says.

CHAPTER 34

A stream of black and flashing blue arrives. An armored personnel carrier bursts through Orlov's gate. SUVs and cars pour in. Two helicopters circle. A SWAT team fans across the lawn. Radios scratch and crackle. Lily and I run to the gate. It feels as if war has broken out in a small kingdom. The tuxes and the evening gowns, hands in the air, file from the house and kneel in rows on the grass, men with guns surrounding them. A helicopter lands by the pool. Two men and a woman, yellow FBI letters on their jackets, get out and run beneath the whirl toward the villa. They point. One of them lifts a phone. A face from beneath a helmet yells from a second-floor window, "Secure." The helicopter near the pools lifts and flies west, and the chaos calms a bit. The sense of danger is gone, but the air is charged and alert, and I can tell by the faces of the FBI agents, who look to the villa and the kneeling rows of frightened extras, that Orlov, as if in a movie, has vanished.

"Long night, Carver?"

"What's going on?"

Azadeh is zipped in a blue FBI windbreaker, her ponytail threaded through a ball cap. Her sunglasses reflect my unshaven face as she waves for Lily and me to walk with her, past blueprints unfurled on a car hood, and through the gate along a line of agents with guns out. We stop on the lawn, beneath the screen and the empty rows of chairs where Juliette Binoche sat hours earlier in her dress, pearls, and tears.

"He's gone."

"Orlov?"

"We watched the gate all night," says Lily. "No one came or went. There's no other way out."

"There's a tunnel."

"*Fuck*," says Lily.

"We didn't know it until a CI tipped us a few days ago. But we weren't positive until right now. Our guys in the house just radioed that it's in the wine cellar, near the room where he kept his paintings."

Azadeh looks to the sky. The second copter circles the estate once more and skims east.

"Orlov had it dug after he got here in the nineties. Brought in a construction crew from Ukraine and then sent them back. No one knew. It goes under the pool and beneath the back wall to the street."

"A man like that is going to keep an out," I say. "We should have known."

"He had a lot of outs," says Azadeh. "We figured he left right after you guys had your movie night. About three-thirty a.m."

"It's almost eleven now."

"You were watching the place, too, right?" says Lily.

"We were going to let your DNA thing play out," says Azadeh, "to see if you could get him for Katrina."

"You still don't have enough on him, do you?" I say. "For the hacking."

"Not prosecutable, but we know."

"If you knew he had a tunnel, why didn't you move?"

"I told you, we only just found out. We didn't know where it came out. We didn't think he'd take off. We've been listening to him. He thought he could beat you, Carver. He actually kind of liked you. You should hear him on the tapes. You made an impression."

"What did he say about Katrina?"

"He never mentioned her one way or the other. I think he sensed we were onto him. We stayed far away and left no trace, but I suspect he knew. This Russian shit with Putin and Mueller's investigation. Maybe something in that came out—some leak or crack his intel picked up."

"Maybe Moscow pulled him," I say.

"Is he still in the city?" says Lily. "Were you watching his plane?"

"His plane didn't go anywhere," says Azadeh. "But another one took off from Van Nuys just after four a.m. Guess who it was registered to?"

Azadeh takes off her sunglasses, looks right at me.

"Holly Martins," she says.

"Who's that?" says Lily.

"You were watching him last night," says Azadeh, pointing to the blank screen. "Up there."

"Joseph Cotten's character in *The Third Man*," I say.

"That's him," says Azadeh.

"*That* was the movie last night?" says Lily.

"Correct."

"Son of a bitch," says Lily.

"Made a life out of it," says Azadeh.

Azadeh was right. She told me days ago that Orlov hid in the films he produced. Comedy, romance, thriller—it didn't matter; they were about loss. He slipped into them and peeked out. It was all there last night on the screen: Juliette Binoche's face, memories of a life he wanted but couldn't have, long-ago fragments he kept twisting and reinventing. Maria. She was his country. He couldn't have her, and he became a man of many lives. The movie he was making was not meant to end; it was a ghost of the imagination.

"Sinking in, huh, Carver?" says Azadeh.

"He's smarter than we are. More disciplined."

"He's not smarter than everyone," says Azadeh.

"What do you mean?" says Lily.

Azadeh sits in a chair, looks to the screen.

"We think he's dead."

"What?"

"Holly Martins's plane last had contact with air-traffic control in New York. It landed on Long Island, refueled, and took off. Minutes later, wreckage falls from the sky around fishing boats off Montauk."

"How can you be sure?"

"We aren't until we find the pieces. The plane, whose ever it was, wasn't at high altitude. The debris fell in a tight pattern. We've got teams and divers out there now."

"If you thought he was gone, why all this here?" I say.

"We didn't know. We just moved. We had knowledge of the tunnel. You were pressing him for DNA. We were scared of losing him."

"I think you did," says Lily.

"Is Armando Torres here?" I say.

"The bodyguard? No. Probably went through the tunnel with him."

"Juliette?"

"She was sleeping in a back bedroom," says Azadeh. "Our guys are questioning her now. I don't think she knew anything. She and Orlov talked a lot on the phone. About the movie. She became as intense about it as he was. She loved the idea of aging incrementally. A little like Richard Linklater did in *Boyhood*. But Orlov was going for something more intense—more European, anyway. The slow fuse of time. A Cold War heartbreak."

"She said all that?" I say.

"In a sense. It was quite important to her."

"Were they lovers?" says Lily.

"Juliette and Orlov?" says Azadeh, looking perplexed at the idea. "No. We have nothing like that. I hadn't even thought of it. I think her character made her too sacred to him, you know? If he touched the flesh of it, it would be ruined all over again."

"You got into his head," says Lily.

"I've listened to hours and hours of him over the past few years. I've read everything about him. Think about it. How can one person hide in so many skins? Be comfortable in each. How do you do that? Who are you inside? What is the voice you hear? You get that, Carver, right?"

"He was a spy first. Everything else was part of the disguise."

"Yes, but to excel at each is incredible."

"He got to you," I say.

Azadeh shakes her head and half smiles.

"I never met him, but yes, he got to me," she says. "My

obsession. I—we—almost had him. We were so close. We knew he was behind it all. One step ahead and hiding in plain sight."

"What if he went through the tunnel but isn't on the plane?" I say. "What if that's a deception too?"

"Could be," says Azadeh. "We hope to find bodies in the sea."

"Even then we might never know."

The sun has burned away the dew. It is almost noon. The shadows are gone, and the movie screen bares its seams and small rips. Most of the tuxes and evening gowns have been questioned and released. They wander over the lawn looking like the extras they are, rented elegance turned back into baristas, waiters, and salesclerks. I wish they were still out by the pool, pretending in their wigs, pencil mustaches, and cheap jewelry. They were pretty at night, making you want to tag along on their whispers. They file through the gate and into a sheriff's bus. Agents carry away cameras, editing monitors, laptops, boxes of wires. Azadeh walks toward the villa. I know how she feels to be so close, so inside an obsession that slips away. Maybe Orlov and Dylan Cross will one day conspire over espressos and brandies on an island off the Croatian coast or in a town square in Sardinia. It wouldn't be impossible; the world's designs and coincidences, though most go unnoticed, are infinite.

Lily is down by the back wall, looking, I imagine, for where Orlov's tunnel comes out beyond the palms and umbrella pines.

I stand by the statue of the peasant girl. She is the color of a gravestone in an old church cemetery. I touch her cheek. She is cool. Lichen has bloomed at her feet, by the fountain water, but she is still young, a child, glancing away with a discreet smile, as if she has overheard a secret. She must be special to Orlov—an artifact from the Old World, stolen in the night, perhaps, from a

Russian village and brought here to stand alone amid jasmine and honeysuckle, calling no attention to herself, yet drawing you to her.

I pull my hand away and walk back toward the lawn, my feet crunching on the loose stone of the curved driveway. An agent carries a painting out of the villa—a portrait of young woman wearing a scarf, black hair blowing, eyes staring at something unseen in the distance. It is Maria. I imagine Orlov painting her many years ago in the room by the wine cellar. I can hear his brushstrokes, the swirl of his colors, how he must have labored to freeze time, to keep a version of her alive. Another agent follows with a portrait of a ballerina stretching along a barre, peering into a mirror that reflects a city spreading behind her. Only part of her is painted. The rest is a sketch, her face unfinished.

CHAPTER 35

Two men pulled from the sea.

Mickey Orlov. Armando Torres.

Trawlers gathered them like fish and sailed for Montauk. This is what Azadeh says through her phone as I stand at my window and listen in darkness. The plane's tail number matches the one listed to Holly Martins. A passport bearing the same name was found floating in the water. The plane, a Bombardier Global Express, exploded in midair. Fishermen heard a blast, saw pieces of sky fall. The bodies, including the pilot and a woman in a blue skirt, were nearly intact, which, Azadeh says in a detached monotone, is unusual. But it does happen. There have been cases, she says, where those blown from a plane have been found hundreds of miles out in the ocean, unbruised, uncut, fully dressed. DNA tests confirm the identities of Orlov and Torres with 99.9 percent certainty. She says this twice, reading the number with slow specificity, as if to harden it in the air.

"We have photographs, too, Carver. It's him."

The words through the phone stop for a moment. I can hear

Azadeh breathing, vaping. She's on her porch in South Pasadena. Alone. Elsa is sleeping. Papers are spread beneath a small lamp on a table that Azadeh keeps by a rattan chair. Her neighbors know that when the porch lamp is on in the dead of night, Agent Azadeh Nazari has a case that has gone bone deep.

"A plane like that doesn't just explode, Carver."

"Maybe our guys did it."

"No. The CIA wanted him arrested, not killed. The great spy exposed. Washington wanted a show. The Democrats certainly did. They'd love to stick it to Putin."

"Trump wouldn't want that. It would have invalidated him."

"The Bureau did. Trust me. The whole point these days *is* to invalidate the last two years."

"Maybe Orlov's own people."

"That's what I'm thinking."

Azadeh hangs up. I splash water on my face, change my shirt, comb my hair. I grab the car keys and head for the 10 and the Pacific Coast Highway to Malibu. The ocean air is faint with the scent of burned-out wildfires that have left hillsides and canyons as black as the night sky. Beyond the windshield, it seems another country, the other California, land of nightmares and charred, skeletal houses. But the road curves, the white threads of waves glow, and the houses that escaped the embers whirling in the gusts stand sturdy and bright in the moonlight. I push the gas and feel the wind, racing north. I turn and rise into the hills. I slow and stop at Stefan's gate. I buzz. Luksala's voice greets me. The gate clicks open, and I drive into the courtyard. Luksala appears, regal and never hurried, like an African tribal leader strolling through a sleeping village.

"How are you, Mr. Sam? Come."

He leads me through the foyer and living room and out back past the pool and across the grass, where two shadows sit in Adirondack chairs, smoking cigarettes and facing the ocean.

"Ah, Sam, welcome," says Stefan. "Up late, huh?"

"Hello, Mr. Sam," says a silhouette I am coming to know well.

"You're not in disguise," I say.

"Not tonight," says Zhanna Smirnov. "Tonight, I am me. A pleasant change. Stefan invited me to dinner. He's a good cook. We had fish and potatoes with rosemary—rosemary tastes like Christmas, no?—and wine from Chile. Now we are full and drinking bourbon and talking to the ocean. Sit, Mr. Sam."

Stefan offers me a cigarette. I take it. Zhanna hands me a bourbon. I sit in the chair between them. We lean back, blowing smoke at the stars. I sip. I look to Zhanna: black jeans, black sweater, a silver necklace, a black leather jacket with buckles and zippers. Stefan is dressed in black too: a thick old cardigan and a ball cap keeping him warm. We listen to the wind and watch distant tankers in the moonlight.

"Do you like this bourbon, Mr. Sam?" says Zhanna. "Stefan keeps telling me to like bourbon."

"You can get used to it," I say.

"It's from Kentucky," says Stefan. "The best is from Kentucky."

"Maybe you give me bottle to take back to Russia," says Zhanna.

I turn to her. "You know about Mickey Orlov," I say.

"Is that question, Mr. Sam?"

"No."

"We heard something on the news over dinner, didn't we, Stefan?"

"Tragic," he says. "I didn't know he had made so many movies."

"Curious that a plane would explode like that," I say.

"Yes," says Zhanna. "I am worried to fly always. Statistically, you are safe, but you are in the air, no? So many things can go wrong. Electrical. Fuel lines. Who knows?"

"Maybe you do," I say.

"You are funny, Mr. Sam. You are a hard worker. Clever man, I think. But now is time to drink and talk to the ocean."

"Katrina's diaries."

"You read them, so you know, Mr. Sam."

"I read only the pages you gave me."

"They were the most important pages," she says.

"You loved her."

"Yes."

"But not enough," I say.

Zhanna looks at me. I can feel her eyes. Stefan leans toward me. The wood of his chair creaks. He gets up and walks toward the hill's edge. He stops, barely discernible from the night—and looks over the water.

"What do you mean, Mr. Sam?"

"To save her."

The words hang, dissolve. Zhanna bites her lip, sips her bourbon. She lights another cigarette, blows an arrow of smoke. She is like Orlov the other day: agitated, showing a sudden break in composure. She regathers herself. Takes a breath, pats my arm, stares into the sky.

"Katrina was unstable," I say. "On drugs. Chaotic. Then Maria told her Orlov was her father. That upset things, didn't it? Orlov had no idea. A ballerina daughter shows up at his studio. It unsettled even him. But it gets worse, right? Katrina threatens to out him. To expose Moscow's election hacking. All of it. At least, what she knew. She didn't know much, but just enough. Dangerous variable. What to do, right?"

I watch the waves.

"This is clever bedtime story, Mr. Sam. Like my father used to tell in Russian when I was a girl. Maria had left by then. She was older. It was just Father and me. Mother died in accident long before. A brother before her. Father made lies real. He made little pretend worlds. They existed by themselves. That is a gift." She pours more bourbon, tips the bottle toward my glass. "Tell me more, Mr. Sam. Please. We are here talking to the ocean. Ocean is full of stories."

"Something had to be done with Katrina," I say.

"And Mikhail Orlov did it," she snaps. She takes a breath, returns to calm. "Obvious, Mr. Sam. The Russian men who came here. The Krause man who is dead. All Mikhail. This is what he does. All his life, like a man starting and blowing out fires."

"No," I say. "I think Orlov wanted Katrina to be his daughter. He was startled, yes. He didn't know what to believe. But he was a romantic, and here she comes, out of the past, out of the only thing that is pure to him. His connection to Maria. He would never have hurt that. He would have tried to control her. Get her help. He wanted a DNA test to be sure. Katrina was outraged at that. But Orlov would have convinced her. She was a threat to his spying, but I think—"

"You think, Mr. Sam. What do you *know*?"

"What can I prove, you mean."

"To know and to prove—they are like opposite sisters, no?"

"Too often."

"I think this time. Mikhail's whole life was for Russia. You think he would betray all that for crazy daughter out of nowhere?"

"Yes."

We drink our bourbon. Stefan sits at the hill's edge, his cigarette ember bright in the distance.

"You did it, didn't you, Zhanna? You killed your niece."

"You know, Mr. Sam, when we met in Brussels, I thought we might be lovers. For a night. I did not know when or where. I just thought it. I think you felt the same way. I can tell these things. Do you feel that way now, Mr. Sam? Here in your America, in your California. This place is paradise with end of days sneaking inside, no? Fires, earthquakes. People sleeping in the street. Maybe this is where world ends. My father would like this. He would tell a great story."

"You didn't answer me."

She laughs.

"Mr. Sam, you are funny."

"What do you do? Who do you work for?"

"I am Russian."

"Yes."

"Then you know."

"But Katrina . . ."

"Speak of her no more, Mr. Sam. I don't want to get angry at you."

"What I know but can't prove is this," I say. "Katrina jeopardized Orlov's operation. She had to disappear. Isn't that a euphemism from your country? Orlov was getting sloppy. Too sentimental. He was obsessed with the film he was making about Maria. He was becoming a liability. The FBI was getting closer. You knew. You knew it all. You were sent to clean it up. A ballerina overdoses. A plane explodes. You made the first look like Orlov did it, and the second like an accident."

"Like perfect package. With bow."

"Putin will give you a medal. The master stroke was Jimmy Krause. That linked Orlov to Katrina's death. How did you get Armando Torres to put Krause with the two big Russians? Moscow, right? Someone called Orlov, someone high up, and said two men were coming and needed a guide to show them around. Orlov doesn't suspect anything. It must happen all the time. Innocent request. Orlov tells Torres to take care of it."

"Please, go on, Mr. Sam. I'm on edge of seat."

"But you had Torres. He was working for you. The whole time. How did you flip him? What did you promise him? That had to take time. Orlov had no idea. You tricked the great spy. But you decided it was too risky if Orlov was arrested for Katrina's death. Too much else could come out."

She stands and turns toward me with her glass. She kneels beside me. I can smell her cigarette, her perfume, her leather. She runs a hand through my hair, presses closer to me. She puts her lips to my ear the same way Dylan Cross did in the moment before she vanished. Zhanna has survived intrigue. She has slipped between worlds and exists beyond comprehension. Outlasted even Orlov. I wonder what she is like alone in the dark, her disguises left at the door. I don't turn. She whispers.

"I am going now, Mr. Sam. Your story is like comic book."

"No."

"Katrina could not be saved. She was not who she was. She was Katrina no more."

"What was she?"

"The truth you cannot prove."

"Orlov?"

"He, too, was not the same. A man gets older, no?"

"Why . . ."

"I did nothing, Mr. Sam. I am here having dinner with a friend in Malibu."

"Does Stefan know?"

"What is there to know?"

"I can arrest you."

She laughs. She stands, kisses me on the forehead.

"No, Mr. Sam. We both know you can't. I am ghost, like Mikhail's movie."

"The FBI, CIA will come."

"One day, perhaps."

She starts to say more but doesn't. She finishes the last swallow of bourbon and walks toward the house. She's in no hurry. I have no hard evidence, and what I know is not enough. I call Azadeh.

"Let her go," she says, and hangs up. I dial Ortiz. Same thing. I turn. No trace of her. Stefan returns from the hill's edge. He sits beside me. We don't say anything for a long time.

We walk to the house. Luksala tells us Zhanna is gone. "A black car came with two men. Two very big men." Stefan pulls another bottle of bourbon from the shelf. He pours three glasses, winking and handing one to Luksala, who heads down the hall to his room at the far end of the house. Stefan lights wood in the fireplace. "It's cold this year, Sam," he says. He puts on music from Serbia. I don't know the lyrics, but the voice is deep and soft.

"Zhanna had Katrina killed."

"I know, Sam."

"And you invite her for dinner."

"I only found out tonight."

"What are you going to do?"

"Do? What do? It's done."

"There's no feeling, then?"

"Katrina and I split long before. There's feeling, Sam. But there are wars you cannot win."

"That doesn't sound like you."

"Tonight, it is me. Tomorrow, who knows? Have another drink, Sam. It is almost light."

Stefan lifts an envelope from the table and hands it to me. It's addressed to "Mr. Sam." I open it and read Katrina's diary entry from the night she died.

> *I don't know if I can do* Giselle. *The body resists her. She must be like air. But I am air no more. I want to be child again. To see the world that way. To be with Suly in a new city. Mikhail wants test that I am daughter. He knows. I can tell. But still. I am scared. I see those men again on the street. Watching. They will come and knock, but I won't let them in. I take a pill. The tender little bite it gives. I look out the window. The men are gone. Wonder where they go. I wish Levon was here to play. I would dance until morning. Sweet, lost boy. Oh, but he can play. To be girl. To be like air. I see her. Zhanna called. She was crying. I have never heard her tears before. She wants to save me but knows she can't. I ask her what this means. She hangs up. I call back, but no answer.*

At the bottom of the page, written in a different hand in fresh ink, is a street name and house number in Joshua Tree.

> *Mr. Sam, the man you want is here.*

CHAPTER 36

Lily and I drive at dawn. The 10 is uninspiring for miles. Chino, Riverside, Redlands, Beaumont, Banning. The outlands stretching away from the kingdom, distant mountains rising in copper ranks—a land you want to speed through. Sun on the windshield, St. Vincent playing low, Lily sleepy and quiet, cold air reaching in from the desert, drawing the car east until the raggedness falls away, and wind turbines, like fields of white propellers, spin in broken unison at the edge of Palm Springs, where we turn north and rise on Route 62 toward Joshua Tree.

"I've only been to the high desert once," says Lily.

"I slept here in a blanket on the ground when I first moved to LA. I counted the stars until I fell asleep." I crack the window and breathe in dry air. "This is where you come when you don't want to be found. Dylan Cross built a church in this desert."

Lily knows this. She lets the sentence disappear. A few minutes pass.

"Butterscotch, bone, and pennies," she says out of nowhere.

"What?"

"The colors of the rocks. Butterscotch, bone, and pennies."

"A volcano or some kind of eruption millions of years ago."

"How does anybody really know?" she says, turning toward me and looking back out the window. "A million years ago—what does that mean? It'd be a good place to run though."

"You back to it?"

"Did a good five the other day. I lifted too. Look."

She makes a muscle, laughs, and pretends to punch me.

"You want to stop for coffee? There's a place."

"No," says Lily. "Let's just find this asshole and see what's what. No backup, right?"

"Just us."

"Like partners."

"A little."

"All right, I'm not going to talk about it. But I'm getting my detective shield, Carver. You're going to have to deal with it." She switches from St. Vincent to Cat Power. "That Zhanna's some chick, huh? The doer."

"Can't prove it."

"One day, maybe. Fucking spies."

"I don't exactly know who she works for."

"Not knowing is probably the smart play."

"Too bad for Katrina."

"And Levon."

"Wonder what will happen to Orlov's movie." She grabs the rearview, tilts it toward her, studies her eyes. She runs a faint thread of color across her lips, tilts it back. "I had a dream about Juliette Binoche the other night."

"Weird one?"

"They're all weird, Carver. She was in a first-communion dress, eating cake and dancing on a lawn filled with fireflies."

I turn onto Quail Springs Road. We drive three and a half miles and turn right on a dirt stretch that leads through yucca, scrub oak, and juniper to a house wedged behind Joshua trees in the lap of a hill.

"I guess this is it," says Lily. "Number's the same."

"No cars. Nobody around."

"Let's do it."

"We knock," I say.

We quiet step toward the front door, guns drawn. Lily peels off around back. I reach the porch. The door's open a quarter of an inch. I peek through and push. Slow. I step in. Lily slips through the back door and into the kitchen. She shakes her head. There's no furniture, just a few rugs and two battered beach chairs. Bottles of Stoli sit on the counter near three empty pizza boxes, overflowing ashtrays, and a deck of cards. The sun is coming through the windows. I look out. The sky is purple-blue, and on the ridge in the distance, a man bundled in a coat walks his dog. We head down the hall. The first two bedrooms are empty. The door at the end is shut. Lily grabs the knob. She nods, turns it. We burst in.

Antonio Garcia sits in a corner on the floor, hands cuffed behind him, legs wrapped in rope and tied like a mummy's. His mouth is duct taped. His black hair falls long and dirty around his face and down to his shoulders. He's crying and sweating. He recognizes me. Lily pulls the tape off; he gasps. Keys to the cuffs and a bowie knife lie on the windowsill. I unlock Garcia and cut the rope away. He stands. Smells foul. He's shaking. He reaches into his pocket for a rubber band and gathers his hair into a ponytail. He's unshaven and drawn. His eye is bruised, his lip cut. He moves with the stiff soreness of someone who took a beating. He brushes his clothes and tries to become himself again, summoning the arrogant flair and irritating gaze of the man I met the morning after Katrina's death.

"Anyone else here?" says Lily.

He shakes his head and swallows.

"They left last night, I think."

"Who?"

"Two giants. Russians. They came to my loft and threw me in a car. Stupid men. Gruff like peasants. Terrible suits—one charcoal black, the other a strange hue of midnight blue. They might have been brothers. I need a toilet." He runs down the hall. I follow and stand outside the bathroom. He comes out patting his wet face with a towel. "They knocked over my mannequins and ripped my costumes. They tore my place up."

The three of us walk to the living room. Garcia sits in a beach chair. I pull the second one up and sit in front of him. Lily leans against the front door.

"You had what they wanted," I say.

"Katrina's diaries," says Garcia. "She asked me to keep them. She must have put them in my loft the night she died. I was returning from Paris. We had chosen a hiding place in a box of rags under the sink. I never read them. They were in Russian, anyway. But still, I never would. She trusted me. She had so few people to trust."

"How many?"

"People?"

"Red books."

"Twelve."

"Why didn't you tell me you had them?" I say.

"You know why." He asks for a cigarette. Lily goes to the ashtray and fishes out a half-finished one. She lights it on the stove and hands it to Garcia. He inhales, makes a face. "They even smoke cheap."

"What did you do with Katrina, Antonio?" I say.

"I should have a lawyer," he says, rolling the cigarette between his fingers, staring at the ember.

"If you want."

"You won't understand." He looks up at me. "No one will."

"Try me."

I cut Lily a glance that says if he asks for a lawyer again, we'll have to let him make a call. He finishes the cigarette. Lily hands him a glass of water. He stands and looks out the window.

"They threw Nishka in the street," he says. "Poor cat."

"You were good to take him in."

"What could I do after Katrina died? She loved that animal. I couldn't abandon him."

"Of course not."

"He won't last long. He doesn't have the temperament to survive the street."

He pushes his face closer to the glass, feels the sun.

"We think we know who killed Katrina," I say.

"Russians?"

"Yes."

"Those two?"

"They probably forced her OD. They were just the doers. It's way beyond them. More complicated."

"Katrina was complicated," he says, dazed, touching his cut lip and bruised eye. "She was glorious. Despite it all, you know." He glances at me and back out the window. "Her body was perfect. I drew her so many times. I have sketchbooks full of her. She would pose, and we would talk through an afternoon. She loved to be drawn." He looks down at his small, callused, nicked hands. "The cellist—what was his name?"

"Levon."

"He had extraordinary hands, like wings."

Lily rolls her eyes, but Garcia doesn't see.

"Were you and Katrina lovers?" says Lily.

"Detective," says Garcia, looking up from his hands to me.

"He's gay," I say.

"I was thinking bi," says Lily.

"Tried that, but not for me," says Garcia, facing the window again.

"Tell me about Katrina," I say.

He says nothing. Outside noises seep in. Two ravens flash across the glass. Garcia leaves the window, sits in the chair. Lily fishes out another cigarette and hands it to him. He starts to cry, wipes a tear away with his palm. I take a breath. Lily does too. If he's going to lawyer up, it's going to be now.

"I didn't want her cut," he says.

"What do you mean?"

"I didn't want anything to damage her body. She died without a mark. I found her in bed, you remember? I told you. I thought she was sleeping. I couldn't imagine her on a tray in a morgue. Being cut open by strangers. They wouldn't have known, wouldn't have appreciated how perfect she was." He inhales, blows smoke. "It came to me in an instant. Even before I left her loft that morning."

"What came to you?"

"The unexplainable."

"Try us."

Lily kneels beside him, takes his cigarette, squeezes his hand, and looks at him the way she can do.

"I wanted to rescue her," he says. "I wanted her to leave this world as beautiful as she entered it. Do you understand?" He looks at both of us, holding our eyes for a second, then stares ahead to the window. "It was so fast and confusing. My mind went back and forth. I listened from across the hall. I heard them zip her into the bag. That awful, crinkly sound. Like taffeta but louder, you know? I don't know how you live with that sound in your life, Detective. They carried her away. I was frantic, racing around my loft, too much tequila. This was one of *the* ballerinas. In a bag, like trash." He breathes in, tries to calm himself. I lean back in my chair, give him space. "Then it came to me, Detective. But how? I watched from the window. The doors to that awful truck closed, and they drove Katrina away."

"Is that when you called Wallace Blackman?" I say.

"So you know a little. Wally and I worked together on a film years ago. A dreadful horror thing. Warlocks. Demons. Too many virgins in a castle. Wally was excellent at special effects. CGI, blowing things up. He's a master. It's important to know people like that in the business. People who, no matter the job, take their craft seriously. Artists. It's an overused word, but it fits some of us. I think so, anyway. Wally liked me. We became friends. He was going through a divorce. I was making costumes at the time for an Edith Wharton film." He stops, sighs. "Will they ever stop making them?"

Lily hands Garcia another glass of water. He doesn't speak for a long while.

"I'm hungry," he says. "Let's go eat. There must be something in town."

"Why don't you finish; then we'll eat," I say.

"Hey," says Lily. "I'll run out and get some sandwiches. Bring back smokes and coffee."

She's gone before Garcia and I can respond.

"I hope she brings tequila," he says. "She's got good bones. Taut muscles. You partners?"

"Starting to look that way."

"Ah, she's your lover. Your voice changed, Detective. Ever so slightly."

I let it pass. I decide to give him a little.

"You remember when I came to your loft and you drew the picture of the woman you had seen Katrina with?"

"Striking, older, right?"

"That one."

"We think she's behind it. She was Katrina's aunt."

"Why?"

"I can't say more. We're still investigating."

"Katrina was always so at ease with her. They were like sisters."

"Did you know Mickey Orlov?"

"Everybody knows Mickey. Well, at least knows *of* him. I almost worked on a few of his films. But the timing never worked out. He's produced a few great movies. Most producers don't even get one. Why do you ask?"

"I saw one of his films the other night at a private screening."

"Was it good?"

"It was unfinished."

"What was it about?"

"A woman with only her memories left?"

"Sometimes they want to take even those."

He looks down at his shirt and pants.

"I'm filthy," he says. "May I take a shower?"

I check the bathroom: one towel, bar of soap, empty cabinets, nothing sharp; a window too small to climb out of.

"Leave the door open," I say. "I'll stand out here."

The shower runs. Steam spirals into the hallway. I can hear him crying, muffled through the water, but the sobs are deep. It's settling around him now, finding its weight, that "unexplainable" moment that changes everything. He'll tell us. In his own way and time. This house must be for sale. There's no sign out front, but it feels like a home between hands. Maybe for an Airbnb. A lot of those in the high desert these days. The water stops. I can hear the towel across his skin, hear him step into his pants, slip on his shirt. A guy like him having to wear the same clothes for days must be a Dantesque kind of hell. He steps into the hall, his hair slick and wet in a ponytail. He seems halfway back to himself.

Lily arrives with two bags.

"Turkey sandwiches, coffee, sushi, cigs, Cokes."

"Tequila?"

"Just Cokes."

"Sushi?" I say.

"Impulse buy," says Lily.

"I like sushi," says Garcia, reaching into the bag.

We eat in silence. Garcia lights a cigarette. I reach for one. Lily shoots me a disappointed glance, but I need a smoke.

"I want to show you something," says Garcia. "Can we drive?"

"What do you want to show us?" says Lily.

"It's best just to go. You'll want to go."

I drive. Garcia's in the passenger seat; Lily's in the back.

We head to the main road. Garcia gets his bearings. We drive east for a few miles toward the Sheep Hole Mountains. Garcia is quiet, exhausted. He cracks the window and smokes. Saying nothing, he points us to dirt roads and flat stretches of desert broken by boulders and hills, wrinkling at places, drawing the eye. The land is at once scoured and shadowed, a vast terrain of smoke trees, cactus, and ocotillo. A fox appears on a boulder. It sits and watches us and disappears when the wind kicks up. It's late afternoon. We turn past the broken wood of an old mining camp and drive deeper into rock formations and ancient swales where rivers once ran. I check the rearview. Nothing but a trail of thinning dust.

"Stop here," says Garcia. "We have to walk a little."

"How far?" says Lily.

"Around those rocks."

"No fucking with us, right?" says Lily.

"No."

We get out of the car. Garcia stays a few steps ahead. He threads us through boulders. I listen to our footsteps across dirt, scraping rocks. We slip through the last formation as if through a keyhole. The land opens up. Nightfall is an hour away, but the colors are changing, glowing like bronze and turning to deeper ocher shades. It feels as if we are pioneers, alone, in communion with the earth. Garcia points to another clump of boulders a hundred yards east. He stops, takes a breath, looks back at me. I have seen that look before. We're close. A gust comes, swirls the dirt, and dies. Another follows. The air stills, colder. Garcia rounds one boulder, passes between two others. Rock walls rise and open to the sky like a house without a roof. He glances down. The last of the light hits ground blackened with ash. Garcia bends and runs his hand over it. Lily and I step closer. Garcia stands, tears in his eyes, ash on his hands.

"Katrina is here," he says. "Here and with the sky."

"Tell us," I say.

He takes a breath, searches for the first sentence.

"We took her from the morgue," he says, a shiver running through him, the blanket I had given him from my trunk wrapped around his shoulders. "I didn't even know if we could. But I had to try. I called Wally right after you left Katrina's loft that morning, Detective. He was a morgue driver for a few years before his special-effects career got going. His dad used to be a fireman, I think. He helped Wally get the job. Wally said it could take at least a day or more before they did an autopsy. We had time. He was excited. Wally gets animated when he's excited, manic almost. He was fascinated. He came to my loft with the uniforms he used to wear. He had a box of movie-set explosives in his van. Wires and gadgets, things I knew nothing about. Wally thought of the plan."

"Why does Wally all of a sudden sign on to it?" I say. "He didn't know Katrina, but you call him, and he comes. I don't know, Antonio."

"He's a thrill junkie. He was a delinquent when he was a boy. He told me he broke into Beverly Hills houses and spray-painted graffiti on the walls. Just to do it. He stole cars and left them in the Palisades. He's still like that. He can be fucking crazy. But he's good too. I don't want to say Wally's not good."

"Good how?"

"He lets your mission become his. Like a soldier."

"Where is he?" says Lily.

"I don't know."

Garcia lights a cigarette, hands me one.

"We waited for night," he says. "We talked and drank tequila. Wally's bigger than I am, so I had to alter the uniform to fit me. Wally walked among my mannequins, pretending he was in a movie. He had no inhibition. We ordered Chinese. Wally grabbed me after we ate. He held me by the shoulders. He said, 'Are you sure?' I said, 'Yes.'" Garcia looks to the ground and then up to the dark rocks. "We drove to the morgue around three a.m. It was quiet. We parked. Wally got out and fastened explosives to two cars at the end of the lot. He had a remote. We pulled our ball caps down. They were police ball caps. Wally knew where the cameras were. We stood to the side of the door. He pressed the remote. A car exploded. People ran out to see. We snuck in. Wally hurried me down a hall. It was chaos. Radios were going off. We went to a room. Wally opened and shut little silver doors. I stood with him, watching faces of the dead slide in and out. And then." He takes a long drag. "Katrina. We lifted her out. She was pale and light, like silk. Nothing had touched her. We put her in one of those terrible bags and rushed into the hall. Wally pressed the remote again. I could hear another explosion outside. We hurried down the hall and out the door. Police cars and fire trucks were coming. We laid Katrina in the van and drove away."

"Just like that," says Lily.

"Nobody stopped us. I kept thinking they would. I kept thinking *this is not real*. It was as if the moment kept taking us deeper in, and we were looking at it from outside ourselves. There was so much confusion. We looked like everyone else. We hurried through the madness. We drove to a parking lot and changed out of the uniforms, into our clothes. Wally threw the uniforms in a dumpster. We went to Ralph's and bought a dozen bags of ice. I waited in the van while Wally went in. He liked being the one in charge. I was alone with Katrina and I remembered how much we liked the nights, just the two of us, telling stories. She once said we were like vagabonds. I told her nothing else would hurt her. Wally came out, and we drove to the Arts District."

"Why?" says Lily.

"I have a storage shed there for my costumes. We lined a crate with plastic. We took Katrina from the bag. We wrapped her in scarves and laid her in the crate. We filled it with ice. We looked at each other. Wally hugged me. 'Now what?' he said."

He falls to his knees and weeps. Lily and I help him up and lead him away from the ash. It is evidence. There will be fragments— bone slivers, teeth. A puzzle in miniature. We sit with him along a rock wall. At first, Garcia didn't know what he'd do with the body. He and Wally kept her on ice for a few days while he scrolled the web, reading about ancient burial rites and cremation and funeral pyres in India and Nepal. He thought it purification of skin and bone—just what he wanted, her *perfect body* to become one with the elements, not cut up for clues beneath fluorescent lights. He wanted her redeemed. He smoked another cigarette and told us a link to a *Rolling Stone* article led him to the death of Gram Parsons. I knew the story. Lily didn't. It's part of music folklore. Parsons was a country-folk-soul singer, a cosmic boy wonder who dressed in rhinestones and found refuge in the high desert. He wrote songs here and kept an entourage that gathered and flowed—misfits with angel voices. He OD'd at the Joshua Tree Inn in 1973. His body was put in a casket and taken to LAX. Hours later, his manager, Phil Kaufman, and another man showed up drunk. They stole the casket, drove it back to Joshua Tree, and set it on fire in the dirt and rock.

"It's what Parsons wanted," said Garcia. "He had told Kaufman once he wished to be cremated and have his ashes spread. Kaufman remembered. I didn't know about Parsons until after we took Katrina from the morgue. That's odd, isn't it? What happened is so alike. Maybe it's this place. The earth and sky. I feel the pull of it, don't you?"

"I'm not as mystical, I guess," says Lily.

"They didn't do a very good job with Parsons," I say. "Not all the body or the coffin burned. It was a mess."

"Wally and I made a better fire," he says. "We built a pyre of dried wood, and Wally had a special-effects accelerant. We sat in the night and watched sparks buzz through the air, like little stars. Wally said that. We drank tequila and smoked a joint. I cried, and Wally held me. The flames played against the rock. Katrina started vanishing. Little by little, we watched the fire swallow her. We stirred the ash. No one saw. No one came. We drove away before dawn."

"How do you know Katrina wanted that?" says Lily.

"I knew."

"Sounds like it's what you wanted," she says.

"For her. It was all for her."

"You're psycho," says Lily.

"I don't expect you to understand," he says, his words coming broken and slow. "You can't. Some days, I can't either. I thought her sacred. There was no space between us. I had never had that with anyone. I didn't want to think of her differently. Of her decay. Is that so crazy? Maybe it is. Maybe I'm crazy." He takes a long hit on his cigarette; the ember lights his face. "I'm tired. I haven't slept. Can I sleep now?"

He sleeps against the rock. I stay with him. Lily drives to

the main road and calls for a forensics team. It is first light when they arrive in white suits, walking around the blackened ground, raking ash for bits of her. Garcia wakes and stands, shivering in the desert winter. He steps toward the men in white suits and stops. He watches them. I stand beside him. The circle is gray-black, but it will return to the color of clay and dirt, become as it was before, as if a fire never happened, and a soul was never set free. In a million years, no one will ever know. Lily stands on the other side of Garcia. We take his arms and lead him toward the car. He looks back one more time. He whispers something, but I don't hear. He turns, and we slip through boulders as the sun crests a hill and light splinters across the land.

CHAPTER 37

Ortiz sits in Demitasse by the big glass window he likes.

"What a nut job," he says.

"I guess they had a connection," I say.

"The human mind, huh, Carver. One scary shit show. Little Antonio Garcia won't be designing costumes for a while. Blackman's gone. In the wind."

"I almost get it," I say.

"What?"

"Garcia's obsession. Devotion. All those faceless mannequins in his loft. He dressed them like he was God. But it all went blurry on him. He had thousands of sketches of Katrina in a closet. In his mind, he couldn't get her right. She was more divine than his talent. That inspired him in a weird way. Always a line off. A slight flaw in how he drew her."

"So he wasn't God."

Mariella brings espressos. Ortiz stirs in a sugar and sips.

"Speaking of obsessions, how's that going?" I say, nodding toward Mariella.

"I told you, it's not like that. I just like knowing she's here."

"Whatever."

"You know about the DNA match, right?"

"I saw the report this morning."

"Katrina was Orlov's daughter."

"I think he knew."

"What must that be like? A whole life coming out of the past at you."

Ortiz folds his hands, leans closer to me.

"Listen," he says, "I'm taking a few months off. I'm feeling it, you know? I gotta recharge. Me and the wife rented a place in Costa Rica. I'm going to fish and drink and watch nothing happen. No dead people. No brass or bullshit politics. I'm just going to be. There's a village and a little church. Looks like a good place."

"You coming back?"

"Might go native; who knows?" He laughs.

"It's a good move. It's been getting to you."

He doesn't say anything. He raises his hand for two more espressos.

"Azadeh still pissed at you?"

"She'll get over it," I say.

"A friend of mine at the FBI says she keeps watching Orlov's unfinished movie."

"Case got to her."

"Zhanna?"

"Like Blackman."

"Never see her again."

"Or if we do, we won't know it."

"I wonder how many passports that broad has."

"Killed her own niece."

"They live in a different world."

Lily pulls up in my car and parks.

"Never saw her in a dress before," says Ortiz. "Nice."

She comes in and sits with us.

"We better get going. Flight's at one."

"You taking him to the airport?" says Ortiz. "Make him Uber."

"I like driving his car," she says.

"Clutch still pop?" says Ortiz.

"Fixed it," I say.

"Give my best to Maggie and your mom," he says.

"I'll be back in a few days. Send me a postcard from paradise."

We leave Ortiz. He lifts his hand for a third espresso. Mariella nods.

"I like you in a dress," I say. "Special occasion, you dropping me off at the airport."

Lily smirks, shifts to third. We hit the 110.

"I gotta do laundry," she says. "All my pants are dirty."

I reach over, touch her hair. Just for a moment.

"When you getting back?" she asks.

"Three, four days. Maybe longer if . . ."

"Is that what Maggie thinks? Time to put her in a home?"

"She doesn't want to. She's tired. She wants me there. She wants us both to decide."

"I'm sorry, Carver."

"Mom was beautiful. She was my protector."

We slide onto the 105. Traffic's light. The sky is broken, winter gray. LAX comes up fast. I pull my bag from the back.

Lily gets out. She comes around and holds me. Kisses me.

"I'll pick you up."

"I'll get an Uber."

"Carver, I'm picking you up."

She drives away, her black hair in the breeze.

CHAPTER 38

The snow falls hard. I hold my mother's hand by the window. I think of her when I was a boy, running on the beach, taking the train with me into New York. How rich and special we felt. The way she twirled in the house when a song she liked came on the radio, and how she'd sit in the kitchen with my father, tending his bruises and cuts with bandages and iodine on mornings after a fight. I can see him wincing and smiling at her in a language known only to them. I remember when we buried him. She squeezed my hand as we stood over the grave. It meant I was not alone. I squeeze her hand now, tight. She doesn't squeeze back. She doesn't speak. She tilts her head toward me, this unrecognizable man who has somehow found his way into her room, and back to the window. Frail and gray. The woman who bore me, the first voice I heard. We sit and watch the snow as dusk falls over Boston. Maggie makes dinner downstairs, the light clatter of forks and spoons, the hiss of radiators. I wipe away a tear.

"It's worse."

"Yes, Sam," says Maggie.

"She didn't eat."

"She eats a little sometimes."

"She's so light," I say.

"It was good you kissed her forehead when we put her to bed. You never know what she might remember. What might spark."

The dinner plates are still on the table. A soft yellow light glows over the sink. Maggie stands, looks out the window.

"The snow must be three feet in that alley. It's still coming down."

She opens the fridge.

"Let's have a beer, Sam."

"Maggie's ritual."

"I've switched to IPA."

"You told me."

She slides me a bottle and a glass.

"Your father never liked anybody to pour his beer. He said it ruined it. I didn't agree with him ever, but he was right about that."

She sits.

"It might be time for a home, Maggie."

"Let's not think about that tonight. You just got here."

"Yes, but we have to face it. It's not just her mind, but her body. She seems barely able to move around."

"We will face it, Sam."

"You've done it all. I haven't helped much."

"Yes, you have. You come when we need you. We talk on the phone all the time. You've been here." She pours her beer. "You like IPA?"

"I do," I say.

She closes her eyes, lets the first sip spread through her.

"That was some case you had," she says. "That poor ballerina. Just imagine."

"I have."

"I feel bad for the spy too."

"Orlov."

"He was a sad man, I think. All those lives. Imagine the stories he could tell. You're too young, but that was quite a time. A clear time. Things mattered more. Of course, back then we didn't know as much about how the world worked. But we knew there were two sides, and we were on the good one. I'm not so sure anymore." She looks into her glass. "I can see him the way you described, watching his movie. What was the actress's name?"

"Juliette Binoche."

"I must have seen her in something."

"What are you reading now?"

"A poorly translated French mystery."

Maggie is older than my mother. She wears her silver hair long, wild, like a girl who won't accept age—not in a vain way, but in an act of defiance, of which she has many. She is tired. Her blue eyes aren't as quick; her voice is still playful, but at times it fades. She reaches over and pats my hand. She did that when I was a boy. She'd wink as if we were conspiring, taking me into her confidence as we set out for the harbor, eating ice cream and making up stories about the tall ships and the man at the newsstand who had a glass eye and ran numbers for a Southie mobster.

"How are the cataracts?"

"Better," she says.

"Hey, I wanted to ask you. What happened to Billy Connor? I saw something in the paper."

"That was a scandal. All those years, just a quiet man. His wife died back in the nineties. Pretty woman, always happy." Maggie sips. "Then I pick up the *Globe* one day, and there's Billy being led out of his house. They say he embezzled more than half a million dollars over thirty years. A little here, a little there from the Sunday collection. Never got too greedy. Just enough not to be missed. But then they got onto him. An altar boy saw him one day. The parish didn't know what to do. No one could believe it."

"He's got to be in his eighties."

"Parish doesn't want him to go to jail," she says. "No one's decided yet what will happen."

"You read about people like that all the time."

"The ones you don't notice are always up to something."

"Maggie's wisdom."

She smiles. "It's true, Sam."

Maggie sits back and pours the last of the bottle into her glass. I'm tired. I go to the sink and splash my face. The snow falls heavy, the alley smooth and white, uncharted. When I was a boy, I'd sit at my bedroom window and watch the snow. I'd see shapes in it: faces, animals, creatures from my imagination. They'd form and swirl away. One night, as my mother and father slept, I dressed and sneaked out the front door into a snowfall. No one was out. I walked to the wharf and watched the snow descend across the black harbor as if it were falling from one dark sky into another. The boats were tied in their slips; snow gathered on sterns and prows. I tilted my face to the sky and stood as quiet as a statue, feeling cold crystal turn to water. I felt my place in the world there, amid the boats and creaking wood. I stood until my toes were numb. I made a boy's prayer inside me and walked home as the yellow lights of snowplows and cinder trucks flashed in the street. An army on the move. I wondered about the men who drove them, shadows breathing ghosts onto windshields, and what they did when dawn came. Was there a secret place they went? Our house was quiet when I got home. I peeled off my hat, coat, and boots and went back to bed, pulling the covers tight, feeling cold and warm at the same time, looking to the window, the snow still falling, and imagining myself an explorer returned from a secret land. I decided never to tell anyone of that night. It was mine.

My phone rings. Azadeh.

"I have to take this, Maggie."

I step out to the back porch.

"She's dead, Carver."

"Who?"

"Zhanna. One perfect bullet to the head. Old school."

"Where?"

"Vienna."

"Who did it?"

"That could be a long list," says Azadeh.

"What are you thinking?"

"Russian intel. Her sister. A lover. Us, but I don't think so. We wanted to keep an eye on her."

"Any intercepts?"

"No."

"Never thought she'd get it like that," I say. "She stayed one move ahead."

"There's always someone more ahead. Could be maybe your friend. Stefan."

"Why do you say that?"

"He arrived in Vienna the day before," says Azadeh.

"They make contact?"

"Don't know."

"He loved Katrina."

"Enough to matter?"

"No idea."

"He got played by Zhanna," says Azadeh. "Everyone did. Maybe he got pissed."

"Where's he now?"

"South Sudan."

"The case isn't solved, but the guilty are dead."

"Take it as a win. A lot of shit gets sorted out on its own. I'm texting you the picture. Sweet dreams."

The photo glows on my phone. Zhanna sits at an open window in a dress. Her high heels are off and scattered to the side, as if she'd had a long day and was taking in the night view. Her head is tilted to the left, a small bloom on her temple. I hold the photo closer and wonder how she would have appeared if we had met again. What she would have said in that devious hymn of a voice. I admired her cunning, how she turned your weakness to her vanity. She was a thousand secrets. I'm glad someone put her down. I stare at her as the snow falls around her, so small in my hand. I breathe in the cold. I am not a boy anymore, but he is out there, beyond the alley light in the distant, dark white.

I open the door and step back into the kitchen.

"Everything okay, Sam?"

"Just work. All good."

Maggie opens the fridge. She holds up two bottles.

"It's still early," she says.

She slides me a new glass.

"I was thinking the other day, Sam. I should have traveled more when I was young."

"You got around."

"I never got to Tunis or Sarajevo."

"Not high on a lot of lists."

"Those are the best kind of places."

"I'll take you one day," I say. "We'll make a big trip."

"I would have held you to that once," she says, running a finger down her glass. "I went out with a man years ago who promised to take me skiing in the mountains outside Sarajevo. He had maps and brochures. But the war happened, and we never made it. He was an engraver. A kind little muscular guy with narrow eyes."

"What happened to him?"

"He moved to Albany and married."

Maggie stands.

"Oh, Sam, I almost forgot . . ."

She walks into the dining room and back.

"Here," she says. "Sara left this for you."

"Sara?"

"The nurse I told you about. The one who helped with your mother."

"What's it say?"

"It's sealed, Sam. I haven't opened it. It's for you."

The envelope is long and white. My name is written in blue ink. *Sam.* I sip my beer, put the glass down, and open it. A picture falls out. I raise it to the light. My mother is sitting by her window. Maggie is on her left, holding flowers, and on her right is a woman in white.

Maggie leans over and looks at the picture.

"That's one of those selfie things," she says. "Sara took it."

"This is Sara?"

"Yes. Lovely girl."

"This . . ."

My voice fades; my heart hits bone. Dylan Cross looks at me from over my mother's shoulder. Her black hair is dyed a deep red. Her face shines with makeup. But her eyes are the same blue flames I was so close to once. It is her in thin disguise, smiling as if she had subsumed my life and was offering it back to me in a captured moment of intimacy. I can't think. I can only see her wandering these rooms, walking the hallways of my childhood. Sara? No. Dylan. She entered this home and robbed me. She collected details and memories from Maggie and disappeared. But the face in the picture is not mocking. The eyes hold no menace. Her smile is not a crime. It is a sly invitation to a game not finished. The picture was taken in the clear light of approaching dusk. My mother's stare is empty and lost. Maggie's eyes are weary with the burden she has carried. It is a photograph of the cruel things to come.

"I don't know what I'll do without her," says Maggie. "Sara was such a help."

"Where is she?"

"She moved."

"Where?"

"She didn't say, just that she found another job. I didn't pry."

"What did she do when she came?"

"I told you. She helped me bathe your mother, comb her hair, rub lotion on her. She helped me clean up a little. She'd have a beer with me sometimes. She asked a lot about you." Maggie touches my hand. "You okay, Sam?"

"Did she leave anything else behind?"

"No. Are you sure you're all right? You seem rattled."

"A little tired, maybe," I say, looking into my beer and then to Maggie, composing myself. "I should have checked out Sara when you first told me about her. You said the hospital sent her."

"As part of in-home care. It's all covered, Sam."

"Do you have the paperwork?"

"No. Sara kept it. You know how I am with that kind of thing. She was a saint. Nothing wrong with Sara."

I look inside the envelope for a letter that isn't there. I tuck the picture into my hip pocket. Maggie and I sit in silence and finish our beers. She gets up, runs a hand through my hair, and kisses me on the cheek. She leaves me and walks up the stairs to her room. Her door closes. The house falls quiet. A trace of Dylan's spirit has not yet vanished. I can sense her. She is out there somewhere, carrying stolen pieces of me. But she has left part of herself behind. A hushed good-night in a warm house. An invisible sliver among us. What to say of such intrusion and violation? So brazen an infraction? Nothing. We will meet again. She will make it so.

I turn the kitchen light off and stand at the sink. The snow in the alley is silver and gray. I search for faces in it but can see none, just a steady, silent fall. I take out my phone and call Lily. No answer.

ACKNOWLEDGMENTS

I thank my agent Jill Marr at the Sandra Dijkstra Literary Agency, my editor Michael Carr, and all the good people at Blackstone Publishing, including Haila Williams, Ciera Cox, and Alenka Linaschke. I am grateful to Lincoln Jones, Theresa Farrell, Amy Jones, and all the dancers at American Contemporary Ballet in Los Angeles. And, as ever, I thank Clare, Aaron, and Hannah for being who they are.